I put the candlestick...on the floor and bore down with both hands and all my strength. For a long moment I feared that the lock was time-set, and that I would not have the strength to move it. Then, grudgingly, with a grating which nearly frightened me into a hasty retreat, there opened a line between the stones I faced.

I bore down harder, dragging at the level, and the crack grew wider. Finally it became an opening the width of my palm. Midway along it showed part of a face, eyes peering into the passage.

Eyes—and there was no mistaking for me even that small fragment of a face. I knew that face. I knew that face well...."

IRON BUTTERFLIES

Andre Norton

FAWCETT CREST • NEW YORK

IRON BUTTERFLIES

Published by Fawcett Crest Books, a unit of CBS Publications, the Consumer Publishing Division of CBS Inc.

Copyright © 1980 by Andre Norton
ALL RIGHTS RESERVED

ISBN: 0-449-24309-5

Printed in the United States of America

First Fawcett Crest Printing: July 1980

10 9 8 7 6 5 4 3 2 1

For Dr. Carol Burnett, without whose encouragement this tale would never have come to be.

Chapter 1

My grandmother died on the last day of March while a raw wind found a way through window crevices to stir curtains she would not have drawn. As had that greatest of queens, that formidable English Elizabeth, Lydia Wyllyses Harrach refused to meet Death a bed-fast victim. Instead she sat in a high-backed chair, upright in her iron-willed pride, ever watching the muddied snow of the lane which led from our manor landing, as if she had some reason to believe what she must face would come from that direction.

She had been tempered, as a craftsman works with his material, by scandal, reputed dishonor, petty spite, until she had become a living legend.

Though I sat beside her during those last hours, she never reached out her hand, nor turned her head in my direction, but ever surveyed the lane. Nor dared I disturb her. Sometimes the intentness of her stare made me shiver and pull my shawl the closer. It was as if by her very will she would summon something—or someone—to appear.

When she at last broke the silence between us, her voice had lost none of its authority.

"Amelia,—" Her tone held command.

"I am here."

"Bring me the box—"

I had sat still so long my feet were numbed and I staggered a little as I arose. There was only one "box"—a small chest I had never seen opened but which was always kept near her, resting even under her pillow at night. When I brought it from the candlestand by the curtained bed, she did not raise her hand to take it. After a moment's hesitation I placed it on the coverlet drawn about her knees.

"Time—not enough time after all—," Her words were hurried, she still watched the road. Then she turned her head slowly, so that intent gaze centered on me. "Yours—" She made the slightest of gestures toward the chest. "Yours also—the rest. There will be a messenger." She paused, then her will helped her to the last. "Your heritage—take what is offered—by right, by right!" Her voice rang out in the repetition of those words. There was, I believed, both the heat of anger and the force of pride in them. Then a shadow of protest crossed her face.

Her body straightened yet more among the supporting pillows. Still her head remained high, she might be wearing a crown instead of the ruffled nightcap. So she met Death at last, refusing him any triumph.

I caught her as she slumped forward and my cry of "Grandmother!" signaled her maid Letty from the other side of the room. Her dark face was creased with a grief closer to simple love than any emotion I could muster. She had shared years and memories I knew nothing of. Now I was an intruder.

"The box, Miss Amelia." Letty pushed the casket on me. Drawing my shawl still closer about me, I went to my own chamber across the hall.

Life at Wyllyses Hundred had never been easy, nor particularly happy. As a child I had accepted the rigid routine of the house without question. Only when I went away to school seven years ago had I discovered that the world beyond our Maryland manor lived in a different fashion. To me the family life as reported by my schoolmates had seemed so exotic as to be unreal. Nor could I adapt to their freedom easily.

At our home no neighbors came calling, we visited no one. My father had died in the second war with England, falling at the Battle of Bladensburg. My mother, a quiet woman, often in pain, and, I realized as I grew older, much in awe of her mother-in-law, had faded out of life soon after, leaving very little impression to remember her by.

Old scandal had blackened our name, that whispers and isolation had taught me. My grandmother had made a strange marriage—wedding with one of the captive Hessian officers billeted in Maryland after the surrender at Saratoga. When the war was over at last, he returned home overseas. Had he promised to send for her? No one living now knew. The story which arose was that the wedding had been a false one, that she was no wife in truth, and her son had no rightful name. Of Captain von Harrach no more was heard.

That her marriage was dubious, that she had chosen an enemy, both branded Lydia Wyllyses and made of her a recluse. Then a further blow struck, her father called to account on the dueling ground a loose-tongued neighbor, killed his man, to live out the rest of his own life a cripple.

It was then my grandmother showed the rare metal of which she was forged. She assumed the duties her father could no longer manage, and she proved to be of so astute and practical a turn of mind that the family prospered. Not only did Wyllyses Hundred become a fruitful and self-sustaining manor, but in addition there were ship holdings and much to do with trade, once our new nation ventured into commerce abroad. In a little, I, in turn, had a part in this. For as my grandmother's hands became crippled with rheumatism, I was pressed in service to write her letters and instructions. Though there were some letters she still painfully penned herself and those I never read.

My life was, judged by that of my contemporaries, an unnatural one. I had no companions of my own age nor did any kind of social meeting ever claim my presence. Perhaps this cloistering saved me from disappointment, for I was far from a beauty and would doubtless have been neglected had I ventured into company. I was too tall for a female, and my body was lanky, though my schooling had not allowed me to remain gawky or awkward in my carriage. My very fair hair was fine, though thick, and would not hold a hint of curl. So I dealt with it in the most sensible way by binding it about my head in braids. My dark straight brows were set above my eyes in such a manner as to make my habitual expression a sober, near scowling one. I was no candle about which male moths would gather.

These lacks ceased to bother me once I had left school. As my grandmother's deputy, I was entrusted through the years with more and more authority in her name. I was interested in my duties. Did she ever think of me as a young girl? She had so encased herself in an armor which could not be broached by emotion that she seemed all powerful, a stable center to my whole world. On that March day when she left me I was like a ship suddenly lacking a steersman.

She had spoken in those last moments of a messenger—a heritage—and the chest. I sat now with my hand on that. The box was old, fashioned of wood which had either turned dark from age, or been stained so. The carving on the lid was very much worn away. But a shaft of the weak spring sun crossed that near-vanished design, so I could see it was a representation of a heraldic shield—but it did not carry the arms of the Wyllyses.

In its lock there was the small key which hitherto my grandmother had always worn on a chain about her neck. Reluctantly I turned that.

Papers had been crammed so tightly within that with the raising of the lid they sprang upward. A letter on top was clearly written by my grandmother and it must have cost her much pain to set down those straggling words, since her hands were near helpless of late. I unfolded the sheet to read.

So my small, safe world cracked, fell apart. These words were no fanciful flight of imagination—they were the truth. Feverishly I dropped the page and shuffled through the rest of the papers—letters, and a piece of parchment with crabbed legal language, signed by an official seal.

Thus I learned of the true Joachim von Harrach, whose blood ran in my own veins—but the name I bore from him was false.

He had been a younger son (the sixth of seven brothers) but still a prince of the arrogant Wittlesbach line, making him kin in turn to that stubborn German-English George who tried to keep us subjects of his will. Quarreling with his father, this prince had fled and joined the Hessians as an officer, leaving behind Hesse-Dohna of which his father was Elector and autocratic ruler. Then there had come deaths—by fever, by hunting accident, by a fall from a horse, and Joachim was ordered home to his kingdom.

It was very easy for his father to sweep away an imprudent marriage. His signature on the parchment did that. There was a proper princess ready and waiting, carefully groomed to her role, a court-solemnized marriage.

Another letter had been rolled inside that document that had made of my grandmother a mistress, my father a bastard. This second sheet was creased and recreased, as if it had not only been read many times, but might also have been fiercely crumpled in a hand and then smoothed again.

I knew the heat of anger as I read it. An offer—a dishonoring offer—to such a woman as Lydia Wyllyses. Yet I knew from my reading of the European newsletters which my grandmother had ordered sent to her regularly, as well as from the German mistress at my school, this but followed a custom common in such German courts. A ruler might have both an official wife of his own rank, and a morganatic one—even two such— To me the protestations of love in this letter were an insult. My hands shook as I threw it from me as I would something poisonous.

Yet there remained the message in her own letter. That I took up to read again. Now I understood what must have been the driving purpose of her life.

All that I have done to make secure our heritage here and have our name prosper was accomplished so that we should carry no further stain. I could not win back Joachim, though I believe that such pressures were brought to bear upon him that, schooled as he was, he could not resist. By the laws of this country I am his legal wife, and I would have acknowledgment of that. To this purpose have I worked—and perhaps it is not now impossible. Should the message which I await now come, I ask it of you, Amelia, that you do what is in your power to win this recognition. You will have an independent fortune and so will not be unable to do as you see fit.

I bind you to no promise, however. Time buries much. If this cause seems of no value to you, then do as you wish. If the promised messenger comes, receive him, hear him out, and then decide. I will not ask more of you—

There was no signature, it was as if at the last the pen had fallen from her hand. My grandmother had never asked anything of me save my aid as a secretary and her deputy. Nor did she now try to tie me by any command from the dead. Yet anger welled in me, not for myself, but on her behalf. Let this messenger come— let me then decide what course to follow. What she asked of me I was hot to give. I would prove indeed that she had been an honorable woman cruelly misused!

Fired by that resolve, I read through the other papers. They were reports for the most part coming from

Hesse-Dohna. There was a terse description of the royal marriage. The only son born of that was dead, killed in Napoleon's wars—one daughter, unmarried, still lived, though there was no other message from Joachim himself. That is, I thought so until I found beneath the papers a piece of yellow-white brocade crossed by a tracery of tarnished gold thread. It seemed to part by itself as I took it up, so there spilled into my lap a necklace with a pendant, the whole dead black in color. Twisted about it was a piece of paper. I unrolled that.

"Lydia—Lydia—Lydia—" Just the name written over and over again, the last time with such force that the pen pierced the paper, leaving a blot like a drop of blood from a wound. The force of that writing—it reached even into my emotion-starved heart. I could not doubt who had written it, nor that he had been racked by deep feeling.

The necklace—it was fashioned by workmanship of the highest order, yet the metal was no more than common iron. Filagree butterflies, their delicate wings formed of threads near fine enough to draw from a spider web, were united by rosettes in which small sparks of light marked, no gems but tiny beads of cut steel.

Almost without conscious thought, I held it about my neck, looking into the mirror of my dressing table. It was eerily beautiful, yet I found it somehow distasteful. Why should the most delicate of insects be represented in the harshest of metals? What kind of mind would devise such a union of opposites?

As I would return it to its wrapping it slipped in my hand and I saw the engraving on the back of the pendant:

"Em get aushet zum Wolh des Faderland."

"Exchanged to the welfare of the Fatherland," I translated.

What did that mean? But that was a mystery without solution for me now. I slipped the chest and all it contained once more safely locked within, under my pillow.

Five days later my grandmother's man of law made my future plain. I was over legal age and Lydia Wyllyses had indeed left me independent. There was another clause which made James Weston frown disapprovingly.

"Should you marry, Miss Harrach, your property will be placed in a trust from which you alone shall benefit. Madam Harrach insisted that you should always have full use of your inheritance with no interference."

This fact, I thought with hidden amusement, should indeed speedily remove the danger of fortune hunters. A wife so independent of her husband was an abomination to be feared. Weston's distaste already appraised me of that. But, as she had promised in her last letter, grandmother had left me free in more ways than one.

There remained only the promised messenger. The most recent reports from Hesse-Dohna (I had taken to reading and rereading the material in the chest from time to time) had been signed P. F. and they gave such detailed accounts of court life that I felt they could not have been penned by any merchant or sea captain, but must be by one who held some responsible position there. I was studying the latest of these after James Weston's departure, when Letty came to me.

"Miss 'Melia, there be a gentleman as says he is expected—and would speak with you—" She stood in the doorway smoothing down her apron. I knew Letty's moods, even more now since the funeral, when she had attached herself to me with the same devotion she had served my grandmother.

He was expected—the messenger! I half arose from my seat and then forced a show of calmness.

"Did he give his name, Letty?"

"No. He just say he have important business with Ole Miss. I tell him she is gone. Then he say he see you."

"Show him into the morning room, Letty."

But she did not move. "Miss 'Melia, you sure you want to see him?"

14

"Why not?"

She crumpled the hem of her apron now. "I got a feelin', child, jus' a feelin'."

I knew Letty's feelings. Too often in the past they had turned out to be warnings. But this time—if it was the messenger— I shook my head at her and she went with a sigh.

As I entered the room I saw only my visitor's back, for he stood at one of the deep-set windows looking out into the garden. He was tall and his well-cut coat of dark green set so smoothly over his shoulders it was like a second skin. But there was a stiffness in his attitude, as if he were a military man about to spring to attention.

"You wished to see me—?" I must have entered very quietly, for until I spoke he did not turn. Now he did swiftly, with an ease which belied his posture of a moment earlier. I had expected a seafarer or one of the merchants who visited the manor at my grandmother's bidding. This was a different class of man entirely.

His face was brown enough to suggest that he did spend much time out under the sun, but the sharpness of the glance with which he favored me was that of a man well used to command. I could not at that moment have declared him either plain or handsome, but there was a character in his face which impressed. His hair was dark and one unruly lock curved down on his forehead not quite far enough to conceal the seam of a scar, one end of which cut his left eyebrow, raising it, to give him a distinctly quizzical look. Now he bowed.

"Miss Harrach?" His voice was deep, carrying the faintest hint of accent.

"I am Miss Harrach."

"I am Pryor Fenwick." He paused as if I should recognize the name. Then he must have guessed from my expression I did not. With a hint of frown he continued:

"Did not Madam Harrach advise you of my coming?"

"As she was dying, sir, she mentioned a messenger she was expecting. The reason was not given me."

"Then you were not told that I was to be your escort to Hesse-Dohna?"

It was my turn to stare. "My grandmother left no such instruction, sir. As for going to Hesse-Dohna—why should I consider such a journey?"

Something in his assurance aroused irritation in me. In fact he had an affect which I could not understand, and one which I distrusted. Now he came toward me and I had to force myself to remain where I was when I wanted nothing more than to retreat.

"How much of the situation do you know?" His question was an abrupt demand. I resented him at that moment with a heat which another part of me found astounding. Unless, as Letty, I was indulging in prophetic "feelings." At that moment, inwardly distraught by these odd feelings, I replied to his question evasively.

"Sir, I must ask you to be a little more plain." I schooled my voice, hoping my composure would appear outwardly unruffled. "Just what am I supposed to know?"

He looked impatiently at me. His frown was now close to a scowl.

"When I spoke of Hesse-Dohna, you showed no surprise. I will wager you know the rest well enough, Miss Harrach."

Pryor Fenwick he had named himself. 'P. F.'—My grandmother's correspondent who was so discreet as to use initials only?

"Sir." I clung to caution, remembering my grandmother's rule of never acting on impulse. "Are you the P. F. who wrote from Axelburg on the tenth of November last?"

He nodded.

"If that be so, in what manner have matters changed since then? Oh, please, be seated, sir." I waved him to a chair and was glad myself to drop upon a small settee nearby, folding my hands quickly in my lap like a school miss, lest they betray me to what I judged a very acute eye by their slight tremble. Was all my grandmother had fought for during the past years come closer to hand now?

"The Electress Caroline died in January." My visitor did not seat himself, rather he rested his strong brown hands on the back of the chair, his dark eyes so searching my face that I had to force myself to meet his gaze with a difficulty which had not moved me in the presence of any man I had met before. "The Elector is in poor health. It has long been his wish to—"

Because he made me so uneasy I interrupted him.

"To right the old wrong, Mr. Fenwick? In what way can he do that? Will he produce another paper inscribed with official seals to admit he did have a lawful wife, a son who was no bastard? Have you been sent to bring me such a paper, Mr. Fenwick?" My voice carried some of the heat of my inner anger.

"He has sent for you, Miss Harrach, having had brought to him the letter from your grandmother. He is old and ill, and he wants to see you—"

He paused as if awaiting some quick agreement from me. But his mention of a letter written by my grandmother struck me silent. Why had she done this—humbled herself (or so it seemed to me then) to write to a man who had so foully and callously used her? It was not in her to do such a thing—I would not believe it. When I made no answer he continued.

"I know that in this country the position of your grandmother was made difficult—"

"How perceptive of you, Mr. Fenwick!" I flared. Was he, a man plainly used to the giving orders, now at a loss because he could not be in command of the situation, that that lay in *my* hands?

"My grandmother, sir, was labeled, after the desertion of her lawful husband, a discarded mistress, his son a man without a name. This was the 'position' in which your Elector chose to place those in which he should have taken pride. My grandmother's father was forced to defend her good name in a duel, he died a cripple as the result. This is *our* position and has been

17

for nearly fifty years. Now why dares he send for me? Also, what is your part in all this?"

Visibly he controlled what was plainly a hot temper. I marked the twitch at the corner of his mouth, the tightening of his lips before he replied.

"I am the Elector's Colonel of the Guard, his trusted messenger, to answer your last question first. He delegated me to correspond with your grandmother—for the situation was such that he could trust but few of those about him. He perhaps chose me because my family came originally from his country, and he believed that this being so the task might be easier. You cannot understand, positioned as you are"—now he was plainly lecturing me—"the demands of duty. The Elector had a duty to his House, to his people—"

"But not to his family?" I interrupted. "You are most informative, Colonel Fenwick. But, having made his choice in the past, why alter it now? How does the death of the Electress change matters?" The strength anger gave me stopped the trembling of my hands. I suddenly realized that they clutched each other so tightly that I was in pain from my own grip.

"As long as Her Royal Highness lived, the Elector could not communicate—" Fenwick half turned from me, I think he was seeking words to force my understanding. "Intrigue flourishes in any court. He—he did what he had taken oath at his father's deathbed to do. Now he is free—but also he is ill. His doctors are not hopeful. But his force of will is such that I think he shall defeat their foreboding—at least long enough to see you.

"The position is this, Miss Harrach. He has not the power to give you any succession to your rightful rank. But he has a private fortune which is his to bequeath where he wills. Most of all he wants to see you because you are what you are—his granddaughter."

"So you propose, sir, that I immediately set forth to meet, overseas, a man I do not know, and of whom I hold no high opinion, to garner a fortune. Sir, thank you for this estimation of my character—I have not heretofore believed greed one of my more pressing sins. A pretty suggestion, sir, and one I find quite insulting!" I arose. "I pray you forgive my leaving you, but this conversation is highly distasteful. Shall we bring this interview to an end?"

He loosed his hold on the chair and made an impatient gesture.

"Miss Harrach, I seem to have presented the case badly. It may be that I was not the proper advocate to be sent. The truth is that I am perhaps the only one in the Elector's confidence concerning this. Since his illness, he has had to depend on others, and court loyalty is a chancy thing. I can tell you only the bald truth, that circumstances over which even a ruler can have no control forced him in the past into actions he bitterly regretted. Now he is free, he needs—he is old, he would make his peace."

There was such a note of intensity in his voice now that I was prevented from voicing my first answer. There flashed into my mind oddly enough the memory of that paper wound about the necklace—its odd effect of a voice crying out in pain.

"But what you ask—that I undertake such a journey with you—"

Again he made that impatient gesture, brushing away my objection.

"Of course we do not travel alone. Gräf and Gräfin von Zreibruken await you in Baltimore. The Gräfin is a distant cousin of your own. Now Miss Harrach I must ask *you* a question— What was the abiding purpose of your grandmother's life?"

I drew in my breath sharply. "But you cannot promise that—that she be recognized—openly—respectfully—"

From within the breast of his smoothly fitting riding coat he brought out a folded paper, or rather a sheet of parchment. He held it out, and such was the force of his gaze, I found myself accepting it, reading what was written in formal script.

19

"My grandmother—but why does this speak of her as a Countess of the Holy Roman Empire? This—"

"Is the first step in establishing her as an equal in rank at court."

"Suitable to be an Elector's wife?" I hoped he caught the sarcasm in my voice. "Unfortunately it comes too late—"

"The title descends to you, since you alone are her heir. The Elector obtained this three months ago, he was not aware she also was ill—or near death. He hoped—" Fenwick shrugged. "Time and fate have never favored him."

I refolded the parchment, recalling that other one in the casket—one took away, one gave. The title would not have meant anything to Lydia Wyllyses—an honorable name was more. Still she had asked this of me—the clearing of that name. What choice did I have anyway? The man was old, ill, and some could stretch it that I had a duty to him. His fortune—that meant nothing. But what might come from the parchment was another matter.

Perhaps my face was more expressive than I wished, or perhaps the Colonel believed that any female was easily brought to the right point of view if a man insisted. For now he said briskly: "It will be necessary to make hast, Countess. The Elector cannot wait long. There is a ship waiting in Baltimore—it will sail in five days—"

"Sir—! What you suggest is impossible!"

"Madam," he snapped, "it is not only possible, it must be, I have said—the Elector is near dying. That is the truth!"

The force with which he spoke then underlined the urgency he apparently felt. Suddenly I was a little breathless, as one being whirled along by a natural force one could not hope to control. A matter of expediency. But five days—! For a moment I felt as helpless as any female who had no control over her own affairs. The Colonel bowed and now did move toward the door.

"I shall speak with your man of business, Mr. Weston. Arrangements for your comfort will be made."

Perversely I wanted to say I would have nothing to do with his "arrangements," that I had no intention of sailing for Hesse-Dohna. Yet I also knew I had already committed myself to this wild adventure.

Chapter 2

♦

I went about the business of settling affairs temporarily at the manor, for, though I knew I was to sail for Europe and the unknown, yet I had no intention of remaining there once my duty to my grandmother's memory was paid in full. Letty demanded to go with me, but I had to point out to her that the difficulties of her traveling where she could not speak the language, where those of her race were not commonly known, were insurmountable. For I knew, through the forceful comments of Madam Manzell, the German governess at my late school, a vast gulf existed between classes in her native land. One of her favorite (and, to me, horror) tales had been of a Grand Duke who had calmly shot a peasant before the eyes of a visitor in order to prove that he *did* have arbitrary life and death powers over all his subjects.

That I myself might be exposed to caste and rank

problems I also expected. My only barrier against such would be the parchment Colonel Fenwick had left in my hands. I had the first taste of what lay before me when, two days later, in the prim and stuffy front parlor of James Weston's home in Baltimore, I met the other two who were to be my traveling companions, the respectability of whom the Colonel had so assured me. The Gräfin interested me the most, since I was supposed to share kinship with her. Madam Manzell's stories had made so much of the self-importance and arrogance of those associated with any court I did not look forward to our introduction with any warmth of feeling.

The Gräf wore the plain clothing of a gentleman. However, so ramrod stiff was his stance that one expected to hear the faint clink of a sword at every movement, a rattle of the spurs with which his civilian boots were not equipped. He was tall, a beanpole of a man, with bristly, close-cropped gray hair. Equally bristly sideburns made stiff brushes before each ear and well down along the chin line. While his nose was like some hawk's rapacious beak, his chin retreated in a weak line back to his cravated throat. He entered a step or so in advance of his wife, gave me a sharp bow, his dark eyes not quite meeting mine.

His lady, however, was very different. In the first place she must have been near to me in age, much younger than her gaunt husband, and as vivacious in manner as he was stiff and aloof. She was small of stature, her figure tending toward the buxom. Curls, as bright as a gold piece straight from the mint, bounched below her beplumed and ribbon bonnet, clustering also around a face wherein blue eyes were wide and would-be innocent. Her small mouth was as round as an unopened rosebud, pink-red. She gave the room a quick glance, as an actress might make herself aware of the stage, and then equalled my curtsy.

"Countess—" Her voice was soft, her English only a little accented. "We are honored to be of service—"

I had no delusions concerning what might be my

reception by the court of Hesse-Dohna. There had been no need for Colonel Fenwick to warn me that there might be more enemies than friends. So, I must from the start, assume the status my grandfather had given me. My curtsy was therefore a shade less deep than hers. And, to her apparent surprise, I replied in German. Her eyes widened as we exchanged polite nothings. I noted, however, that the rigid Gräf and his lady waited for me to be seated before they themselves took the chairs I indicated.

Colonel Fenwick, who had escorted them to make the introductions, again took a place near a window, half turning away, as if he would like to escape. I drew my shawl close, feeling again a chill such as I had on the day of my grandmother's death. But I had made my choice and must abide by it.

The Colonel and the Gräf remained only for a few minutes and then asked permission to withdraw, leaving me with the Gräfin. She was apparently one of those women whose waking hours must be ever filled with conversation, to whom silence was a dire thing. For she prattled on now, not as one nervously striving to fill up a silence, but because that was her nature.

Her conversation dealt with the ship on which we were booked to sail, the nature of its accommodations. I discovered speedily that it was only necessary for me to murmur at intervals a yes or no or to nod. However, she finally came to fewer words and looked at me more directly and critically—or so I believed her stare to be.

"Lady von Zrebruken"—now I used my native tongue—"you will excuse me in that I find my situation now to be 'most strange and unusual—perhaps even a little frightening—"

She nodded vigorously until the magenta plumes on her plum velvet bonnet (her color choices made my eyes ache—if what she wore was high court fashion I feared my wardrobe would be indeed counted drab) swayed back and forth.

"Therefore"—now I prepared to play the role I had planned for myself during those few days since this action had been forced on me—"I shall depend upon you for assistance. Colonel Fenwick has told me that we are in some way kin—?"

Her answer came in a gush, by all appearances she was delighted by my attitude.

"But of course." She, too, now spoke English. "My father was of the Family." Her smile, it seemed to me, for I watched her closely, was no longer that of a pretty, frivolous woman, instead it held a shadow of slyness. "Of the family," she repeated. "His Serene Highness, Prince Axel, was my mother's protector, you understand. He was the Elector's brother who was killed at Waterloo."

So the Gräfin was also the result of an irregular alliance. It would seem that the ruling House of Hesse-Dohna was given to such. I nodded as if this fact had already been known to me.

"It was most kind of the Elector to choose you to make such a lengthy journey in order to accompany me."

"To do so is not only our duty, my lady, it is a pleasure. Ach, you shall like our country, so beautiful, the people so kind—Axelburg such a fine city! We have the opera, the fine gardens—the Treasure House of His Highness. He allows even the commoners to visit that on feast days to see the splendor of his collection. You will not believe such exists until you see it!"

I would believe nothing concerning Hesse-Dohna until I saw it for myself, I decided. During the two days that followed, the Gräfin was never far from my side, though I did not see much of the Gräf, nor of Colonel Fenwick. To my astonishment—and dismay—I found myself regretting the absence of the latter. To me he was a figure of sane security in my quickly changing world.

On the day we embarked I was still unhappy from my parting with Letty, with the life I had always known. I could not but be aware that this was a reckless venture and I had no real friend at hand. The Gräfin insisted that I share the attentions of her own sour-faced and silent maid, averring that as soon as possible I must have a proper attendant.

But I wanted none of Katrine's breed, her very presence in my small cabin could dampen my spirits. Nor did I, on deck, watch the last of my country. I doubted my courage at the crucial moment. Rather I faced downriver toward the sea, and so became aware of someone beside me as I felt the deck swing under my feet and strove to adapt my body to that surge.

"A brisk wind, perhaps too chill for you, my lady—"

Brisk it was. I had to hold to the rim of my bonnet. But I managed to turn my head a fraction to look at Colonel Fenwick. He had put aside the high-crowned hat of fashion, wore a knitted cap pulled down about his ears, and the jacket of a seaman. Now he looked more at home and at ease than I had ever seen him.

"Too cold? But this is my first time a-sea and I would not miss the beginning of a new adventure."

He looked at that moment even more quizzical than his scar gave him reason, and I had a sudden suspicion that he might deem me using some trick of flirtation. Again anger flared in me. The Gräfin's chatter and her lord's stiff silence had made me yearn for some easy exchange of conversation, but now I would not allow myself to think that I might find such with the Colonel.

"You have a taste than for adventure, my lady?" His voice was as chill as the spray which now and then touched a fingertip to my cheek.

"Does not everyone, sir? You must allow that this is an adventure to me—"

He no longer met my eyes, staring instead moodily at the sea.

"Watch yourself!"

Those two words came from his lips with a force as if they had been torn forth against his will. Before I could frame a question he was gone, his long strides taking him aft.

Surprisingly the Gräfin proved to be a better sailor than her husband. While he kept to his cabin she fluttered about, enjoying heartily the special delicacies our party had brought. I learned not only to endure her constant chatter, but from the flow of trivia strove to pick out information concerning Hesse-Dohna which might be of value to me.

It was plain that the late Electress had not been beloved. She combined, to a high degree, irascibility, pride of blood, and a dislike for being the consort of a relatively minor prince. She had done her duty though, produced an heir and two daughters, of whom she took little notice. When her son had been killed, her chagrin had made her take to her bed. Not, I gathered, from any excess of grief, but in sheer rage that the title would now pass to a junior branch of the family she despised.

In spite of his wife's notorious temper the Elector had always treated her with courtesy. The fact that he had not installed any favorite had been remarked upon as an oddity of character unique in his class. Instead he spent his energies on the gathering of what the Gräfin termed his "treasure." A tower of the palace in Axelburg had been gutted, its interior rebuilt in the form of a single large room on each floor. These became the repositories for the wonders which were either created by his orders, or acquired by his agents roaming Europe.

There was a lacquer room, its walls covered with panels providing niches which housed figures of precious metal, ivory, gems. A silver room was next, to display the plate which had been gathered by his predecessors and added to by his own efforts.

All these the Gräfin dwelt upon greedily. Her fingers sometimes moved as if she actually fingered the riches, while her absorption with such details made me remember the strange butterfly necklace my grandmother had left me.

If the Elector Joachim possessed such riches, why had he sent his American wife a piece wrought of the most common of metals? Not wishing to reveal to the Gräfin what I now carried in a secret pocket sewed into my petticoat, I strove to word a question which might in some manner solve that mystery.

My answer came during her tales of the Napoleonic period, of how the court had had to flee, and the treasure had been successfully hidden. For she launched into the description of how in many of the courts, their treasuries drained empty (though nothing of course was done to destroy the superb Hesse-Dohna collection), an urgent appeal had been made to the women of the nobility. Those who turned in their jewelry to fund the common cause received in return iron jewelry specially designed by artists, each piece bearing the notation I had read on the pendant. These were worn with great pride, as a man might display a battle decoration.

Was it because of this "honor" that my grandmother had received the necklace, a furtive recognition of her meaning to the Elector? Or had he been sure she would never have accepted from him any real jewelry of price?

Besides this dwelling on the Elector's treasure, I gathered from the Gräfin a picture of the court which was in no way reassuring. Exaggerated formality of manners when dealing with inferiors in rank, mingled with sottish behavior of men who had few curbs placed upon their wills. Intrigue and spying, maneuvering to better one's position or secure the downfall of an enemy appeared to be the major occupations of all concerned.

I had to fortify myself many times over with the thought of my grandmother's appeal to my sense of duty to keep me from planning to cut short this journey and return to my own country before I ever saw the boundaries of Hesse-Dohna.

So distracted I was by this distaste for what might lie ahead that I did not really heed the first time the Gräfin introduced the name of Von Werthern into her conversation, though she began to repeat it so much that I was forced finally to listen more carefully to her comments upon the amazing virtues of this member of the inner court circle.

It would appear from the Gräfin's summing up that this young man possessed every known attribute of a romantic hero. So fervent were her praises that I began to suspect her own interest in the Baron was perhaps more than just that of kin as she professed herself to be. He was so handsome as to command instantly, upon first meeting, the full attention of every female, his manners (to me) sounded like those of a well-experienced seducer. But it seemed that he was also a fighting man, a noted horseman, hunter, duelist—a paragon such as would send any female of sensibility into sighing and swooning.

That she would express her preference for him so openly and so often surprised me a little. Was she in love with him to the point that she *must* discuss him merely to satisfy herself? Was she thus infatuated to the point that she would not care if I were to repeat some of the remarks made to me?

On the morning we at last landed after a tedious voyage and were setting out on the last stage of our journey, she produced with a coy affectation, as I thought, of secrecy, a miniature of this Apollo.

The painted face was handsome enough; though to me the eyes did not have a very pleasant expression. He was clothed (the miniature was a bust portrait) in an exceedingly ornate uniform, with a number of orders among the gold lace and cords which rivaled the bright yellow of his hair. I managed to voice a few generalities in answer to the Gräfin's demands for my opinion, but to me he was lacking in appeal.

I was still reluctantly holding this miniature, which she had pushed into my hand, when Colonel Fenwick came with the message our traveling coach was ready. Glad of an excuse, I offered the painting back to my companion and then saw the Colonel glance at it. His face was without expression for a moment. Then he directed at me a look which made me feel, in an odd and disturbed way, as if I had been judged and found wanting. Perhaps he believed that I was encouraging the Gräfin in her infatuation. Certainly *he* had made no attempt to know me better during the voyage, keeping to himself, while the Gräfin had been ever at my elbow. To him I could be just another empty-minded female—just a responsibility he would be glad to be rid of as soon as we arrived.

Now I found myself resenting that impression. I would have liked very much to have made plain to him that this visit to Hesse-Dohna meant only one thing to me and I wanted nothing from it except the word of a reputedly dying man—that my grandmother be given at last the honorable position in the sight of the world she had always deserved.

As he turned away abruptly the Gräfin pursed her lips in a pout.

"He presumes too much," she said. "Because his father took service with the Elector, knew him years ago in America, and His Highness is his godfather, he believes himself to be a person of consequence. What is he truly but a hireling, a mercenary! You—" She paused a moment and then continued, "Your country-men would have none of his family once—they considered them traitors, drove them out after your revolution. So some of them sold their swords overseas. He shall find what is thought of his kind—soon!"

That the Colonel was of Tory descent I had had hinted to me before I left Maryland—when I had had a private interview with Mr. Weston who gave me, at my request, a sum in gold I carried in secret, being prudent enough to want funds if I should need them. But Tories no longer were the ogres of one's childhood. Thus I had thought no more of him than that he was an exile who had at last found a place for himself.

Only the present spiteful note in the Gräfin's voice might have been uttered by one of my own country-women a generation ago. It was hard, ugly, out of character—making her for an instant something else than she had continually presented herself to be.

Our progress across land was hardly more comfortable than the voyage and far more constricted. The Gräfin and I, with Katrine seated with her back to the horses, were immured for hours in a great lumbering coach which dipped, rattled, swayed from pothole to pothole on ill-kept roads. The Colonel and the Gräf had the better of it, for they rode horseback and kept ahead, with the uniformed escort, of our rocking prison. Another detachment of guards behind added to the small train of carriages and wagons, some transporting luggage, others servants which had been waiting for us.

It was the duty of some of these to forge well ahead each morning, take over an inn, getting rid of lesser travelers thinking to shelter therein, prepare the beds with our own linen, cook our meals, have all ready for our arrival. That we used only inns surprised me, for the custom of my own country was to visit the nearest manor or plantation along one's route, strangers being welcomed with openhanded hospitality. But, I decided, European customs were perhaps different.

At last, having survived the queasiness brought on by the imprisonment in the coach, the dullness of long days of riding behind drawn or nearly drawn curtains (for the Gräfin had protested on our setting out that too much light gave her headaches), we clattered in the early dusk into the cobbled streets of Axelburg itself.

The Gräfin, who had been drowsing during most of the last dreary day, now jerked back the nearest curtain. I could see lamps shining and a bit of house wall here and there. The coach grated to a stop and there came a blaze of dazzling light as the door was opened, the steps let down, and a number of liveried servants moved to greet us.

As I stretched my cramped limbs and looked about I saw we had pulled into a walled courtyard and the imposing house before us was no inn. The Gräfin twitched her skirts into order and made me the most formal of curtsies.

"My lady," she spoke in English, "please to enter. This is Gutterhof, our home."

The house was at least three stories high and, in spite of many lights in the windows, had the heavy look of a fortress rather than a home. But the fact we were at the end of our journey made me welcome this first sight of one of Axelburg's ancient houses, ugly and slightly menacing though it seemed. Within I had a confused impression of a large hall through which we followed a lackey holding a branched candlestick. He was quickly joined by a discreetly but richly dressed older woman, while one wearing the apron of a maid fell in behind as I was escorted with some pomp up a staircase and down another but narrower hall. Until at length I was ushered with ceremony into a cavernous room where even four candelabra such as the footman carried made very little way against corner shadows.

It was a chamber of what seemed to me royal ostentation. The bed itself was a hugh cavern, half walled by curtains supported by carven posts, possessing a canopy surmounted at its peak by a shield upheld by fantastical beasts over which the candlelight flickered so dimly their fierce eyes, claws, and other portions of their gilded anatomy only showed at intervals.

The curtains, the thick carpet underfoot, those heavy drapes which must conceal windows somewhere behind their folds were all of a time dulled blue. What could be seen of the walls showed panels painted with sprays of flowers wreathed and intertwined as if to suggest a jungle or a forest such as sheltered Sleeping Beauty in the old tales.

There was a dressing table of delicate ivory and gold which might have strayed in by mistake, then been too frightened to escape. For it huddled well back from the bed. Some chairs, a few throne-backed in keeping with an earlier age, others more modern, stood about here and there accompanied by small and large tables.

The lackey had bowed himself out. Now the silk-clad older woman, who might have been sister to Katrine so frozen and correct was her expression, informed me that food and drink was on its way and Truda, indicating the maid, who stood with her hands concealed under her apron, was entirely at the service of the gracious and highborn lady.

I thanked her and she withdrew in a crablike fashion, making three curtsies, each slightly less deep, before she disappeared through the door. So I was remained with Truda, and any one less like Letty I could not imagine. At that moment I was near overcome by a wave of bitter homesickness. I wanted to be in my own room, in my proper place, so much I could have wailed aloud like a child abandoned in a stark boarding school.

The room did not smell musty, but I felt as if I could not draw a deep breath here. That massive bed appeared to threaten rather than invite one to rest—

Nonsense! I must curb my imagination. It was nothing but a bed, and the girl facing me, her eyes cast down, her face blank, had no reason to greet me as a friend. Her face was round, almost childish, while her hair had been so tightly braided, and those braids fastened back under a half-cap, that the hair appeared near pulled from its roots about her forehead.

"There is hot water?" I broke the silence between us.

She started and for the first time her eyes met mine. She colored and gestured toward a screen. "But, yes, gracious lady. Water—all else for your comfort. Please to look, if all is not right, then I am to do your will."

The screen, which was taller than my head, masked a fire on a hearth which was wide enough to be like an alcove. Flames burned bright and hot. There stood a bath and beside it a row of water cans—from others set on the hearth spirals of steam arose. I gave a sigh of relief. Such luxury had not been a part of the service in any of the inns.

Later, some of the ache and stiffness soaked out of me, my damp hair which had been expertly washed by Truda, and brushed and blotted near dry with towels before being coiled up loosely, I sat down, clad in the warmest of my chamber robes, to eat. So soothed was I that even the bed now ceased to wear its forbidding aspect.

The food was very good, a clear soup, duckling with peas, tartlets filled with fruit, cheese, a trifle smothered in rich cream. I drank sparingly of some wine and perhaps that added to my sleepiness, for I yawned and yawned again.

But I was not too weary to keep close to hand the packet which I had guarded closely during this whole journey. When I settled in the bed, finding it somewhat awkward to edge to the center, I pushed that beneath my pillows. The gold I had begged from Weston, the parchment Colonel Fenwick had brought me, my grandmother's last letter, and the necklace, a talisman to keep my mind firmly on my mission here, formed my secret hoard.

The screen which had hidden the hearth was folded away so I could see the flames. Truda would have drawn the bed curtains, but that I refused. Watching the fire, I drifted into sleep at last.

I was not too tired to dream.

Once more I was back in my grandmother's room, sitting with my shawl about me, even as I had on the day of her death. There she was also, but no pillows backed her now. She sat proudly erect, her eyes holding mine. Though her pale lips did not move, there was that in her gaze which was urgent, demanding, striving to tell me something. I was cold, not chilled by the room, but with an ice of fear which filled me, prevented me from speaking or moving.

Then the walls behind my grandmother's chair changed. From the familiar patterned paper I had always known, they showed gray—they were formed of stone blocks. There was no longer light from any window.

For the windows had narrowed into slits through which only pallid gleams reached us two. Still I sat and stared at my grandmother and she back at me, struggling, I knew, to communicate. I saw one hand rise from her lap, rise so slowly that it was manifest she put into that action the greatest of efforts, or the dregs of some fast-failing energy.

Between her white fingers swung a vividly black chain, moving slowly back and forth as might the pen-

dulum of a clock remorselessly counting out vital minutes, hours. I knew what she held was the string of
iron butterflies. Their delicate charm was lost, they
could be rather the silhouettes of ill-omened bats, or
some other creatures of an evil, haunted night.

So very slowly her hand moved, but the chain swung
faster and faster, until it was a whirling blur. Then it
flew free of her grasp—spun through the air toward
me, as if it were a knife blade aimed at my throat. Still
I could not move, or cry out, but was held in the vise
of that ice-cold fear. So great was the terror which now
filled me that I felt my heart could not continue to beat
but would burst apart in my breast.

I made the greatest effort of my life and somehow
brought up my arm, holding it as a shield against the
threatening whirl of the still-spinning chain. Only that
never touched my skin. Instead my eyes blinked open—
I lay looking up into the reaches of a vast dark cavern.

Chapter 3

Lying in a cavern? I was sweat drenched, tangled within
the heavy bedclothes of the great state bed. I turned
my head and saw, on what seemed a distant night table,
a guttering candle set in a safeguard which had the
form of a castle—or rather a tower—through the slit
windows of which shone the failing light.

The fire had near burned itself out, only a few dull

oals remained. I pulled up on the wide pillows, my hands at my throat, pushing aside the frill of my nightgown, rubbing the skin to assure myself that that whirling black of the butterflies had not struck.

My grandmother—no, even in the dream I was certain she had not flung that threat at me. The chain itself had appeared to take on purpose—She had been striving to warn—surely that was so!

Yet I needed no warning. I had been rash in coming here, too sure of myself. Now I had stepped outside all that I knew and understood. There was no one I could call upon. The Gräfin? I had no trust in her. The Gräf— had seen so little of him and what I had did not impress me. The Elector? A man about whom I really knew nothing good, with whom I had no bond except the accident of birth.

I clutched the edge of the bedclothes with my wet hands. My thoughts traveled on. What of Colonel Fenwick.

He was the Elector's man, a very loyal one—of that fact I could be entirely certain. So the Elector's wishes would rule with him.

My fingers slid beneath the pillows, closed upon the packet I had concealed there. There was a need to make sure that the necklace still lay in hiding. I was too fanciful, no piece of jewelry could do more than just induce a nightmare.

Packet in hand I slid across the vast surface of the bed and climbed out, my feet bare on the carpet of the dais on which it was enthroned. The season without these walls might be early summer now, but in this room the air of winter held with the fire near dead. I did not wait to pick up my robe, rather I went to that power-imprisoned candle, scorched my fingers lifting off the shield. That was of no moment now, I must assure myself the packet was intact.

The cord was firm. I picked at its knots, spread out the parchment, and then the roll of brocade. Even in this very limited light the necklace was startling clear.

I did not lift it from its soft bedding, only assured myself that this could never be the weapon I had dreamed it. Before this I had never considered myself burdened with a morbid imagination, yet at that moment nothing would have led me to place the circlet against my throat. Instead my mind dwelled upon that desperate appeal which I had read in my grandmother's eyes. A warning?

Such was pure superstition. Had I been so influenced by Letty that her lore of signs and potents was overriding good sense? I rewrapped the necklace, repacked it with that paper which made of me a Countess—a state I had no desire to grace—and padded back to bed.

Resolutely I pushed the packet once more beneath my pillow and forced myself to stretch out. I had not replaced the tower cover of the candle and I turned my head to watch that tiny beacon of light.

It was my firm intention to remain awake, not to summon any more dreams. But my tired body betrayed me and I do not know when I slipped once more into that place where nightmares lurked. However, those no more troubled me. Or, if they did, I did not remember them when I became aware that someone moved about not too far away and I opened my eyes to uncurtained windows and golden sunlight, warm and welcoming.

In that sunshine the room, which had appeared so filled with foreboding, was altered, though it lost none of its princely dignity. There were mirrors on some of the walls, their gilt frames as ornate as the leafy, flowered panels I had seen the night before. One corner was filled with a huge painted and tiled stove. A solid wardrobe faced it from across the room. Gilded cupids frolicked across that, and smaller ones formed the door handles.

The chamber was indeed a strange collection of old and new. The state bed was clearly of the past, several centuries past. While, save for a chair or two in the same massive style, the rest of the furniture was of a later date.

At a scratching sound from the door, Truda tripped

across my range of view to open that, take in a tray which she brought to one of the larger tables. It bore a silver pot of fanciful design, its handle being a queer dragon beast clinging to the side, its head raised to peer into the interior. The rest were covered dishes.

I had already washed in warm water, but I was still in my chamber robe as I seated myself to breakfast. Truda's answers to my attempts at friendly conversation were strained, nor did she ever look at me directly. I was not used to being so rebuffed, though I guessed that the proper custom here was to ignore the humanity of servants—to consider them only hands and feet to provide one with attention.

As I drank the thick chocolate Truda poured me, I wondered if their masters and mistresses must not sometimes appear to them as dolls, to be dressed and then set into another world altogether. Used as I was to the manor, where the most minute details of daily life were open and known, this stiff separation made me uneasy. Whereas Letty, as she bustled about my room, would have had a tongue busy with reports on a dozen or so small matters she deemed it necessary for me to know, this girl crept as noiselessly as possible, flushed when I spoke to her, took on a ghostlike character I found disturbing.

She had already unpacked my clothing, hanging my gowns in the wardrobe, dealing efficiently with my other belongings. Now she stood not too far away, ready to raise the cover from the plates, to display bread cut into finger-sized bites and already buttered, a small pot of dark red jam, a selection of pastries. I thought longingly of the good home-cured ham and other more sustaining viands which would have been served me usually, provider meant to sustain one through a busy day.

How did a Countess of the Holy Roman Empire spend her days? Certainly, I decided, not at a desk writing out a series of instructions to men of business, nor in riding around fields to check the crops, visiting dairy, kitchen, still room, the hands' quarters—all those duties I knew so well. Would boredom itself conquer my sense of duty? I was never meant to sit with idle hands and empty mind.

My watch reported the hour of nine. At home I would have been already two hours busy. But here— In my survey of the room I had not seen a single book, nor any other aid to finding employment.

Cup still in hand, I went to the nearest window, curious about Axelburg, or what I might see of it. I already knew from the Gräfin's chatter, that the Elector Adolf (my great-grandfather, that is) had torn apart with ruthless energy his ancestral palace and rebuilt it, by vast labor at untold expense, in the style of an inferior cópy of Versailles, so that it stretched out from the old city (the VERY old city) in the form of a fan.

This morning I could see beyond a cluster of gabled roofs and some towers which must mark churches the rise of the palace. Notable as a part of that were two towers, totally at odds with the rest of the roofline, one at either end of the structure.

Those were all that remained of the original building and the Gräfin had explained the reason for their survival. Elector Adolf—though he had prided himself on foward-looking views and had patronized several men of the newer learning—had also sheltered a certain Count Ladislaw Varkoff of mysterious origin. He had acted the part of the Elector's private prophet and several of his predictions had proven surprisingly accurate. His main claim to fame had been a stern warning that, were either of the ancient watchtowers of the previous castle-palace destroyed, the ruling family of Hesse-Dohna itself would come to an abrupt end. Thus the towers remained to frown at the frivolities which the Elector used to decorate his new home.

The Gräfin had pointed out that my grandfather's gutting of the interior of the west tower had indeed been followed by the death of his only direct heir. Now the rule would pass to a cadet House of supposedly inferior standing.

I became aware of Truda hovering nearby and asked what she wanted.

"What gown does the gracious and highborn lady desire? The Gräfin awaits her in the gold room—" This was the longest speech she had made and one she voiced so hurriedly that her words slurred. I half expected her to give a visible sigh of relief as she ended.

What gown indeed? For the first time I seriously considered the contents of that wardrobe. Though my grandmother had made a point of seeing that we were dressed in the best of fashion available, by the time any style found its way from Paris or London to Baltimore it was already probably well out of date. Judging by the Gräfin's daily wear, I already appeared most drab and dowdy. I had not missed the glances she had turned upon me when she believed herself unobserved. However, I had no intention of spending any of my guarded secret store of money on dress. I could use my plea of being still in mourning to cover my deficiencies yet awhile.

"The gray silk with the lilac ribbons—"

Now I was sure of Truda's questioning side glance.

"I am in mourning," I said flatly. Perhaps the highborn ladies of her experience would have given no explanation, but such came natural to me. There were times in the past when I had had heated arguments with Letty over the suitability of this or that gown.

The gray silk was produced and I had some difficulty in persuading Truda I was not a doll to be dressed but could put on garments by my own efforts. The gown was indeed plain, with a ruffle of discreet lace high about my throat and only a procession of small, precise bows down the bodice, and narrow puffed-ribbon banding to weight the flare of the skirt. In this stately room I was now a stray from another world, perhaps a humble governess peering daringly into the mirrors of her mistress.

Under my orders Truda coiled up my hair in the sensible crown of braids I always wore. My reflection told me I looked neat and respectable. Only, was either term the proper one to be applied to the granddaughter of a ruling prince? Neatness was a virtue, but respectability in my present surrounding was, by the Gräfin's hints and lively comments, not an attribute much cultivated at court.

A lackey, with powdered hair and a crested coat bearing bunches of ribbons on either shoulder, bowed me out and ushered me as a guide though several corridors, down the main flight of stairs again, to bring me at last to a door he threw open with a flourish.

The sun was very bright across a thickly beflowered carpet which set a whole garden underfoot. There was no gloom here, the furniture was all white and gold, covered with golden velvet. The carvings on the wall panels had also been gilded, so that the wreaths of impossibly plump fruits glittered.

In contrast to the spill of brilliance around her the Gräfin appeared in a light shade of blue. To my eyes that dress was more elaborate than any which might have been worn to a Maryland ball. The neckline was very low and the guimpe which filled it was only a hint of modest covering, being of a fine net which concealed nothing of the rise of her full breasts.

She wore a heavy necklace over this gauzy shield and there were jeweled drops in her ears. In addition a sparkling buckle latched a ribbon belt which accented the smallness of her waist, meant also, I presumed, to draw attention to those higher mounds where nature had been so generous. To my eyes there was a vulgarity in such a show which made me vow inwardly that if she represented the high fashion of Hesse-Dohna, then I would remain a dowd by choice.

"Dear Countess!" She jumped up as might a vivacious girl, hurrying toward me with both hands outstretched, as if I were her dearest friend. I did not miss the shadow of dismay in the blue eyes which surveyed me from head to foot. "I trust you rested well. Does Truda satisfy you? She has been well instructed, I assure you. She knows even the latest styles of hair dressing—"

"She is most deft and pleasant." I could not escape the stab of irritation at that suggestion that I was no good advertisement of Truda's skills. "But, as you must remember, Gräfin, I am in mourning—"

"But you cannot keep to that—not here!" Her sharp protest startled me. "It is not the way of the court. Private mourning must not exist when one goes into public. You will come to understand our ways soon."

"When I meet the Elector?" I wanted to know just how soon I could carry out the purpose which had brought me here. "Just when can that be arranged, Gräfin?"

"Please," she pouted, "let us not be always so stiff with one another. We are kinswomen, I want us to be friends also. Let me be Luise—not always 'Gräfin.' It will be so pleasant, as you shall see. His Highness"—her face turned sober—"your meeting with him must be most carefully arranged. He is ill, his doctors forbid excitement for him. There are others who might make trouble. We must wait—"

Her words now did not agree with what Colonel Fenwick had told me of the need for haste, his insistence that the Elector's health was so precarious that I must travel at bone-racking speed to reach the bedside of a dying man before it was too late. I had not seen the Colonel since my arrival. Of course he was not a member of this household, but I had thought that he would keep in closer communication with me—some message— It struck me then that I had no idea at all how I might get in touch with him should the need arise.

"We shall be told at once when it is possible," the Gräfin continued. "This is a most private matter, you understand. Only a very few people close to the Elector know of his earlier marriage at all—fewer still that he has moved now to have it declared a legal morganatic one—"

I looked at her steadily. "By the laws of my country

he has had only *one* legal marriage—that which united him to my grandmother. My father was his single legal heir—"

The Gräfin threw up her plump white hands in a gesture which might express either surprise, or some exasperation at my dullness. "The laws of your country mean nothing here, that you must understand. Also"— there was a very distinct sharpness in her tone—"there are those who would not wish the Elector to show any favor, even at this late date to—" She hesitated.

"A dubious descendant?" I finished for her.

"But that you truly are not—you are of the Blood!" She nodded her head emphatically. "Has not the Elector already procured for you the title of Countess of the Empire? As such you can take a high position. But you have to fear the will of the Princess Adelaide. She is his only remaining daughter, and she never married. She was too much of a Wittlesbach to take a lesser match than a ruling prince, and no greater one was offered. Though"—she laughed maliciously—"when they hastened to marry off King George's sons so that there might be a heir, she fancied her right to be one of those choices. Now she has consoled herself with religion and has been appointed Lady Abbess of Guern— though she spends more time at court striving, as she avers, to convert her father to pious ways, than she does at her abbey."

I wondered why the Gräfin had never been moved during her babbling concerning the court to mention before this particular obstacle in my path. I was about to break my self-imposed rule of not asking blunt questions when the door of the golden room opened and one of the lackeys announced:

"Baron von Werthern."

The man, who entered with the ease of one perfectly at home, indeed bore some resemblance to that miniature the Gräfin had so coyly displayed. But the artist had flattered him by thinning down the pouchiness of his jowls, setting his small eyes farther apart. He might be termed good-looking, or possibly so—in a coarse

42

way; and he carried his thick body with more grace than one would expect. Also the uniform he wore lent him eye-catching attention. He crossed the room in a stride far heavier than that of Colonel Fenwick and raised the Gräfin's hand to thick lips.

"Konrad! But we thought you on maneuvers." She became all fluttering eyelashes and smiles. "What a magnificent surprise!"

Surprise it was not, I was sure. She was already turning to me.

"Gräfin von Harrach, may I present Baron Konrad von Werthern." She spoke as if calling my attention to some treasure as great as any guarded in the Elector's famous tower.

"Gracious lady." Now he bowed to me. His English was guttural, far more accented than the Gräfin's. "We have been waiting impatiently for your arrival."

I curtsied as I would to any gentleman upon introduction. But I did not extend my hand. I felt distaste at the very thought of having his lips touch my flesh. He was eyeing me in a bold way which I disliked almost as much.

Having lived most of my life in such a reclusive fashion, I had very little knowledge of the ways of men, and I certainly never expected to awaken instant admiration in a stranger. Neither had I thought to be surveyed as if I were a slave on an auction block—which was the only way I could describe the look which the Baron turned on me. I withdrew to the settee and met that stare coolly with I hoped some of my grandmother's quelling cast of countenance.

The Gräfin broke into feverish chatter, as if the result of this introduction was not what she had expected. Did she believe her friend so completely overpowering in his person that I would goggle at him bemused? I was perplexed now as to whether it would be considered the discreet action for me to withdraw, leaving her to entertain her favored guest in private.

Before I could put my desire into effect, as if she sensed my intention, she was on the settee beside me,

43

one of my hands caught in hers as an anchorage. Perhaps I was to serve as a chaperon, or maybe it was my drabness she desired to enhance her own sparkling affinity with that vividly bright room!

I was given little time to dwell on either suggestion, for the Baron deliberately moved a chair close to *my* side of the settee, seating himself, and leaning a little forward to address a series of pompous and dull questions.

Had I found our traveling unduly fatiguing? What was my impression of Axelburg? Each time he waited for my reply as an instructor might wait for the proper answer from a dull pupil. I was certain that he was playing some sort of a role and his real emotion was that of boredom. The Gräfin kept glancing from one to the other of us as she might watch some absorbing action in a play. Nor did she appear in the least irritated that her cavalier was focusing his full attention on me.

I replied shortly concerning the bare facts of our journey. As for Axelburg, I spoke the entire truth.

"Of that, sir, I have seen so little I have not gained any reliable impression of it."

He appeared to brighten a little. "That can be changed, Countess. It would give me, for one, the greatest of pleasures to make known to you our city. A city of which we are justly proud." His stilted speech had the ring of sarcasm to me, and I did not like the way he kept leaning farther and farther forward in his seat as if to give the impression that we two were speaking privately. I felt rather than saw Gräfin Luise stir. Was she now about to call her cavalier back to his rightful allegiance?

"It would be of all things a great pleasure for you, Amelia." (For the first time she used my name familiarly and I resented it.) "So we shall arrange it. But, of course, not at present. Remember Konrad, the Countess von Harrach must remain in—or rather shall we say stay here quietly—until she has been received by His Highness and his will be known."

It came to me as sharply then as if the gemmed dagger ornament which pinned up the Gräfin's tall top-knot of curls had been drawn and presented as a weapon in truth. Foolishly I had walked into this house, this city—this—*trap!*

I had been so intent upon my own reasons for coming here that I had never, until this moment, seen what might lie on the other side of my plan. This was a strange country in which I was unknown, of which I was ignorant. Could I accept *anything* which had been told me? Perhaps in parts—to someone— The Elector—maybe—I was of value, or Colonel Fenwick and the von Zreibrukens would not have been dispatched to bring me. But had I value as a tool, a piece to be played in some intrigue? My first fear was heated by slow anger—not only at those about me—but at myself—and my folly. I had to use full control not to rise and go to the door, strive to pass through it and out of this old house, just to see if I could in truth be allowed that freedom. Out of my gathering anger I answered the Gräfin with all the care I could summon and in the calmest tone I knew.

"Since I am unknown, what would it matter? If I chose to see something of the city, who would recognize me?" It was a test question, the best I could devise at such short notice.

I saw the edge of her white teeth show as they closed for a second or two on her full underlip. She gave the appearance of one thinking deeply, but not as if my suspicions had any roots.

Then she laughed. "But you speak the truth, Amelia! Who indeed would recognize you here. It is true, is it not, Konrad, that our secret has been very well kept? That you have heard no rumors, no speculations? Has that hen-witted lady who waits on our Reverend Abbess asked any questions lately? You will discover, Amelia"—she swung back to me, not waiting for any answers from him—"that the court lives on rumors as hungry men seize upon meat. Dullness is our greatest burden, we hold it at bay with tittle-tattle, whether it

45

be true or not. A story can run the length of the city as swiftly as a swallow flies. So—Konrad, reassure us— what has been said—what may you have heard?"

He smiled. "Ah, Luise, there is no rumor as yet. The secret has been so well kept that I could almost be led to believe that someone has invoked the aid of a potent hexenmeister to seal lips—"

She shivered and, to my surprise, looked decidedly sober and shaken, even if this was the very answer she had wanted, but the Baron was continuing.

"It is truly accepted by all that our so-worthy Colonel was summoned to attend a dying kinsman in the land from which his family was exiled, while you and the Gräf went south to consult a noted physician concerning his gout. You, at least, have been sorely missed, dear lady, the dullness of which you have just complained has been like a gray cloud in our sky. I will not deny there have been some—shall we say—speculations, which as a gentleman I could not think of repeating to you. But of your real errand no, no hint at all!" He had begun his speech in a tone which might have been meant to be lumbering playfulness, but his ending was soberly emphatic, and he was gazing earnestly at the Gräfin as if it was very important that she believe his reassurance.

She put on her lighthearted airs again. "So—then if I have brought a new-made friend back with me, why should it not be right and proper for me to show her some of the sights? If my friend is in mourning, she will not be expected to accompany me into society as yet. Does it not arrange itself to our wishes after all?"

"Well enough." But the Baron did not smile. "However, it is to be wondered what the worthy Colonel might say to your plans."

"Him!" She snapped her fingers. "What can he do if we say nothing about our desire but simply do as we wish? He would not dare to draw attention to us outside, lest that which he is pledged to keep secret does become a matter upon which the gossipers remark. Always he has been one to take too much on himself,

46

nd more since the Elector has recently shown even
more dependence on him. Tell me why, Konrad." Her
voice had the bite of annoyance now. "How and why
his—this foreign adventurer, who is no more than a
mercenary, a hireling, if one speaks the full truth, has
become so great an intimate of His Highness? You
poke of a hexenmeister just now, I tell you this one
eems to possess such powers!"

"It remains"—the Baron's voice was heavy, and now
a little cold, as if he had no liking for her frankness—
that the Colonel does have the full favor of the Elector.
You know what efforts the Abbess has made in the
past, and, before her, Her Highness, the late Electress,
o deny him the confidence of His Highness. What came
f all their intriguing, save smarting defeat? As long
as he holds his position of trust, you would not be wise
o cross him in any matter."

I felt as if they had forgotten me, and I listened
agerly to learn, even from their tones, some hint of
hings I must learn. So Colonel Fenwick was currently
n the highest favor—but he was not liked by these
wo. Also he had had and did have other enemies. Was
he fact that I had been brought to Axelburg a move
n the Colonel's game, someone to be used to make
ertain his own safety? His master might well have
ent him, but once here—what part did or could the
Colonel devise for me?

If he understood he was so disliked, and he must—
or I knew he was not a fool—why had he chosen the
Gräfin to be my companion? Or had she, on the other
and, been the selection of another and he given no
hoice concerning that?

Luise had claimed kinship with me, and with the
Elector, even though it rested on no legal relationship.
She had never, during all her gossiping, spoken of the
Elector himself except with the most respect, plain as
he had been about his late wife and his daughter.

I clasped my hands very tightly together, as I had
n my first meeting with the Colonel, hoped that my
ace might hold no more than a look of inquiry or polite

interest. I was not made for intrigue. It frightened, then angered me again. I held to that anger as a sailor might hold to a lifeline. For from it I knew now I could draw strength. From this moment I must think mainly of myself, of what I could do to walk safely through a maze of what might be both doubt and deceit.

Chapter 4

*The Gräfin sat up straighter, her rounded chin ex-*pressed, to my eyes, a shadow of sullen obstinacy.

"The Colonel has not seen fit to favor us with any attention since our arrival. I do not think that he would dare to say that we must stay within our own house— if we make no great parade of going out. But—yes—is it not perfect! Tomorrow is Liberation Day and the treasure tower is then open to respectable visitors. Or has the illness of His Highness altered that custom?" She appealed to the Baron.

"There has been no edict to that fact—"

"Then we shall go! Oh, not in a marked carriage. Also, we shall dress as plain as any burgomeister's family—you shall see!" She laughed. "Amelia and I shall be two good friends from the country—wide-eyed provincials, a little dazzled by all the splendors of Axelburg. I shall not even take Katrine. She is too well known, having carried messages for me these many years. No, nor shall you go with us, Konrad"—her eyes resumed a flirtive side glance—"for you could not possibly hide in any coat sober enough to make you nameless. Just the two of us—for who will expect ladies of rank to be without attendants?—thus we can pass as country cousins, open-mouthed and eyed.

"And, Amelia, it is to be above all things a real adventure! There is always a crowd of the common sort—town worthies and the like—who bring their stodgy relatives to see the wonders. We shall go in the early afternoon when the press is the greatest. You must see the sights of Hesse-Dohna, especially the Great Treasure!"

To me such an expedition was more than just a chance to view my grandfather's collection. Now I would be able to learn what lay beyond these walls. If there might be any way to help myself to some independence, it could only lie through such knowledge.

"I do not like the idea—" the Baron began.

"Only because you cannot be a part of it. Confess it, Konrad, is that not the truth? What harm can come from what we would do? No other one but Fenwick has seen the Countess, and I shall myself take such care not to be recognized as you will not believe!" She touched the tip of her upturned nose. "Shall I even set a wart here, Konrad, pencil a wrinkle here and here?" The finger now sped from the corner of one eye to the other. "Oh, I shall put on years, and Amelia might even be my daughter. It is a famous plan!"

She gave a little bound on the settee—like a school girl envisioning a picnic. Some of the overflow of her mood reached me—enough to make me eager to try the venture for more reasons than one.

The Gräfin's idea of disguise appeared mainly to be the forsaking of a riotously plumed bonnet for one trimmed with a cluster of ribbon loops and a quite large nosegay of flowers. Her muslin dress (for the day turned out to be overwarm) was sprigged and beruffled wherever there was space for any trimming to be applied.

Seated beside her, my far more simple white dress with only black ribbon trimming and a straw cottage bonnet, I might well have presented the appearance of a superior servant, perhaps even a personal maid.

Save that here in Hesse-Dohna even Katrine went clad in what could only be a form of peasant dress, full skirted, aproned, and with a blouse worked in bands of blue and red stitchery. Out of the carriage window I now saw many versions of this same garb. The stitchery might vary in color and pattern, the skirt be slightly longer or shorter, hair might be braided with ribbons, lying across the shoulders, or else drawn severely up, to be hidden under a tall muslin cap which had a close resemblance to the helmet of a grenadier.

We did not travel in a crested carriage—as the Gräfin had promised—rather in a small, plain barouch. The trip was necessarily a slow one, since the streets of Axelburg were, for the most part, narrow, the pavement cobbled; so we jolted about, and both of us needed to keep a firm grip on looped sidestraps at hand's reach.

Many of the houses were picked out with colored paint, dabbed either over the carving which edged the eaves and framed doors and windows, or on the walls themselves. Such had faded, but the brilliant sunlight brought it back to life, while many of the buildings we rocked by possessed flower boxes set along upper window sills, filled with blooms.

Yet, in spite of all this color, there was something overawingly ancient about those houses, a strangeness which hinted to me of a darker past. I did not know what made that particular fantasy grow in my mind. However, once it had, I was able to sight the sooner the grotesque bits of carving which were ugly—leering, fanged faces, twisted bodies, beasts such as certainly never had walked this earth, save through the troubled nightmare of those who slept ill.

Our coachman continually cried out hoarsely, cracking out with his whip, to clear our passage. Now and then the Gräfin caught at my arm, raising her voice to be heard above his clamor so she might call my attention to this or that landmark. There were even two churches so imposing that they might well claim the distinction of cathedrals.

The larger was also carved and adorned with all manner of elaborate stonework. It stood in a market square, and because of the throng gathered there, we could not approach it closely. To my surprise, the carriage halted and the Gräfin loosed her hold on the strap to point to the taller of the church's towers.

What she might be saying was lost in a sudden clamor of bells. A door high up on the wall of the tower opened and along an outside ledge there marched a procession of small figures. At least those appeared small from where we sat, but they must have been of respectable size or we would not have seen them at all. First came a knight in heavy armor, his head hidden by a helm on which crouched a mythical beast. One hand held the reins of his mount, but looped in the other, which had fallen to his side, were a number of chains. These trailed out behind him dragging a group of prisoners. By their odd garb and headgear they appeared to be of another nationality or even race than their conqueror. Some tottered as men might who were close to the end of their strength. Others crept on hands and knees, the artist who had portrayed them being a master at conveying their helpless agony.

Forward went the horseman, behind him dragged the captives, while the bells tolled, seeming more to suggest an overwhelming defeat than a triumph. Another door opened and the procession vanished within it. The Gräfin looked at me proudly.

"The Prince Axel," she announced, "our own ancestor. So he returned from battle when the infidels threatened Hesse-Dohna long ago. Our people do not forget. He was a great prince, we have much to be proud that we share his blood." There was pride mirrored in her face. The spectacle over, she rapped the edge of the driver's seat with her parasol and we drove on.

"This is Axel's city, much of it arose by his order. He had the Kriche of the Captives built—it took most of his lifetime before the last stone was laid. It was his grandson who brought a man from Nuremburg to make the Prince's procession so his great deeds would never be forgotten. The Princes of our house are all buried in the crypt and only royal brides can be married there."

"A most unusual sight," I commented, but thought to myself that the unknown artist had certainly emphasized the cruelty of the times in his treatment of the captives.

There was the beginning of a frown on the Gräfin's face.

"How strange you must be—you people of the colonies. Does no feeling of pride rise in you seeing evidence of the greatness from which you spring?"

"There are no longer American colonies," I returned sharply. "We are a nation free of any foreign tie—"

"Ah, now I have, as some say, trod upon your toes! But, Amelia, this is now your home, is that not so? Do you not feel a part of it?" She made a sweeping gesture with one hand. "So sober you always are! Look, is not this a pleasure to the eye. See the flowers, the happy faces—listen, there is singing!"

We were almost out of the confusion of the market square, and I had to admit that the color, the air of festivity did impress me, in spite of my struggle to remain an onlooker only. Seated on benches outside an obvious tavern, some young men were singing lustily a roaring air which did touch some emotion, so I could imagine soldiers marching from a victory.

"A war song—" I spoke my impression aloud.

The Gräfin nodded. "It speaks of the Fatherland, of battles fought and won. Does it not make the blood race—even if one is only a female? Ah, now our ride becomes more smooth—"

Our carriage had emerged from the older part of town onto a wide avenue where the pavement was meant for faster travel. Before us spread the fan of the palace, its windows glittering in the sun, a spread of formal garden edging it with green behind a fencing of fanciful wrought iron. A wide gate faced the avenue down which we, and a number of other carriages proceeded. Only one leaf of that was not open and I remembered another scrap of custom—only a reigning prince himself could drive through a completely open gate, or enter double doors with both thrown wide at once to admit his august presence.

We did not head for the impressive great entrance of the main block of the palace, but turned right, to where the East Tower raised against the blue of the sky. Seen closer, that remnant of a dangerous and rougher past looked even more out of keeping.

The rudely dressed stone of the walls did not match with the formal grace which had been wedded to it. It remained a grim reminder suggesting dungeons, darkness— Again I felt the fleeting touch of fear. Part of my dream flashed into mind—the cover of the nightlight in my bedroom—had it not been fashioned in a shape not unlike the tower?

Gathered around the door was the crowd the Gräfin had foreseen, the bright scarlet jackets of sentries standing out here and there. It was, of course, folly to think I might see Colonel Fenwick here. Yet for a moment I had the oddest wish that one of those brilliant coats might be his, and he would be waiting for us.

In spite of all her frills and curls it was perfectly true that the Gräfin would attract no attention. For a number of the females were tricked out in even more elaborate costumes. My own plain garb was far more noticeable, though I saw others in the line formed to be admitted who were no more fashionable than I.

As the line of sightseers made a decorous way between the soldiers and into the interior of the tower, we stepped from the brilliance of day into a dazzle of another light. By the aid of this it was easy to see the Elector did possess more than one kind of protection for his treasure house, willing though he might be for his subjects to come and admire.

The slit windows of the room had been closed with sheets of metal very closely fitted to the old stone. Before these, as well as on brackets of fanciful design all along the walls, were set burning lamps. There were so many of these they rivaled the sun outside.

Also our passage was limited to a confined space by walls of bars, unpleasantly suggesting, in spite of the fact they were gilded, those of a prison cell. Behind these on either side appeared the first examples of the "treasure."

These objects were more appropriate to the general setting than those other fabulous rooms the Gräfin had described to me. For here, on mounted stands, was armor certainly never intended to be worn in actual combat, for it was so inlaid with gold and set with gems as to seem fitting only for use on state occasions by some fairy tale prince. There were display racks of swords, the hilts of which sparkled with jewels, the scabbards wrought of gold and more gleaming stones. Nor were pistols and guns missing, though again they were begemmed masterpieces of inlay. Helmets, which more resembled crowns than protective covering for a fighter, were mounted on dead-eyed marble busts. It was as if danger could only be faced by the rulers of Hesse-Dohna when they wore their ransoms on their persons.

The number of burning lamps and the crowding of the spectators so heated the room, I felt a breathless desire to gain more air. However, there was no turning back, for more ranks of visitors shuffled on one's heels. I strove to push away not only the sense of imprisonment which gripped me, but to reach the foot of the stair ahead.

It seemed the Gräfin found little here worth her attention and by some nimbleness of foot we began to climb, to come out once more on a bar-walled corridor down the middle of a chamber of red and gold walls, the famous lacquer room.

The passage was much narrower here, and once or twice the Gräfin fell a little behind. I could see already that visitors could proceed no farther today, for, though there was another stair, that had been closed off by a grill gate. When the sightseers reached that point they went to the left, through an archway which much connect with the palace itself.

The Gräfin plucked at my sleeve, slowing my pace. At that moment I wanted nothing more than to be out of this place. But she continued to urge that I look at this or that wonder. In other circumstances I might well have lingered by my own desire. But the precious objects seemed to me to be so crowded together, the heat of the lamps so great, that I felt both blinded and stifled. I had only a confused impression of cups and coffers cut in strange forms out of crystal or malachite, or even more precious materials, so embellished by further ornamentation that what lay beneath was three-quarters hidden. There were strange, even grotesquely ugly figures fashioned in the same way. Far too much to remember or enjoy looking at. In fact the whole display impressed me with being as tasteless as the beplumed bonnets the Gräfin delighted in.

Just before we reached the grill gate where all must turn, we did come upon something which caught my eye and slowed my steps, bringing from me a gasp of pure wonder.

A wide table stood just behind the bar wall and it was backed by a series of mirrors to amplify and repeat what lay before them until one could believe that one had been transformed to the size of a giant now viewing a miniature scene of real life.

Plainly a court had been duplicated in full magnificence. Enameled and begemmed figures, so gracefully and intricately made, so expressive in their tiny faces as to suggest that each was a replica of a living person executed by a master artist, had their places there. On a dais under a crimson canopy there were two thrones, each holding a seated figure. That of a man had his head turned toward his companion, one hand raised to beckon to several others who stood below the steps of the throne platform. Each of these bore either a cushion or a tray on which rested, in minute detail, tiny jewelry, boxes, crystal carvings.

The woman to whom this array of gifts was being offered wore, in beautiful cream and gold-tinted enamel, a faithful representation of the court dress of more than a hundred years earlier. Her small face had a proud, almost sullen cast (how very gifted had been the man who had fashioned her figure, for I felt that I would have recognized her immediately had I met her in life). She sat with her hands lying loosely on the golden billows of her full skirt. A stomacher of diamonds, so small that they could only have been chips of chips, was only part of her jewels. There was a circlet of delicate filigree, set with the same stones, on her fair head, a necklace about her long throat, lying across shoulders and breast nearly bare in the extreme décolleté fashion of that day.

Below the two rulers, and beyond those bearing gifts, were gathered members of the court, plus soldiers at stiff attention. However, one was hardly aware of them, for one's eyes returned to the two on the thrones. There was something oddly appealing in the attitude of the man. His shoulder-length curled hair fell forward but did not entirely shadow his face. If the woman was perfect in her frozen poise of boredom, the artist had not so flattered the king or prince. His features were harsh, and again must have been faithful representation of a once-living man. I had a queer feeling that though he was attempting to win his lady with gifts (perhaps he had already learned the unpleasant lesson that she was best so approached), he was clumsy and maladroit, that he was unhappy and to be pitied. It was so real—this miniature court—

Again the Gräfin tugged at my arm. "The birthday of the Electress Ludovika." Her voice pulled me out of the fantasy which had begun to build within my mind. "Her last birthday—"

"Did she die so young—?"

The Gräfin's hold upon my arm became a pinch, so hurtful I gasped. She did not let go but rather pushed me past the table. I could not shake free without arousing the attention of those about us. She, too, glanced hurriedly right and left, as if she had feared my innocent question had been overheard.

We had reached the turn point at the stair gate and I caught a glimpse of movement beyond that. As I looked more intently at the barrier I met eyes I knew. Colonel Fenwick, wearing a most elaborate uniform jacket, in spite of the heat a befurred dolman slung cloaklike over one shoulder, stood there. His hand went up on the grill as if he wanted to jerk it open, and the look on his face was so grim that it startled me as much as had the pinch the Gräfin had delivered. There was no mistaking his anger.

But he did not speak, and I had no intention of doing so. I hurried past, propelled by the urging of my companion, into a side corridor. Here were no bars to keep us in line and the crowd thinned out, so we walked a little apart. I made an effort and disengaged myself from the Gräfin's clutch.

"What is the matter?" I demanded with some force. Had she seen the Colonel? I believed not, at least she had given no sign of having done so.

Instead she looked about her, as if fearing notice still. Then she shook her head emphatically, so that I gathered I was not going to receive any answer at present, though perversely I determined upon having one. There was something about that fantastic court display which seemed to have disturbed her—or else my question had. Yet that had been the most common and reasonable one. The Gräfin had announced that it was the scene of some Electress's last birthday. But the woman on the throne had been quite young—so she must have died. How could a fact which must lie a hundred years or more in the past seem so upsetting?

I was certain by now she had not sighted the Colonel. No, she had been so intent on getting me away that she had never glanced toward the gated stairway. The colonel himself? His anger had been plain—I could almost have said I felt the flame of it through his gaze at me. He had been both surprised and furious at our appearance there.

We wasted no time strolling through that portion of the gardens which had also been opened to the public on this holiday. Once we were in the carriage, though the horses had to be kept to a walk, such was a press of the crowd, I turned to the Gräfin and asked with firmness:

"What happened?"

She did not pretend not to understand, but she was very sober of face. I think at that moment she wished nothing more than to forget my question. Since it was plain that I must have a reply, she said after a long pause.

"To speak of the Electress's death—that is not done—ever! Any one hearing you ask such a question would know you were not of Hesse-Dohna. Her story—it is very well known—it is retold to every girl—it is flung into the face of every wife by her husband sometime during marriage as a warning—a dreadful warning—"

The Gräfin was very serious, more so than I had ever remembered having seen her since our first meeting.

"She was very beautiful, the Electress Ludovika. It was well know that her marriage to Konrad-Axel was not of her choosing. He was a soldier, a man who cared nothing for the things she enjoyed. He was older, not handsome, nor soft and charming of speech. To him she was all beauty and goodness, though anyone with true sight could see that she hated him, hated Hesse-Dohna, longed only to escape.

"It was said that she dared to exile him from her bed, using the assurance of her physician, or her favorite lady, that she ailed. But she was also a woman of strong passions, you understand. What she would not give the Elector, as was her duty, she granted elsewhere. This, too, was a whisper which grew louder and louder.

"She had her creatures, also, people who kept to the shadows, who obeyed only her orders, no matter what those might be. Twice those in high places who would have opened the Elector's eyes died—very quickly and
58

not without pain. It was said that one of her people was a true hexenmeister and knew not only powers of evil he could summon to protect her, but worse lore—that of vile plants and other substances which could kill. So she went her own way, doing as she wished. The Elector was much away with his troops and did not know.

"At last she grew so free of any fear of him that she openly took, before all the court, a new favorite. He was an Italian, a worker in gold—not even of noble birth. It was he who fashioned that birthday scene. They say that he was so handsome that common women thought him an angel come out of heaven. But it was also true he did not want the Electress's favor, he had a wife which he loved. Then that wife died.

"Perhaps losing her sent him mad, or else, as it was afterward hinted, the Electress had him fed a potion which was to bring him to her bed, but which, instead, disordered his wits. For when the Elector returned from his campaign, this man sought him out and told his story. At first Konrad-Axel deemed him only a madman and would have had him shot for besmirching the name of his lady. But others, having gathered courage, added to the goldsmith's story. He died, yes, but his story did not die.

"The Elector moved quickly. His men, soldiers loyal to him, not corrupted by the fears of the court, took prisoner all the Electress's creatures in a single night and put them to the question. Under such torture they broke and spoke of murder and evil, though the hexenmeister was defiant to the last and died cursing Konrad-Axel when they burned him for the warlock he proudly said he was.

"Ludovika, screaming, was dragged from her apartments in the palace. She could not be put to death, though she was certainly a murderess many times over. But her birth was too high, she had kinsmen the Elector could not stand against should they choose to defend her. Thus he passed a sentence of death-in-life on her. They took her to the fortress castle of Wallenstein and therein she disappeared from the world. Outside the walls below one tower they built a scaffold as a warning that she was dead for her crimes as far as the world was concerned."

I shivered. It was a story which held a kind of horror and the Gräfin repeated it in a voice lacking her usual affections, rather as if she were reciting something she had memorized from some roll written long ago.

"But why did the Elector keep that scene, reminding himself and all who saw it? I should have thought he would have had it destroyed!"

"Not so! He very much wanted that the memory of her would be kept ever before himself and his people as a warning. It was to him a pledge of justice that not even one who was royal was above punishment. His marriage with Ludovika was dissolved. He married again—he must have an heir. But when his new wife came to him he kept the birthday scene on a table in her chamber, so she must look upon it daily. However, she was of another nature and such a lesson was not needed, for she was a Wratenburg of a most pious line. In her time all the pleasures of the court disappeared and they say that all who were in the palace went to church once a day and kept Lent at the table near all year round."

"So now the scene is part of the treasure—"

The Gräfin did not make any comment. I wondered if a part of the tale she had just told had not carried an implication which might be striking home concerning her own conduct. If she was, as I had come to suspect, unduly interested in the Baron, then perhaps the example of the fate of the murderous and adultrous Electress might well mean something more than an unpleasant story.

"They say she still walks—"

Her words broke through my train of thought— For a moment I did not catch their meaning. Then—a ghost! Surely in this enlightened age one did not believe in haunting! Such ideas could only be found in novels— say one of Mrs. Radcliffe's, with the bleeding nuns, secret passages, and skull-headed tormentors of beautiful and luckless heroines.

The Gräfin looked down at her hands and those were clasped so tightly that the kid of her gloves stretched dangerously taut across the knuckles.

"What did she feel?" My companion's voice was barely above a whisper, yet the words reached me over the clamor in the streets. "What did she think? Shut up there—in the dark and the cold?" The Gräfin shivered. "There was that sentry last year—Wallenstein is still partly garrisoned—and he swore he saw her face at the tower window. She dabbled in evil things. They say that she even had that hexenmeister to her bed and that is why he served her to the death. There were things she might have learned from him—"

I refused to allow such tales to disturb me. Though I could well believe that such stories might grow up about Wallenstein after the days of Ludovika. Witches had indeed been burned in this blood-soaked land—and there were other evil tales—of man-beast interchanges, for example. No, this was the nineteenth century! I refused to plunge back into the shadows of the past!

"She is long dead," I pointed out. "There are no witches. Come, Luise." I hesitated over her name but used it to draw her out of that strange mood which seemed to hold her. "You and I both know this is nonsense."

For a moment there was a sullen droop to her lips, as if she resented my common sense. Then she laughed.

"Yes, but you have not seen Wallenstein." Once more she shivered. "It is such a place as one can believe houses ghosts and witches. But—as you say, it is not of our concern. Tell me, Amelia, what did you think of the treasure? It is a pity we could not ascend to the silver room. Perhaps the Elector was visiting that today. They say that since his illness, he often has his chair wheeled along the upper corridors and sits sometimes for hours looking at his collection."

I thought of the Colonel on the stairway leading to the upper section of the tower. She might be right in that guess. So I had been that close to the grandfather I did not know? When would we ever really meet?

Chapter 5

It was as if the telling of the Electress Ludovika's story had in some manner changed my companion. Her usual vivacious chatter was stilled. She stared straight before her, not as if she saw outwardly at all, but rather regarded some grim picture her own thoughts supplied. By the time we had returned to the Von Zreibruken house she spoke only to plead a headache and left me in the great hall, wondering about the state of her own conscience.

I followed her upstairs at a slower pace and, as I put off my bonnet in the chamber, which, even in the full glow of the sun, had far too many lurking shadows, I looked into the somewhat cloudy surface of the dressing table mirror.

Not that my reflection interested me. Rather I was recalling the details of that marvelous work of art— the birthday of the Electress. The words the Gräfin had uttered haunted me. What *had* it meant for a woman so indulged and pampered, so sure of her charm and power to be immured for life in an ill-omened fortress? Perhaps execution would have been by far kinder. How long had she dragged out a miserable existence there, memory always with her? The shadows of this room here and now were in keeping with my thoughts, seemed to draw in closer behind me.

I must push aside such fancies! They were induced by this room, by Axelburg itself. These shadows might not be the ghosts of common ignorant report, but still they chilled one.

Resting my chin upon my fists, I resolutely fought my imagination. Until I had come here I had always believed myself a sensible person, not to be seduced by any fancy. Yet now—no, I was not some superstitious fool!

I would not look at shadows— My face in the mirror seemed overpale. Though why should that not be so? It had now been weeks since I had been in the full sun, riding out each day to oversee the manor work, having the healthy color of one living a well-regulated life. I reached through the slit in my skirt, seeking that inner pocket where I carried my packet. From it I freed the butterfly necklace.

The miniature Electress Ludovika had been offered gems beyond counting. I had only this chain of iron. On impulse I pulled loose the prim-cut, fine muslin collar set modestly about the throat of my dress. Rolling that back to an indecorous degree (such display of breast and shoulder as was no more than common with the Gräfin), I fastened the necklace. The chain showed very black against my skin, the filagree butterflies leaping to the eye as if they were real insects poised to fly at any moment. On the warmth of my breast and throat the metal felt cold and harsh, yet I did not remove it.

Rather I examined what I saw with an intent survey quite unlike my usual checking upon my clothing to make sure I was neat and properly attired. The sleeves of my dress ballooned properly, if not to the exaggerated width of the fashions I had seen this afternoon. My waist was small, my bell-shaped skirt flared. Perhaps this dull color did not become me—I might have looked better in rose or green—but that did not greatly matter.

Why—I saw my dark brows draw together in such a frown as a governess might turn upon some flighty miss in her charge—why was I now so conscious of my appearance? Was it that black chain about my throat, the pendant well down between the beginning curves of my breasts, which made me more aware of my shortcomings of person? I did not envy the Gräfin in the least—but I wished—

There was a flush rising on my too-pale cheeks. I would not allow myself to face what had caused that flicker of thought.

A scratching at the door startled me. I swung away from the mirror forgetting my disarray of clothing. At my call Truda came in. She dropped a curtsy as she said:

"Will the gracious lady be pleased to receive a visitor? He urges that it is very necessary that he speak with the Countess at once—"

She was plainly flustered, even a little apprehensive, as if she expected some blame in the matter. Nor did I need to be told the name of who waited me. Perhaps I had unconsciously been prepared for this ever since I returned to the house. I hurriedly rebuttoned my muslin collar, and stowed the packet away into hiding, I would wear the necklace, even in hiding. It seemed to me to be as much a pledge of identity as the parchment. Yes, I would wear it now, not only to bolster my pride, but to build my courage. Head high, I went swiftly through corridors, down the stairs to the yellow room.

Colonel Fenwick did not stand by the window this time, and he was much more dramatic figure in his regimentals—still wearing the crimson and gold of his court uniform. However, above the stiff collar of his jacket his face was as grim as it had been when I had caught that sight of him in the palace. I wondered briefly if the Colonel ever did smile and what he would ook like if he were not always prepared to berate some unfortunate mortal for an error of judgment, behavior, or both.

"You have a message for me?" It could be that what he brought was the summons I had so ardently expected since my arrival in Axelburg.

"Whose idea was it for you to appear at the palace today?" He ignored my question, demanded an answer to one of his own. As if all which mattered in the world was his own affairs.

"Does it matter? There is no reason for my identity to be known here at present." I summoned my coolest tone. As usual his effect upon me was disturbing. My hand actually twitched. I realized, with amazement at my own feelings, that my first desire had been to slap his flint-hard face, make him aware of me—me, a person—not just a piece to be played in some royal intrigue. That realization of my wholly alien reaction shook me so I must have missed some of his reply.

"—your presence here is already known—where it may do the most harm! We do not know who is responsible for loosing that information, but this is a delicate business and must not be bungled. As long as the Elector remains so helpless and dependent upon others we have to take the greatest care." Now the Colonel went striding back and forth across the flower garden of the carpet, not regarding me at all.

I seated myself with what composure I was able to summon. Now that I believed I had my own strange emotions under control, I was better able to see that he was indeed greatly concerned. He ceased pacing and swung around.

"To have to depend wholly on others, and some he fears to trust. Do you realize what that can mean? A message can be circumvented, changed, conveniently forgotten—if it is given to the wrong person. There are those who would do anything to prevent his seeing you." He stopped and rubbed his fingers across his chin. Though his eyes were still on me, I was sure that I was not what he saw. Was he weighing in his mind some new revelation, or warning? As the silence lengthened I was uneasy enough to be the first to break it.

"Because of the treasure?" I wanted to add that I had no desire to possess what I had seen that day, that all that splendor had no meaning for me. It was too rich to belong to any one person. I could accept all my grandmother had willed me and take pride in my American possessions, for I understood them. But the vast wealth displayed in that tower was meaningless.

"The treasure." He repeated my last words with a contemptuous curl of lip which again made me tightly rein in my temper. "So that is it—you wished to see what might be your dazzling inheritance—"

I arose swiftly to face him. "There is no reason for such an exchange of unpleasantries between us, sir. It is plain you have come here for some definite purpose. If it was to berate me, then I question *your* authority to stand in judgment upon either my manners or my motives!"

One of his fists clenched tightly and I saw a muscle in his cheek twitch. His jaw was set as if restraining what I guessed might be an outbreak of a hot temper. Then, after another long moment of silence, his fingers uncurled and he shook his head. Again not at me, I believed, but at some thought.

"Countess." His words were chill and delivered with a formality which gave them extra weight. He could not be really doing what I had challenged him that he had come for—to deliver judgment—or was it in part a warning? "Countess, it is true that you cannot know what lies behind"—now he gave a quick glance around the room as if its pretty fripperies disgusted him—"the surface of what you have seen here. Let me make plain what is of the utmost importance—"

"Sir, I will be most obliged if you do or say what you have come to do." I made stiff reply.

His next move startled me, for, having sent a distinctly quelling look in my direction, he crossed the room, not with those exasperated strides which he had earlier made, but with a lightness of step I would not have thought possible. One hand closed on the latch of the door, and he actually set his right ear to the panels, plainly listening.

Back he came with the same noiseless tread, passed me to unfasten the long window giving on the outside. Then he gestured that I was to join him, stepping aside to wave me onto a balcony which overhung a small walled garden I had not even known existed. When we were both outside he closed the window door with a snap.

My antagonism had been momentarily lost in a need for understanding. It was plain that he believed we might be overheard or spied upon while inside. But if the Gräfin had been selected for my traveling companion and present chaperon, why should her home be a place of lurking suspicion?

"You have reason to mistrust anyone within this household, sir?"

His hand closed upon the balcony railing so close to mine that his cape-dolman brushed my shoulder.

"If you are wise, my lady," he spoke English now, "you will mistrust every place—and everyone—within Axelburg!"

"Including you, sir?"

He made no answer to that, instead he spoke swiftly, as if he must say the greatest number of words in the least possible time.

"I do not know what you may have been told of what is happening here. The Elector has had another stroke—it has left him speechless. What he would communicate he must write, convey by signs. As yet those about him are mainly wary and dare not contradict his orders—his direct orders. However, as I have said, much can be done to thwart him by misunderstanding, forgetting—As long as I have access to him, and he still insists that be so, his wishes can be carried out. There is a good chance that I may soon be barred from his presence.

"Have they said anything to you about the Princess Adelaide, she who was appointed an Abbess?"

"The Elector's daughter? Yes, the Gräfin spoke of her."

"She is attempting to take charge, has brought in two nursing sisters. They could keep him wholly incommunicado if she succeeds. She is still a little afraid of him—or his authority—and so far has not taken the final step. I am doing what I can to arrange a meeting for him with you. It must be very soon, he is failing. Perhaps even another day—or night—and he will be too sick to withstand those vultures—they will have him prisoner in his own apartments, every door guarded. Therefore we have decided upon tonight!"

"But how—do I just drive up to the palace—?"

He made one of those gestures of impatience I had come to know so well.

"Make some excuse—do not dine with the family. Have a headache—cannot all you females summon a headache at will?" His voice was as impatient as his hands. "I have a man under my command who comes from the same village as your maid, he knows her well. She will admit him. Wear a cloak with a hood, draw that up to hide you well. Kristopher will show you this." He twisted a ring on his finger so that I could see the dark red gem of its setting was carved intaglio with a design. "You will follow his instructions—"

This might be one of those improbable romantic novels, still I could see that he was entirely serious. I found myself actually nodding agreement, as if he had done no more than suggest a sedate ride through a park.

"And—" He pointed to my throat.

Remembering my recent experiments, my hands flew to my collar. It was still lacking the top two buttons closed, so that part of the necklace must be visible.

"Be sure, my lady," he was continuing, "that you wear that."

What did he know of the necklace which had been the hidden possession of my grandmother for so long? Or was it, like the ring Fenwick himself had just shown me, meant to be a passport of identification?

"Very well—"

He had not waited for my words of agreement. Instead he flung open the door behind us and, I think, would have manhandled me within with the same vigor which the Gräfin had used to draw me away from the display in the treasure tower had I not been more nimble in withdrawing into the parlor. He closed the balcony door not a moment too soon, for the opposite door opened and the Gräfin swept in.

Her full lips shaped a smile, but the eyes above those appeared to me both narrowed and watchful.

"Colonel Fenwick! I am most sorry I was not informed that you had come. I must speak most sharply to Franz for being so remiss—"

"Gracious lady," he dropped into the usage of the honorific terms, but there was, I believed, something mocking in that salutation. "I came here to inform you all that what was done today was most unwise. As you are well aware, the Countess"—he indicated me with the slightest of nods—"was not to appear in public until after His Highness made clear his decision concerning her. If you had been recognized—if you *were* recognized—who knows where this story has already spread."

She pouted, but I could have well told her that Colonel Fenwick was not the man to be impressed by any airs and graces. "No one save you, and I, and Ulrich, know she is here. Who could have known her for who she is?"

"You and the Gräf, *and* Baron von Werthern."

She turned her face a little away. For all the roundness of her chin its present lift expressed stubbornness and she passed him with deliberation to seat herself, folding her hands in her lap.

"Dear Konrad is my cousin, he is not only in the favor of His Highness, as well you know, Colonel, but he is also in a way kin to Amelia. He has shown the greatest discretion—and he was made aware of this matter some time ago."

"There are far too many aware," the Colonel snapped. "As for today—I have been sent with orders."

"And those? Also are they verbal only? It is said that

His Highness has suffered new afflictions and must now write his wishes. Do, for your own sake, make sure of any orders, Colonel, lest you be forced to answer for your actions at a later period—to those not at all sympathetic with your methods."

"The orders are from His Highness, you may take my word, or disregard that at your own peril." His voice was smooth and cold. "The Countess is to remain in seclusion until he gives instructions otherwise. There are to be no more such imprudent actions as that of today."

She glanced at him quickly and then away again.

"One will, of course, obey His Highness's commands. But when will Amelia be granted a meeting then?"

"That is His Highness's decision only," the Colonel replied quellingly. "By your leave, ladies." He sketched a bow which was hardly enough to express civility and was out of the door before the Gräfin could speak again. We heard now only the ring of his spurred boot heels on the floor of the hall without.

The Gräfin made a face. "Such a boor as he is! Or perhaps he wishes to show us how strong he thinks he may be against the day when the Elector can no longer protect him. What is Fenwick but an adventurer who sells his sword? Why does he believe he may stamp about ordering this and that as if we were conscripts on parade before him? Do not allow yourself to be disturbed by him, dear Amelia, he is not one of *us*, nor can he ever aspire to be more than he is today—a messenger. And soon he will be less—"

On her full underlip her pink tongue tip showed for an instant. I did not need much sensitivity to understand that strong emotions did abide under the Gräfin's doll-like surface and that some of these were concerned with Colonel Fenwick.

"It is strange—oh, do come and sit down here, my dear. You stand there so tall and straight-backed you also remind me now of the Colonel!" She patted the settee in invitation I thought better not to disregard. "Yes, it is strange that His Highness has not already
70

sent for you. If his health is as precarious as rumor tells us—and Konrad has heard some disturbing things— then it would seem he must desire to see you as soon as possible. I do not like this—someone may be making mischief!" She stared straight into my face as if trying to read some answer there. Undoubtedly she could well suspect, having found the Colonel with me alone, that I had learned more than her Baron had told her, and from perhaps a far more reliable source. When I said nothing, the Gräfin continued.

"She has been very much at the palace—the Princess Adelaide, bringing all those black-robed females to look down their crooked noses and squawk their pious prayers aloud like crows. She is not going to stay in her abbey now—no, she pushes to see her father make due repentance for his sins, mainly those which affect her the most! I have never trusted her—ready to thrust that long nose of hers into all private affairs, mainly those which do *not* in the least concern her!" She spoke so hotly that I was sure the Gräfin had had her own difficulties with the Princess and still smarted from some passage at arms before or since that redoubtable female had entered the bosom of the church.

"But if it is she who is making trouble— No, there are plenty at court who will not take kindly to her meddling. If only His Highness would send for you and settle it all!

"He will—he must. Konrad is busy about the matter now—and he has influence. Yes, Konrad will have a solution."

I noticed that she never mentioned the Gräf as one to be consulted in difficulties. But neither did I put any dependence on Konrad von Werthern. Never before had it been so necessary for me to consider my own words and acts with such care. The Colonel's suggested headache might become real, I decided, before this day was entirely over.

But now I sat and listened to the Gräfin's continued string of speculations—sometimes making as noncommittal a comment as I could summon. Her various out-linings of this peril or that, or some to-be-hoped-for resolution flowed steadily on. I tried to make myself attend to her words, hoping to sift out what might be of future benefit to me. Only I found my thoughts turning more and more to the action the Colonel had ordered me into that night.

He had never asked my agreement to his plan, he had simply stated that this was what I must do. Now I framed in my mind several very sharp and telling rebuttals to his arrogant assumption that I was under his orders. Those came too late, I was committed to the venture, though a sensible female would have retired to her chamber, locked her door, and stayed voluntary prisoner until morning. The trouble was that I was, in some ways, no longer a sensible female.

At last I interjected into the Gräfin's monologue my excuse of a headache, and then had some trouble extricating myself from an instant reaction of solicitude, though once within my chamber I was grateful for the suitable-for-an-invalid tray Truda brought, for I found myself most healthily hungry.

I did have in my wardrobe just such a cloak as the Colonel had mentioned. It was a shabby thing, faded in color to a uniform drabness, but I kept it for its excellent protection in bad weather.

How else did one dress to meet an unknown grandfather who was also a reigning monarch? My sober collection of half-mourning gowns seemed, as I examined them one by one, most inferior to such an occasion. That the court was used to elaborate toilets I knew. But—the fact that I was in mourning—that so the memory of my grandmother was ever in sight, as well as in my mind—perhaps that was the best move I could make now.

I chose a dress of cream white trimmed in black ribbons. The night was sultry and if I were to go muffled in a cloak, I did not want to smother. I sought my sewing bag and, using my embroidery scissors, I cut the stitches which held the high-necked guimpe in place. With that gone the dress appeared far more in

72

the formal fashion, though I felt very bare of neck and shoulder after I had hooked myself into the bodice. The iron necklace helped a little and its effect was startling—I looked someone very different from Miss Harrach of Wyllyses Hundred. I might not be clad in brilliant satin with an overflow of jewels, but I did have something— For the first time I realized that perhaps a pretty face was not the only thing to attract another's eyes.

I am not given to blushing, but now the direction in which my unruly thoughts had turned did bring color to my cheeks. I caught up the cloak and, with that across my lap, seated myself out of the range of the betraying mirror to wait.

Waiting, for me, has never been easy; now, in this room, it made me fidget. I kept feeling that I was under observation from some unseen source and I had to summon all my composure not to rise and pick up one of the candles, pull aside the curtains of the bed, peer into each and every pool of shadow to assure myself that I *was* entirely alone. I gave a start and a little cry when a scratching at the door announced Truda's long-awaited arrival.

She told me that the Gräf and the Gräfin were at dinner and most of the servants so busied with the serving of that that she could guide me out. We went down a smaller hall to a narrow staircase. There I had to keep close hold on the rail, so steep were the steps. There was another hall to traverse, then we came out a very small side door into what was plainly a corner of the stable yard.

There a figure loomed out of the dusk and held one hand into the limited beam of a single lantern—just long enough for me to see the Colonel's ring. Truda vanished before I followed the stranger among a number of smaller buildings, to pass through a second gate. Beyond that I was handed into a closed carriage, the curtains of which were tightly drawn.

It seemed to me that the drive was a long one, surely when I had gone with the Gräfin this afternoon we had

73

not made so many turns. I tried to guess from the sounds I could hear if we were cross the square of the market again, but those which reached me were so muffled they meant nothing. At long last the carriage came to a stop, the door opened, the steps were let down, and I was handed out.

Here there was not even a lantern to give a light. The moon was rising, but its rays did not reach into the shadows where we were. Another figure came from the dark, a hand was slipped beneath my right arm. I again was startled and gave a gasp which was answered by an angry whisper and there was no mistaking the note of authority in *that*.

"Hold to me for guidance," the Colonel ordered. "We cannot show any light here."

I surrendered to him as we crossed a strip of pavement against which pressed a wall of darkened brush. There was another door waiting—slightly ajar—then I was inside where there was the odor of polish, a trace of tobacco smoke.

"Stairs here." Again that authoritative whisper.

I had already discovered that by stubbing a toe somewhat painfully against the first one. We went slowly, I having to be confident that my guide would not allow me to stumble. We made a turn and now I sighted a faint glow above which gave me the power to press on a little faster.

So we reached a wide hall. Some distance away was a table on which sat a four-branched caldelabra all candles aflame. In the light of that stood a sentry. The man stared straight ahead—in his utter motionless stance he might have been one of the wooden toys much favored by small boys. He did not even blink as the Colonel, without a glance at him, opened the guarded door.

Within was a blaze of light, so sudden it dazzled me a little. My cloak was swept away from my shoulders, and I could be glad of that for the heat of the room was as great as if I had stepped directly onto a hearth before a roaring fire.

74

"The Countess von Harrach!" Colonel Fenwick's voice was hardly above the whisper he had used since our meeting below, yet it seemed to ring both in my head and in that stiflingly hot room.

My bedazzled eyes had adjusted. If I had thought that my bedchamber in the von Zreibruken house was large and imposing, this chamber was twice its size and certainly three times its peer in magnificence. Nor were the hangings here shabby and the furniture out of place.

I faced directly the great bed, tented with a crimson canopy now looped back. It was set on a two-step dais, and between me and its foot was a carven, gilded railing, as if to further emphasize the importance of its occupant and the necessity that he be set apart from all inferiors.

Pillows had been heaped high to support that occupant, and, as I looked directly at him at last, the rest of the room vanished from my attention. Curiosity had brought me here, now something else, more urgent and important drew me forward of my own accord, until my hands rested on the top of the balustrade and my eyes saw only the man who was watching me in turn with such a burning, demanding gaze that I could not have broken that eye bond between us, even if I had wished.

Chapter 6

I do not know what I had expected to see when I at last
confronted this man who had shamed my family, made
my grandmother the formidable and stern woman she
was. By sheer will I kept my horror to myself—or hoped
that I did in that moment. My grandmother had met
death her noble face unmarred, her carriage that of a
triumphant queen. What I looked upon was the wreck
of what must have been once a handsome and com-
manding man.

One side of his pale face was flaccid, the muscles so
changed that the eyelid was drawn nearly shut, the
mouth loose. From the corner of that dribbled moisture.
He wore no nightcap and his hair, near the color of the
pillows which supported him, was still abundant. The
upper part of his body, muffled in a rich robe of crimson
gallooned with gold, must once have been powerful;
now his shrunken flesh and outthrust bones under that
show of rich color would have given the lie to those
who still thought him to be a force in the world—if it
were not for his other eye with its piercing gaze.

Slowly, as if he must fight for every fraction of an
inch, he raised his right hand from the spread of fur-
bordered velvet lying as a coverlet across his inert body.
Seeing that gesture made with such infinite struggle,

my first shrinking from him vanished. I found myself wanting to give him aid. Still I sensed that there was in him the same determination and need for independence which my grandmother had shown. He would use what he could of his ailing body to the end.

A hand tightened about my own arm. The Colonel drew me from the foot of that throne bed, urged me around the side, bringing me as close to my grandfather as the width of the bed would allow. I was facing still that living eye, for with the same slow force as had brought up his hand, so did he shift his head on the pillows so he might watch my advance.

His lips moved, arching apart a fraction on the living side of his face. His struggle to speak was manifest. But there came no sound. If that was a signal, the Colonel moved. He loosed his hold on me, laid on the bed a tablet of paper and placed carefully between the fingers of the up-raised hand a pen.

The hand jerked into position, and the pen moved, leaving behind a broken scrawl which ran crookedly. Once the hand had come to a rest the Colonel whipped away the tablet, tore free the upper page, and set the pad in place again. The page he held out to me, while that fiercely demanding eye blinked, releasing me from its imprisoning stare.

I could make out the words I discovered, distorted as the writing was. It was in English—perhaps he believed I could not understand any other language.

"Lydia—" I was not aware that I was reading the scrawl aloud. "Always—Lydia—no one else—oath I gave held me here—but always Lydia—"

I thought of the paper I had found about the necklace I now wore—of that name repeated on it with such force as to near penetrate the surface on which it had been written. I did not think that this was a lie. To my surprise I felt a smarting in my eyes, the rise of emotion.

Perhaps a cynic might say that what Elector Joachim now felt was different from his emotions during his days of rule, that he had accepted his "duty" then philosophically and without fighting custom. A cynic could believe this, yes. But I, watching the effort which had written those words, meeting the stare of that one eye, had to believe.

He was writing again with the same painful effort. The Colonel took up the second sheet and passed it to me.

"What of son—my true son?"

I answered his question. "My father was killed, fighting for his country."

The eye closed, once more the lips strove to work, to shape some word. Never did the stubborn determination leave that ruined face. He looked up at me again and I felt as if I were being weighed, measured. Then he wrote:

"Well done. You—Lydia—like Lydia—" The pen fell from his fingers and the Colonel quickly bent to set it back again. But he did not add to what he had written, not yet—instead he held that measuring look upon me, studying my face with such intensity that I felt as if my very mind was open to his reading, that he knew my every thought, good or bad, kind or petty. It was such an examination as I had never undergone before, nor would I have believed until that moment that a single eye could convey such meaning.

Perhaps because he was near to the end of existence there was given him at that moment some power of unspoken communication no one of us who was not bound by his fate could understand. Never afterward could I say how long I stood there, held by his survey of me. But I believed that I also learned something of which I was ever after sure. For all the circumstances, for all the anger I had felt for him, my grandfather had truly been worthy of the woman he had seemed to desert and repudiate. I would never know the barriers intrigue and duty had raised between them, but they were well matched in courage, in strength and—in love. Not perhaps what that word means to most—no, this was an emotion which had been deeper, stronger,

78

little of the body perhaps, but much of the mind and spirit.

For the third time he wrote and the message was passed to me, it was longer this time and he had to pause several times. There were beads of moisture on his forehead, the sense of concentration which radiated from him impressed me as much as had his gaze. He was forcing his body to obey his will in a passion of need.

"My blood—Lydia's. I had to know. Safe—make you safe—will make sure—safe—wait for plan—he will help—do not trust—"

The pen fell, he had sunk back in his cushions, that speaking eye closed. As the Colonel removed paper and pen I dared to move, leaning over the edge of the bed, I reached out and took that now lax hand into both of mine, wishing that clasp to make him understand that I knew the truth of what he had tried to tell me.

His flesh was cold, but the fingers did not remain flaccid, instead they tightened in mine with determination. Moved by an emotion I did not try to understand, I raised his hand to my lips and kissed it.

His eye opened, his lips writhed in a last attempt to speak. I read the frustration, the horror of his own helplessness.

"Grandfather," I said softly. "I know—"

How I wished at that moment we had a day, a week, or perhaps even an hour— This was not the Elector lying here, it was Joachim von Harrach who had once found another life, perhaps far more peaceful and happy, in another land and another time.

"See," I pointed to the necklace I wore. "She gave it to me—wanted me to know— In the end—now—she understands—everything."

It was not my imagination, I felt his grip tighten even more in mine. Once more his gaze was demanding. He needed something and I thought I knew what it was.

"She told me to come," I said slowly and distinctly. "She wanted this—for us to meet."

79

His head moved a fraction in what could only be a nod. Then he turned a little away from me to look at the man by my side. The gaze he directed on the Colonel was a speaking one, even as had been that between us earlier, though what message he would convey by it I could not guess.

There was a sudden sound from the door. My grandfather's hand turned in mine, sought freedom. I laid it down on his breast. The Colonel's grip fell on my shoulder and he drew me back from the bed.

"Come!" His voice was a whisper. He drew me on toward a tall screen at the other side of the room. I was pushed behind this with little ceremony just as the outer door opened with some force.

A gray-haired man, wearing a coat which was not the usual servant's livery but which bore a crest on the shoulder, and a loop of gold cord bearing a medallion resting on his chest, slipped inside and glanced about the room. It seemed to me that he sent an extra searching glance in the direction of the screen and I was certain that he gave the slightest of nods before he turned back toward the door.

He crossed quickly then to the side of my grandfather's bed and took up the Elector's hand, setting his fingers to the pulse at the wrist with a professional ease, while the Elector turned his head back to face the door itself. There had been a perfunctory scratching there and now it opened with some force.

A lackey stood nimbly aside when there swept into the room, irritation expressed in her moon-round face, in the flurry of her veil and the swing of her ground-length gray skirt, a woman who carried herself with all the arrogance of one who has had to defer to very few during a long and well-provisioned life. She looked about now, not even giving a glance to the sick man, and demanded in a strident voice:

"Where is Krantz, where is Sister Katherine? And where is Luc? They were not to leave His Highness for any reason!"

I felt the pressure of the Colonel's hand which he

had not lifted from my shoulder even after we had gained this place of temporary concealment. However, I did not need that warning, for such I was sure he was attempting to convey. My heart was beating fast, but not with any fear, just excitement. That this was my half-aunt, the Abbess Adelaide, I had already guessed.

"Your Reverence." The man at the bed placed the Elector's hand on the furred coverlet. He bowed with deference, but his jaw had a stubborn cast. "His Highness is not to be so disturbed for any reason. He himself issued orders that he wished to be alone—"

"*He* issued orders? How? Since the good God has seen fit to strike silent his tongue. And one can read anything in the scrawls which someone can urge him into writing! I demand—"

Her voice arose steadily, it was an unpleasant rasping voice and I conjectured that in the past she had often gotten her own way by a judicious use of it. Perhaps it was an inheritance from her mother, that much disliked Electress of uncertain temper and overwhelming arrogance.

For the first time there was a sound from the bed. Though he had struggled to speak to me, he had not uttered this croak which he now brought by some effort from his throat. The Abbess was silenced, she stared in amazement, then something which might have been a shadow of fear crossed her face. He mouthed that sound again, his hand was up—his finger pointed to the door behind her.

There issued a silent battle of wills, for the Elector did not try to speak again. However, it was manifest that he *was* in full control of his mind, if not his body, and that he *was* giving an order now—one which he determined she would obey. Perhaps she wished in turn to prove that she was at least able to stand up to him, for she did not move to withdraw. Then the man spoke sharply:

"Your Reverence, it is not well to excite His Highness. Your presence here is obviously not beneficial to him."

Her mouth opened as if she would shout him into oblivion, then slowly closed again. The look with which she favored him was truly venomous. Without another word, nor a glance toward the man in the bed, she turned her back on the two of them and stumped heavily out of the room. In a flash that man was across the chamber in her wake and had closed the door firmly, standing with his back against it as if he half expected the Elector's daughter to think better of her retreat and strive to enter again.

The Colonel was also on the move, bringing me with him out of hiding. For the last time I heard that guttural sound from the bed. The Elector's hand was again pointing, not toward the door through which the Abbess had gone, but to the left.

Colonel Fenwick nodded, stopped long enough to catch up the bundle of my cloak—which luckily the Abbess had not chanced to notice. I waited for a moment, longing for a little more time—maybe to touch again that cold hand. There was a need still in me to speak some reassuring word, to let him know—what—? I was not sure, but I felt that there was something which I might do to ease him if I could only be given a chance. But the Elector's eye was closed, his hand was again being held by his attendant, who did not even glance in our direction, while the Colonel had me again by the arm.

We passed behind another screen which matched its fellow across the room and my companion opened a door behind that. So we came into another room, near as large as the bedchamber but far less well lit. In fact there were only two small candles there.

Both sat on a table, and pulled up to that was a chair in which rested an elderly man. His hair was a mere circlet of white about the dome of a large head, but as he looked at us I saw a vast white mustache bristling outward from his upper lip. As the man back in the Elector's room he wore a badged coat.

Now he arose, getting up with some difficulty and having to pull on the edge of the table to gain his feet.

He did not look at the Colonel but rather studied me from under brows nearly as jutting and bristly as his mustache. Without a word he caught up the candles, one in each age-spotted hand, and limped closer. For a long moment he studied my face, and then gave so low a bow I feared his creaking joints might never allow him to straighten up again. Once he must have stood quite tall, but he was much bent now.

"Highborn." It was plain he attempted to keep his voice to the faintest of whispers, but that task was near beyond his ability. "Welcome, welcome, Highness—" For the second time he bowed.

"Franzel," the Colonel demanded his attention with a sharp tone, "we must be away—now!"

The old man started as if he had hardly been aware of my companion until he spoke.

"Away—" he repeated bemusedly as one in a dream.

The Colonel took him by the shoulder and gave him a shake, so that one candle he held dropped a gout of wax on the carpet.

"Wake up, man! Yes, away—by *his* orders—"

"The door, then, yes, certainly the door!" The old man looked like one throwing off a dream. One of the candles he replaced on the table. With the other in hand he moved, more quickly than I would have believed possible a moment earlier, to the wall beyond. With his free hand he ran fingers along a ridge of carving, a thick twist of vine and leaf. What trick he worked I could not see, for his back was now between me and the wall.

Within a second a panel slipped open and Franzel stood aside, offering his candle to the Colonel, who squeezed his tall frame through the door never meant for one of his inches. The old man beckoned and I followed. As I passed him Franzel once more bowed very low, as if I were a queen entering a throne room. I hesitated, the man I did not know, nor his relationship to my grandfather. It was only obvious that his good will was mine. So I murmured words of thanks before

83

I answered an impatient hiss from beyond and entered what lay beyond.

Behind us the panel slipped shut once more. The way it protected was a very narrow one, smelling of dust, and dank, stagnant air. We had gone only a few paces along before the Colonel whispered back over his shoulder.

"Take my hand. Here is a stair and we must proceed with caution." The light of his candle did show stone steps, very narrow, descending into a well of deep dark. Going slowly down step by step, his hand clasping mine, gave me confidence.

The feeling that the walls about us were closing together, that we were about to be crushed, buried, in this secret place, made me giddy, but I could not throw it off. I felt that each step left me as unsteady as if I trod the heaving deck of a storm-tossed ship. It was only that firm grip about my cold fingers that anchored me to reality, helped me to keep my growing panic under control. I had always feared dark and closed-in spaces since I was a small child, and my courage at this moment was sadly lacking. The stale air did not seem to give me a full breath, and that added to my surge of panic.

"We come to another passage here." My guide did not turn his head, though I so longed that he would. I needed more reassurance than he had given me now. It was as if I were not a person, merely part of a duty he was oath-bound to carry out. Only he had spoken the truth, the stairs were behind us, we edged through a second passage as crampingly narrow as the one above, but running straight.

My cloaked shoulders brushed the dank walls on either side, stirring up that rank odor and the dust which near choked me. Ahead the Colonel had to sidle in some places sideways in order to negotiate this path at all.

We came to an abrupt stop, facing what looked in the faint candlelight to be a blank wall. The Colonel passed our light back to me.

"Hold this," he ordered, "give me all the light you can over my shoulder."

Wax had dropped in hot dribbles down the sides of the carved stick. I steadied the flame as best I could and watched his hands go out, his fingers skim over the surface of the wall. There was no vine carving here to conceal a catch, nothing even to hint that a doorway might exist. A moment later my companion uttered a grunt of satisfaction. His two thumbs pressed heavily against a stone set at the height of his own firm chin, he was grinding his flesh against the stone with concentration.

This time there came a sound, a rasping. I gasped and there was a second exasperated grunt from the Colonel. But the blocks sank back a fraction and there appeared along the seemingly firm stone the outline of a door, one which we both must stoop to use. The Colonel now set his shoulder against the outlined panel and exerted more strength. Reluctantly it gave, and we felt cool, fresh night air. Instantly my companion grasped the candle and blew out the flame. With his hand again on mine I was drawn into the open where I could see moonlight broken by the limbs of trees in what could only be a garden.

For a moment the Colonel remained where he was, standing in the shadow of a bush, and pulling me in beside him. I could hear his breathing fast and deep. I had an odd flash of thought that he was testing the air about as might a hound of the chase—striving to sense so the way we must now follow. We lingered for a very long moment and, in spite of my heavy cloak which I had now drawn very tightly about me, I was shivering, more with uneasiness than the chill of the night.

The moon showed us nothing moving. It made plain, however, the stark bulk of one of the ancient towers against the night sky—carrying a threat which came from the past into the present.

No! I was allowing the events of this night to influence my imagination far too much. I was Amelia Harrach—myself! Now that I had left that awesome old man enthroned in his bed I could forget that a meaningless title had been pressed upon me. I could perhaps even forget there was any tie of blood between us. Only I could not. It was as if he had laid some spell on me, so that I knew I would never forget a fraction of our meeting. In some strange way I could never be exactly the same person I had been before his one fiercely bright eye had searched—reached—measured me. I am come here only by my grandmother's wish—feeling nothing within me which was kin to the ruler of Hesse-Dohna. Now, though I had seen him physically helpless, I was tied to his undoubtable spirit and courage.

No and no! I would not be his Countess! I would never be a part of this life!

The Colonel broke through my confused thinking. "We are in the east garden." He kept his voice very low. "So we must now bear to the north toward the lake—there is a postern gate there." Once more he took my hand and we went so, like wandering children, along the path he wove, skulking from one patch of shadow to the next.

Once or twice I glanced back at the bulk of the palace. Faint glimmers of light showed in some windows, but otherwise there was no sign of life. Around us night insects chirped, there was rustling in the beds and borders. Once I saw a bird swoop in a silent, deadly dive, and heard a thin, squeaking scream cut off in mid-note as the feathered hunter made his kill.

We passed by a series of stone-bordered basins feeding runnels of water from one to another. So to a door—hidden by an arch supporting a luxuriant spread of vine. A latch clicked sharply in the night—then we stepped through onto a pavement wide enough for a carriage but also walled upon the far side. Along this, lighted lanterns hung at regular intervals.

From the man by my side came a low but carrying whistle. Moments later I heard the sound of hooves, slowly, as if the horse moved at little better than a walk. There came into view that curtained carriage which had brought me here. I was put within it, given no more time to exchange a single word with the man who had been my escort throughout my adventure.

Huddling within the folds of my cape, still shivering, I tried to set my thoughts in sensible order. It was true that I had been acknowledged by the Elector, yes, but so far only secretly, with but Colonel Fenwick as witness. We might both claim the truth of what had happened and not be believed. In fact the whole meeting had been carried out under such a veil of secrecy that I did not see that I had gained in truth what I had come for—looking at it coldly and shutting out of my mind as best I could the extraordinary influence the dying man had had on my emotions. It was still left to him to signify whether our relationship would ever be openly acknowledged, and I knew that I must never discuss what I had done—especially with the Gräfin.

In this matter, my hands clenched hard upon the folds of my cloak, and I caught my lower lip between my teeth, I was alone. Who dared I trust? That old, old man, for all his force of personality and spirit, might well be dead before morning. And the orders and wishes of the dead then depend only on the will of the living. It could be denied easily that I had ever seen him, that he had acknowledged me.

The Gräfin's suggestion of the treasure being willed to me—that I never considered as a possibility. Perhaps it was some dream of her own. That it would fall into my hands even if the Elector so desired—that I was sure would never be allowed. I did not want it. What I had come for—the vindication of my grandmother— a public vindication!— I began to realize might never be mine at all, even though I valued that above all the wealth of Hesse-Dohna thrown into a single heap.

Perhaps it all could have been done—Lydia Wyllyses's rights made plain and public—if the Elector had not been struck down. He was still, in spite of his crippling, a man of strong purpose, as witness his dealing with his unpleasant daughter's invasion of his sickroom. But, as the Colonel had warned me, his needs must depend far too much now on the aid of others. I shook my head in warning to myself, I must be prepared for failure.

Yet I remained glad that I had seen him, even in his weakness. Seen, and somehow felt, that bond between us which we had never had time to explore. Perhaps another meeting—a spark of hope sprung to life in my mind. I pinned that hope to his display of courage and will and would hold to it.

The return to the Zreibruken house took less time than my trip to the palace, perhaps the hour being so much later and the streets less busy, we returned by a straighter route. I descended again in the stable yard and a man whose face was only a blur escorted me to the door, rapped twice, and was gone before I could thank him. Truda opened the door, a single candle in her hand, a thick shawl about her. She made a sign to come quickly and sped along the inner ways of the house as if she feared a patrol of watchmen were about to capture sight of us.

Within my own chamber, the door tightly closed, she did not follow me farther into the room, rather stood, as the Colonel had once done in this house, her ear to the paneling, listening. There was a shadow of fear on her young face. Then she did come close to me and whispered:

"Gracious lady, the Gräfin—she has been twice to this door within the hour to ask how you did. I said you slept. And one of the footmen, Heinrich, he has been along the corridor several times—though he has no business here—it is as if he is a sentry."

"How did you—?"

Truda smiled nervously. "Gracious lady, each time I spoke of your bad head and that I had made you a tisane to keep you sleeping until the pain was gone— a herb drink I had learned of my mother. Also I did other things— See?"

She passed beyond me and held the candle higher so that it shown partly into the cavern of the bed. I gasped as I allowed my cloak to fall.

There was a sleeper there—in my place!

Truda grasped the cover, twisted it away from that form. There were pillows placed in line, crowned by a lace cap into which a silken scarf had been stuffed to give it the roundness of a head. Her smile was full as she looked to me for approbation.

"Most clever!" I gave her that at once. "I have much to thank your quick wits for, Truda."

"Gracious lady, I ask only to serve you." She curtsied. "See—I have told them that I, too, sleep here tonight so that I am within call if you need me." She waved the candle about to display a huddle of blankets on the dais at the foot of the bed. "In the older days it was always so with the maids—they must be ever there if their ladies needed them. I am from the country where they still follow the old ways, the Gräfin knows this. She would not think my actions strange."

The Colonel had chosen his aid within this house well. I had been considering the matter of trust during my return from the palace. Had I perhaps now found my answer—or at least part of it—here in the person of this girl? Could I place in Truda the same reliance that I would have in Letty and expect the same perfect loyalty and help in return? How I longed to believe that I could! Yet I must not do now in haste—and my inner need—something which I might well come to regret bitterly in the future.

Chapter 7

*My sleep was haunted by dreams that I could not re-*member when I was brought awake by a roll of sound so loud and insistent that I sat up in bed listening and shivering. Bells—the tolling of bells! Their clamor came from every side—not sounding an alarm, I decided after a moment of dazed listening, rather they peeled solemnly as in mourning.

I slipped out of bed and sped to the nearest window. Outside the gray of dawn was lightening into early day. As I pushed open the casement the bell song was near deafening, the same sad notes repeated over and over.

There could be only one cause for such tolling. The Elector was dead and all the churches in Axelburg so announced his departure from this world. One cannot force sorrow. The complete emptiness I had felt at my grandmother's death did not visit me now. Only—I found myself wishing I had been given some chance to know better that man I had seen in the great state bed, whom I had only met when he must have been already dying. What I had sensed in him might have led us both to—

I shook my head at my own thoughts. Joachim-Ernest, Elector of Hesse-Dohna, had been little to me in life. What could I feel for him now but this disappointment? I had no strong tie with him. Slowly I drew the casement shut and tried to think sensibly and coherently of what this would mean to me.

There would never now be any public recognition such as my grandmother's letter, the promises made to me, had brought me overseas to claim. Therefore it followed that the sooner I was out of Axelburg, the better it might be.

In spite of all the Gräfin's hints and the suggestions made by Colonel Fenwick, I wanted nothing but what was denied me now by death. If my grandfather had been so ill-advised as to mention me in some will or other official paper, I might even be in trouble. I had no illusions concerning the reaction of the Abbess-Princess Adelaide, and perhaps other members of the Family, to my existence. Those intriguers, whom my grandfather had been able to keep at bay when he still lived, would now be vultures seeking the kill and I would be a likely victim if I made myself known.

I could, under the circumstances as they now were, I was sure, depend very little on the Gräfin and her silent husband, of whom I had seen so little. As for the Colonel—I need only recall the Gräfin's disparaging words concerning him. With his patron gone it might well be that he would be stripped of all power, perhaps even in trouble himself.

The sooner I was out of Axelburg, of Hesse-Dohna— the better. It was now my problem to see how I might contrive that flight. I had been brought here by ways planned by the dead man; I had no ready access to even a carriage in which to cross the city, let alone the country—and the other countries and principalities which now might lie between me and the sea. I did have money—but I was not even sure there was any means of public conveyance such as a stage. A young female traveling alone could hope for no better than scant tolerance, might well expect insult and even danger.

I huddled into my chamber robe and sat down, trying

to think, as my grandmother had early impressed upon me, sensibly and with care, weighing one chance against another. If I could reach Hamburg, I could, I was almost certain, find passage on some ship bound for a port in my own country. But between me and Hamburg lay how many miles, at least one frontier to be crossed. Germany was divided, despite the heavy-handed remapping of Napoleon, into a number of independent states, most under highly autocratic rulers.

Nor was I sure even what route a possible stage might follow. I clenched my hands to still their sudden shaking as I faced firmly the fact that I was without any resources save my own wits and the gold I had.

Money could buy much, but it could also spark betrayal. I must move with the utmost care. Only, where did I start? The Colonel? Surely at this moment he would be highly embroiled in the changes brought about by the Elector's death. There was only one other—the girl Truda, though what use to me an untraveled peasant girl might be now I could not tell.

I made myself rise, tried to forget the constant tolling of the bells, and crossed the room to tug at the bellcord. However, it was not Truda who opened my door moments later.

Perhaps she had been knocking and the bells had drowned out the sound, but the Gräfin came in hurriedly. She was wearing a beruffled and lace-festooned chamber robe, most of her hair bundled up under a baggy cap. Even in this dimmer morning light her face showed wrinkles and lines not heretofore visible, so I guessed she had not waited for any ministrations by her maid. Her expression was one of avid eagerness.

"Amelia!" Before I could move she caught both of my hands in hers, and, had I not instinctively retreated a step, I think she would have embraced me. "Amelia, he is dead! Is it not a tragedy? Not to have seen him— not at all—? But we know what he wished, what he must have decided for you!"

She was actually able to summon tears to trickle

down her plump cheeks. Her eyes, though, watched me with a sly searching.

"I am sorry for his people. From what I have heard he was a good ruler." To find the right words was difficult; I knew that I must never betray my adventure of the night before. "I am sorry also that we did not meet—"

"Not to see you, a child of his own blood for whom he had such plans, never to welcome you!" She dropped her hold on me, for I had not responded to her gesture. Now she actually wrung her hands together. "This is a hard loss, Amelia, such a sad, sad thing!"

"Perhaps it is all for the best," I returned quickly, seeing a small opening to begin to press my own decision. "I do not think I would have been welcome at court, Luise. From all you have told me there were many obstacles to be overcome there."

She shook her head. "How can you now be so cold, so calm? Do you not truly understand? You are of his blood—they have always sworn that he cherished memories of his American family and accepted the Electress only because she was forced on him through duty. He was always a stranger to his family—did he not run away as a boy and become an officer in another army serving in your own country? For one of his line that was so unusual a happening as to be near unbelievable. Surely had he been able to see you—know you—your position here would have been so assured that no one would have dared so much as lose a whisper concerning you. No one would have dared stand against his will!"

"But they can now," I pointed out. "Since my reason for coming here is now at an end, do you not think it best I retire quietly to my own home? The new Elector, whoever he must be, surely will *not* stand ready to welcome an obscure stranger, who, according to the reckoning of your law, represents only the result of an unfortunate scandal?"

"Rudolf-Ernst? He has not even been seen in Axelburg for twenty years. The Electress would not let him show his face here after he refused her Franizka—the younger daughter, as a wife! No wonder, a more ugly princess never existed—pudding faced and so fond of the table that she near had to turn sidewise to get through a door. She ate herself to death, they say, and one can believe that.

"Yes, he will be coming fast now. However, he was ever in awe of the Elector, and easily swayed. Also he has no liking for the Princess Adelaide, nor any who give *her* service." She paused, pursing her lips. I believe she was thinking furiously.

"Until the will is made public, dear Amelia, you must make no plans. The Elector was always secretive about his affairs—he had to be with that she-dragon ever at his elbow, her spies as much about him as she could station them. No one knows what he intended to do with his personal fortune, except"—she watched me with searching care—"when he sent for you we could well guess. There is the treasure which was wholly his to dispose of, you know. However, in one thing you are very right, my dear. Perhaps it would be well now to be doubly circumspect, to keep from the eyes of some at court. Yes, it might even be wise to leave Axelburg for the present."

I was wary. Though I wanted nothing more than to leave this city, I desired that journey to be on my own terms, and for only one reason—to go home. Hesse-Dohna had no claims on me. However, I doubted that the Gräfin would further any complete withdrawal.

"The Kesterhof!" She clapped her hands together as if she had solved some difficult problem. "It will be the perfect answer! Only a day's travel from here—and it is most comfortable since the Gräf had the improvements made three years ago. You shall go to the Kesterhof!"

"What is that?" Feverishly I tried to think of some good reason why I could deny the Gräfin the right to make any decisions for me.

"A hunting lodge—or it was until the forest was
94

devastated during the wars. The Gräf has had it made into a country house for us. He was in England—bah, what a cold and rain-filled country that is." She shivered delicately. "There he was much impressed that the English nobles lived at least half the year on their own land and so had more loyalty from their people. As well they should, seeing as how they accepted discomfort such as you would not believe were he to tell you!

"So he had the Kesterhof made into such a house, smaller, you understand, but it is his pleasure to play the British nobleman there. Yes, you must go to the Kesterhof." She pinched her lower lip between thumb and forefinger, her eyes darting about the room as if in search of some means to convey me there instantly.

"*We* cannot leave also. It would not be right under the circumstances—the Gräf has certain duties. However, for you it will be perfect. There is no one there save the servants, and all of them are entirely loyal to the Gräf. If he orders that no one shall speak of you— that will be so."

I did not like the sound of that at all. Yet what objection could I raise? Especially when I had a strong feeling that it was imperative for me now to be out of Axelburg. The Elector had ruled to the moment of his death, but now there were many ready to fish in the troubled waters left by his going.

Also—were I alone—except for the servants—I might have a chance to lay my own plans, learn what I must do to help myself. It would give me precious time to see what could be done. The Gräfin apparently accepted the idea that I was in perfect agreement with her suggestion, for she rang my chamber bell with even greater vigor.

"You must be on your way as soon as possible," she continued. "All the roads into the city will soon be crowded—so many will be coming to witness the lying in state—the arrival of His Highness for the encryptment of his cousin. It would not do for you to attract attention at present. No—that might even be dangerous." She looked at me most seriously as she uttered that last warning.

When Truda arrived my hostess took charge of the preparations for my journey, giving a spate of swift orders so fast I could not see how the maid could separate one from another. She then hastened away, promising to see that I was not only served with a traveler's fortifying breakfast, but that a luncheon basket would also be packed, and one of the Gräf's servants sent on ahead to order the Kesterhof made ready for a guest.

Sure that she had at last left the room, I turned from the braiding of my hair, Truda being well occupied with the packing, to speak.

"Truda, have you any way of reaching your friend, he who knows Colonel Fenwick?"

For a moment I was not sure that she had heard me, for she went on smoothing a dress into folds which would leave it the least creased. Then, without looking at me directly, she said in a voice so near a whisper I had to give all my attention to hear at all.

"Gracious lady, he is of the guard. They will be on full duty—supplying sentries to do honor to His Highness's lying in state."

"There is no possible way then for you to reach the Colonel through his help?"

She gave a last touch to the dress she had put in the trunk—never looking at me.

"Gracious lady, one might try. But no message could be given openly. Such might have to pass through several hands and some one of those might wish to speak of it elsewhere."

Court intrigue again. If their masters vied with each other in such murky employment, how could any servant resist being pulled in? I could well understand the danger of any message of mine, no matter how innocent, being reported to those who might not yet know of my existence but would relish learning of it.

"I want only one thing, Truda, that the Colonel knows where I am going."

He had not sought me out except in obeyance of

rders. With his patron dead would my situation mean
nything at all to him? I could not allow myself to build
n such a thin foundation. Also—with the Elector dead
nd the hostility the Gräfin had shown freely, would
.is own position be such as he could or would come to
ny aid should I have need? Still—somehow I felt that
t was only to him that I could turn with any hope. He
vas the kind of man who, having once given his word,
vould never break that no matter what obstacles arose.
3ut—how far did his word stretch now to cover my
uture?

Last night he had gotten me in and out of the palace
vith an expertise which I accepted as a talent of his
vhich could be depended upon. Now—when I did not
:now what might face me—I was certain that I must
n some way keep in touch with him—even if that came
:o be very difficult indeed. How I wished that at that
·ery moment I might ask his advice. For, even if he
leemed me of no value, save wherein I touched the
.ffairs of his late master, yet I could depend upon forth-
·ight truth from him, and perhaps him alone. I was
.mazed at my reaching such a conclusion even as I
nade it. For what did I know of this man beyond bits
.nd pieces I had garnered from his actions as I viewed
hem, and remarks made about him. Yet it remained
hat I waited now for Truda's answer with real impa-
ience.

"That much perhaps can be done."

I had not known how fully I depended upon the girl
intil she gave that cautious answer. Would she be comng with me? I asked that bluntly.

"They have not told me. Perhaps they will allow it
f you ask, gracious lady."

Did she want to accompany me? Obedience and sub-
ervience had been so drilled into her that she might
:o and yet hold hidden resentment to work against me
ater. In a strange household, wherein the rest of the
.ervants were entirely loyal to the Gräf, as the Gräfin
iad already made so clear, I needed at least one person
vho might be persuaded to consider my interests first—

and Truda would never have played the part she had last night if she had been wholly the Gräfin's woman.

"Truda—" I dared not be as plain with her as I could with Letty, with any of the people I had known from my birth. "I wish you to come with me, but only if you yourself also desire that. I would not take you against your will."

For the first time she looked at me directly. I could read nothing in her expression, at that moment she was as stolid appearing as the heavy furniture about her.

"It is for me to serve the gracious lady in any way she wishes."

Just as I had no clue from her face, neither could I read anything in her voice. How I wished that at that moment the faculty for reading thoughts would descend upon me. Was my demand too selfish a one? How did I know what personal ties she might have here and which she would long to hold to? I needed some help so badly! I, who never thought I would admit that, or that I had been a fool in allowing myself to be so cut off here in Hesse-Dohna.

"I shall speak to the Gräfin." I made my decision. It could be no worse than the one which had brought me to Axelburg. What I held in mind the strongest was that Truda had some connection with Colonel Fenwick.

"It is as the gracious lady wishes." Truda resumed her packing.

The Gräfin, now suitably dressed in court mourning, made a second entrance into my bedchamber shortly after, followed by a footman with a tray. As I sipped lukewarm chocolate and ate the rolls which accompanied that, my hostess never stopped talking, mainly about the duties now engrossing the Gräf, who had been one of those selected to escort the new Elector from his place of semiexile to Axelburg. Her face was flushed and her eyes sparkling. It would seem that this hour of grief meant new and horizon-widening action for the Von Zreibrukens.

"He agrees"—she spoke of the Gräf—"concerning

the wisdom of your going to the Kesterhof. It shall not be for long, dear Amelia, I assure you! Once all is carefully prepared you shall return—and in such triumph! Then you shall take your rightful place—you shall see!"

I thought it best not to point out that I had already decided where my rightful place was, and it was not staying in Axelburg as the butt of envy and perhaps active enmity. Now I did cut into her stream of speech with my request for Truda's company into this temporary exile.

"But of course," she agreed at once. "You could not possibly travel without a maid. There is the staff at Kesterhof, but none trained as bodyservants. Truda does very well, Katrine tells me. She is not a peasant—her father owns the inn at Himmerfels and she would not be in service but she is the third daughter and wishes to earn her dowry. Ah"—she consulted a jeweled watch, the chain of which hung about her neck—"it already grows late. You must be on your way, my dear. I shall send you messages daily so you will know all that occurs. It will not be long before you can join us again!"

I noted that the closed carriage awaiting me did not bear any crest on the door, and the coachman and footman wore no livery, only discreet black coats. The Gräfin had said her farewells in the great hall, and when Truda and I were inside the coach I saw the window shades were down, even as had been those in the carriage which had taken me to the palace the night before. It would seem that my exit from the city was to be made as inconspicuous as possible.

So we drove away in a half gloom, the tolling of the bells still making such a clamor that we could not have talked had we wanted to. I longed to ask Truda if she had been able to dispatch my message to the Colonel, but I would have to wait.

The carriage kept to the ill-paved streets of the older part of town, for we were tossed about and our pace was hardly faster than a brisk walk. Outside, through the clamor of the bells, I could hear a multitude of voices, as if a crowd gathered.

Then, after what seemed at last an hour of such rattling with stops and starts in plenty, the carriage picked up speed and we were shaken about until I felt distinctly queasy. I dared at last to pull aside the curtain nearest to hand, and found I was looking at a stretch of ragged turf backed by a rise of tangled brush. Plainly we had left the city behind. Here even the bells were muted, though we had not altogether escaped their incessant tolling.

Seeing that there appeared to be no reason now for traveling in a closed coach stifling for air, I asked Truda to raise the curtains and give us a view of the countryside. I could see few farms, though we did catch a glimpse now and then of a distant roof or a rutted track turning off into the underbrush. There was a wild look about this country, as if we traveled through a land which was mainly deserted by men. Even the fields we passed were largely unplanted, covered instead with a choking growth of wild tangle, as if fast slipping back into the hands of nature again. When I commented on this Truda had an answer.

"It is all because of the wars, gracious lady. There was much fighting here." She shivered. "Sometimes yet they find what is left of dead men. Many farms were destroyed, burned—the people killed or else driven away. None were left to work the land as once it was."

"But the wars." I was sure that she meant the great devastation which had rolled over this land in Napoleon's day. "Those were done years ago. Surely by now people would have returned—"

Once more that stolid, secretive look returned to her fresh face. Perhaps it was a warning against my probing farther. But she did reply.

"This was never very good land, gracious lady. Once it was all forest—kept for hunting. There was a burning, and in the bad days much of the wood was cut down to feed stoves—sold in Axelburg during the winter. Also—" She hesitated so long that I dared to ask:

"Also what, Truda?"

"It has always been said that the land hereabouts is unfortunate, gracious lady. Men in the past have worked out their hearts trying to bring it to fruitfulness. In return they gained only death or ill fate. It has been cursed, they say, so even from the old times."

I knew that she was not telling me all. From the stories of Madam Manzell at school I had heard that the cruelest of forestry laws had prevailed in many of these countries. A peasant had no respite if deer ate his growing crops, the wild boars and pigs raided his fields. There would be the torture of wicked mantraps set to capture any poacher. If this had been forestland, the farmers could well have suffered greatly from the laws and the whims of the noble or nobles claiming rulership here.

Now that she had mentioned "forest" I could indeed sight stumps of larger trees among the saplings and brush. A few of these, reduced to blackened trunks, stood gaunt black ghosts of another day. It was a desolate country and I liked it less and less.

We drew up twice at inns to change horses. Those places were plainly poor shelters, only a man or two in their stable yards, who hurried about their tasks, barked at by our coachman. I noted that they did not look toward the carriage as natural curiosity might bring them to do, nor did, at either stop, anyone come from the inn itself to ask if we would have any refreshments. The doors remained shut, no head showed at any window.

Truda and I shared the contents of the luncheon basket, though I had to urge her to accept such food and then she took only a small share of the plainest. Nor would she drink any of the wine which was packed with it.

The road began to climb and our pace slowed. Here there were further signs of devastation, more tall standing dead trees, outcrops of dark stone. Once we stopped at a place where a small stream gushed into a basin formed crudely of rocks where the horses were allowed to drink. There I insisted on getting out and walked up and down to stretch my cramped limbs.

No one of my escort wanted this, but I used a manner of authority to silence their protests and went a little along a ledge of bare rock to look out over this countryside, somber and grim as it seemed to me. The road was not well cared for, though gravel had been dumped into the deepest of the ruts, and the brush cut back on either verge. We had halted on the highest point of a hill and from here the way curved down into a valley, this one well forested, green and alive. To the right from where I stood—running in a northerly direction, the land rose steeply to a near mountainous height. Part way up that steep slope was a building of greater size than any farmhouse or inn.

I had no spyglass through which to see it in detail, but I gained an impression that it could be close to a ruin. The lines of its forbidding bulk held the dark threat of a robber baron's keep, the stones which formed those walls of an unusually harsh gray, unsoftened by any growth of vine. I wondered what it was and whether it might still be inhabited—by more than the ghosts of an evil past.

Truda followed me, staying at my heels. I tried to believe that her constant companionship was out of loyalty to me, an offering of protection, not because she had been set the task of gaoler. I pointed to the building on the mountain side and asked her its name.

"It—that is Wallenstein, gracious lady." After one swift glance in the direction I indicated, she turned her head sharply away and did not look again.

Wallenstein! The ill-fated fortress prison into which the erring Ludovika had disappeared so long ago, to be swiftly and conveniently forgotten except as an example of all which was false and sinful. The Gräfin's words flashed back into my mind. What had it been like for that pleasure-loving, highly selfish young woman to be immured in that pile for the rest of her life? It was the dark castle of some story ogre and not of the real world I knew at all.

The Gräfin had mentioned there was still a garrison stationed there. For what purpose? Was it still a prison, perhaps one like the Bastille of unsavory memory, kept for prisoners of state? I longed to ask such questions, but it was plain Truda would not talk willingly about the place and I had no desire to try her patience too high.

We creaked and rattled on down the slope into the valley where the trees closed in about us, keeping out the afternoon sun, so we traveled through a green gloom where the sounds made by the coach were a noisy intrusion. There appeared to be no flowers—no color anywhere—only the green of smothering leaves, the brown-black of gnarled bark. I did not sight nor hear a single bird. We were caught up in this monstrous tapestry of a woodland, the only living things.

It was sudden when we broke into the open again. The heat and light of the sun were intensified by the time we had spent among the trees. Here was a building ahead. I had crowded close to the left-hand window beside me, striving to see what I could of it. This was no fortress suggestive of a castle, though it had greater bulk than I somehow expected. The first floor was stone-walled, but above that was wood and there was an upper balcony which seemed to run straight across the house at that level.

The eaves, the balcony, even the wide window frames were all carven and must once have been painted, even as were the houses of the older part of Axelburg, for the sun pointed out dim blue, red, green, and tarnished gold. Flower boxes had been placed at intervals along the balcony and these were filled with plants, some in full bloom.

Chapter 8

Preparations had been made to receive us. The wide front door was open and lined up at one side of that was a number of servants. Most of the men wore a simple livery, all bearing the Von Zreibruken crest on shoulder or breast. The women were in peasant dress, with deep blue, green, or rust-brown skirts swirling full to just above their ankles, flower-embroidered aprons, blouses with full sleeves, their hair drawn up to be hidden under caps from the peaks of which floated bunches of ribbons.

Among the welcomers I recognized one of the footmen from the townhouse and not far from him stood a woman in a plain black dress who wore jet earrings and a cross pendant from a necklace of the same stone. Her cap was of black lace and below it her face bore a forbidding likeness to one I knew well. It might be Katrine grown several years older who came forward to curtsy to me.

The woman in black was introduced by the footman I knew as Frau Werfel, the housekeeper. She did not smile as she dismissed the rest of the company with an abrupt gesture.

"If the gracious lady will be so kind as to follow—" Even her crow-crack voice could be Katrine's. I did not answer her invitation at once, rather I stood where I was for a moment to survey what I could see of the Kesterhof.

In spite of the weather-faded paint, the massed flower boxes, the house gave no appearance of warmth or welcome, though, in contrast to that evil fortress castle we had viewed from the heights, it might be termed a pleasant lodging. Had I once more been maneuvered into choosing wrongly?

However, since no one can foresee the future, I had to live day by day, doing the best that I could in the time immediately to hand.

Once we were inside, Frau Werfel made continued excuses for the house as she ushered me along. Those were mechanical, I was sure, delivered as a matter of form. It was plain that the Kesterhof was held to a high standard of neatness and order, though it certainly lacked the age-dimmed magnificence of the townhouse.

Its history of a beginning as a hunting lodge was plain, for the walls of the main hall were literally covered, from shoulder height upward, with the horns, or entire mounted heads, of long dead beasts. The glaring glass eyes of wild boars seemed to follow one along in a desire for vengeance, the upcurling tusks at their snouts, glistening yellow-white as if freshly polished— as perhaps they might have been.

The vast room had a stone manteled fireplace at one end, empty of wood now, since it was summer. Though the hall remained chill, the dank cold hung as heavy as a forgotten tapestry. To one side a staircase reached upward. That was far less imposing, also, than that of the townhouse, but it was enclosed with a paneling as high as the balustrade on the outer side and shoulder tall against the wall. This was of very dark wood and so intricately carved that it was difficult to perceive at first that each of the wide panels in turn pictured some episode of a never-ending hunt, mostly the cruel conclusions with men butchering some stricken creature.

Judging by the garments worn by those hunters, I believed that the artist who had wrought this had either derived his inspiration from very old pictures or perhaps the carvings themselves had come into being some three or four hundred years in the past.

Once up on the second floor, however, the Kesterhof underwent an abrupt change. The walls here were not festooned with trophies of the chase, nor were they carven, rather they were covered with a rich, crimson damask-appearing silk. Stationed precisely the same distance from one another along the corridor were chairs upholstered in velvet of the same bright shade a table or two balanced on gracefully turned legs of white picked out in gold. It reminded me a little of the palace—yet the red was too heavy, the gold too visible to be altogether to my liking. I thought it represented in a way the Gräfin when she was most overdressed and to me the most lacking in taste.

I was shown into a room not far from the head of the stairs which was no state chamber but rather akin to the golden sitting room which the Gräfin had made her own back in Axelburg. The furniture was of the latest fashion and upholstered in pale green with bouquets of flowers. Their muted shades of rose, cream, and lavender were repeated in the rug, and again on the long brocade curtains which half overhung others of lace. There were a wealth of small curiosities all about, on tables, mantel, and in a cabinet or two. Figurines, vases (without flowers), boxes meant to hold sweetmeats or other trifles, crowded one another in this very feminine room.

A half-open door showed a bedroom beyond, where the bed was curtained with green patterned in gold, the rest of the furnishings as rich.

Yet there was nothing here to make one welcome. Rather it made me feel an intruder into quarters already claimed by another who would sooner or later arrive to exhibit annoyance at finding me already installed. I nearly turned to Frau Werfel to suggest another suite might be better, and then realized the folly of my own feelings. So instead I thanked her and she took my words for dismissal, whisking away in a whisper of skirts.

My trunks were brought up and Truda went about unpacking with the same quiet skill she had used in putting in what she now shook out. I sought the nearest window to draw aside the edge of the drapery and the lace panel beneath that to peer out.

Below was a courtyard surrounded by a wall, even as the one at the townhouse. It was cobble paved and fronted on, at the far side, by stables. Beyond that I could see treetops, many of them so tall they must be of the original forest preserve when this had been a lodge.

Still farther out, across that greenery, were heights reaching up and up, like that stark mountainous wall on which perched that fortress-castle of ill omen. All this suggested wild country in sharp contrast to the room in which I stood. Somehow I did not like the look of that outer land. By coming here I had made myself entirely dependent upon those in this household—I knew that and it made me uneasy.

Truda worked swiftly, with concentration upon what she did, as if to establish a wall between us. She had said very little during our journey, in spite of my attempts to break through the barrier of rank and gain some knowledge of the girl herself. I longed passionately at that moment for Letty with her constant flow of chatter and her dear friendliness.

Reluctantly I untied my bonnet ribbons and dropped that headwear on a small table, shook out the crumpled folds of my skirt. I would never be at home here, or, I was very sure, anywhere within Hesse-Dohna. At that moment I longed to stop Truda, tell her to repack, that we had no intention of remaining under this roof. It crossed my mind that I must learn soon just how much freedom of movement I really had.

First I must discover what was of most importance at the moment and caution made me approach that in a roundabout way.

"Truda, before we left—did you have time to say goodbye?"

How quick of wit was she? Would she recognize my need to know if my message had been passed along.

Though she never looked up from her work, she did answer promptly.

"Yes, gracious lady." Brief but not quite to the point. However, I thought I could not expect more.

I sat down on one of the small chairs, a little surprised at my sudden sense of relief. For, even as she had said that, she had also nodded, and that double affirmation I took as assurance she had done all she could to let the Colonel know what had become of me.

That there was also a warning in her answer I guessed. I looked about, at those silk-covered walls with their gold-framed pictures of flowers, of young girls wearing the clothing of my grandmother's day and frolicking in gardens, or conducting flirtations with bewigged and satin-coated gentlemen. Could such walls have—ears? They made me impatient, those carefree picture maidens—impatient and a little more uneasy at what they might just conceal. I shook my head, trying to lose those fantastical thoughts of peepholes—of spying. I must certainly calm my nerves and cease peopling my world with such dark imaginings.

With Truda's aid I changed from my plain traveling dress into one suitable for the house. Then I resolutely decided that I must indeed put to the test what was my position here—that of an honored and carefree guest—or—that of a to-be-watched charge. I left my sun and light filled room for the comparative darkness of the paneled staircase.

As if she were one of the figures on that path of the cathedral clock, released not by the chiming of an hour but at the sound of my steps, Frau Werfel appeared at the foot of the stairs before I gained the horn-trimmed hall. She dipped a curtsy, her hands encased in black lace mits, clasped at waist level, her sour face impassive as she asked:

"The gracious lady desires?"

108

"This is a very old house, is it not, Frau Werfel?" I began my campaign obliquely. If the woman was as house proud as the evidence would make it seem, perhaps I could so open communication with her.

"Part of it is near five hundred years old, gracious lady. It has been added to, and his lordship's father had some alterations made. Then his present lordship was pleased to make many more. Since the great forest is near gone and there has been little hunting since the war, the changes are marked."

"You say that the forest is gone. But from my window I saw a number of trees—we drove through what appeared to be dense wood on our way here."

"A wood, yes, gracious lady. But there is no longer enough such cover for true hunting. His lordship has ordered replanting, also that as many of the old trees as possible be preserved. But it will never again be as it once was."

She had not moved from her position, nor had she suggested any tour of the house. I gathered my courage and said firmly: "I find so ancient a place most interesting, Frau Werfel. Would it be possible to see more of those older parts—?"

Her expression did not change. I could not guess whether or not she was pleased, or if she was being pushed into action against her will. Once more she made a stiff curtsy as she replied: "If the gracious lady will then but follow me—"

Gloom appeared to fill the older rooms. The hall with all its trophies was the largest of these. Those chambers opening off of it were also paneled in dark wood, the windows so narrow as to suggest they had been installed for a fortress. Perhaps in those wild early days every nobleman's dwelling place must have been so secured against attack. From my listening during my school days to Madam Manzell's store of often gruesome accounts I knew that open warfare between one baron and another had not only been the usual way of life, but had existed in these lands long after there had been a semblance of common law and order elsewhere.

There had been no attempt to widen these windows but glass had been inserted into their stone frames. The light they admitted was very little, especially since it was now close to dusk. Frau Werfel produced from a sideboard a twin candlestick, but even those candles could not give me more than a shadow-filled impression of sparsely furnished, low-ceiling boxes of rooms which bore no relation to the modern chambers on the next floor.

Trophies, though not as thickly mounted as those in the great hall, continued to be the main decorations, though here and there was a fan of hunting knives and short swords, or a pair of crossbows, on the walls. There was a cold forbidding feeling which was more chilling than any draft from under an ill-fitting door. Outside summer might nod in flowers and sunlight, here was frost and winter's blight.

Frau Werfel, contrary to what I expected, voiced little or no comments about the rooms or their history. Her attitude was one of strained patience and would have quickly withered anyone less determined than I. She made no attempt to show me into the servants area or the kitchen and I had no reason to request that, for by the rules of noble society I could have no possible interest in what went on there, beyond the fact that the service itself was not interrupted.

At length, having seen a fourth dull, dark chamber which was a duplicate of three before, I had to surrender. It was, Frau Werfel astutely informed me, the custom of the house now to use only those upper rooms which had been modified by the present Gräf, and that my dinner would be served above and not in one of these dreary lower chambers.

I reclimbed to my sitting room little wiser than I had been when I descended, and more than a little dismayed at what I had seen. The rooms themselves had a very dampening effect upon the spirits. Truda had completed her unpacking and was gone. As soon as the door closed behind me I sped across the room nd pushed aside drapery and curtains to look out once again.

That balcony which ran immediately below the window must have some exit. At the moment I was a little reluctant to scramble through the window itself, but thought that I could see a door at least two rooms farther on. So I went back to the outer hall and counted doorways. The room with the balcony door was so masculine in its furnishings that I half expected the Gräf himself to rise from behind the desk there and forbid my entrance. However it was empty, save for the rather more massive furniture, another trophy of antique pistols arranged fanwise on one wall, and a portrait of a hawk-nosed, grim-eyed man in the elaborately curled wig of another day. He wore a breastplate of gold-chased metal over a velvet doublet and one hand gripped the hilt of his scabbarded sword, while he stared malevolently down at me, his eyes so well painted that they appeared to both challenge and follow my actions.

The latch of the balcony door turned easily under my hand and I stepped out on that upper way. It ran, I discovered, around three sides of the Kesterhof, not present at the back of the house which faced a remnant of the original forest, as repelling in the quickly-falling dusk as a solid wall.

There was life about below. I saw and heard grooms at their business in the stable yard, and lights began to shine out from the back of the house. Still that life was not mine and I felt that I was like one at a play observing a scene but still waiting for the main characters to appear and the real action begin.

Though this was summer and the day had been warm, with the descent of the sun behind one of the heights guarding the Kesterhof I was shivering. Seeing little below in that fast-fading light that was of any advantage to me, I went within, passing once again through the study. Though the room was now filled with gathering shadows, those angry eyes of the portrait were still alive and watching. I wondered whom it represented. The Gräf was stiff, somewhat grim of countenance, aloof—but he had very little in him of the power which seemed to radiate from this man of an earlier day—that aura of power which, by some magic, the artist had caught with paint and canvas.

I stood before it for a long moment, intrigued by the feeling that there was some resemblance in the painted face to someone. Not the Gräf—then who? The mouth—that stretch of plump lips almost too small to be in proportion to the rest of the face. The mouth— Under my eyes the lips seemed to purse the least bit and it flashed into my mind where I had seen that mouth. The Baron von Werthern! Except that the fleshy folds of his face had none of the strength pictured here.

What had the Gräfin claimed for him? She had, I was sure I remembered, spoken of him as a kinsman. Only I had thought that relationship to be on her side, not that of the Gräf's line, though in the nobility of a country as small as this one, the marriage possibilities must be greatly limited, and there would have been doubtless many unions closer knit within the ranks than would exist elsewhere. It could well be that even the Gräf and the Gräfin were akin by more than the marriage tie.

I did not like what I read into that portrait. There was plainly arrogance there, the arrogance born in one who had never had his will questioned. With that arrogance were signs of its natural companion cruelty. Defiantly now I turned my back firmly upon those watching eyes and marched out of the room. Though curiosity tugged still at me. I wished even more that Frau Werfel was the very opposite of the character she had shown me, as open and talkative as Letty would have been about "the family."

My dinner was served in still another room of the upper floor, one into which I was ushered by a footman, who then took his place behind my chair as I ate in formal loneliness, presenting one covered dish after another as a second servitor or two brought them into the room. That procession of dishes seemed without end, and, though I was hungry when I entered, I had learned to take no more than a token serving from any one dish and still was unable to do even that before we reached the final course of cheese and fruit.

There were three candelabra, all bearing lighted tapers, along the table, the flames reflected from crystal and high gloss finish of the china. Between them stood figurines in the form of fantastical beasts, each standing on its hind legs, its forepaws or hoofs supporting a shield quartered, and sometimes even further divided, to display greater number of armorial bearings. That they were meant to bring notice of the prestige of the family was plain. I found such a show illuminating in a way. It was as if those who demanded it were uncertain of their own importance and must thus make very sure that that was displayed on every possible occasion. Somehow—the fanciful idea came to me as I toyed with a cluster of cherries which had been my selection from the gilt basket of fruit—somehow my gentleman of the portrait would never have seen the necessity to so underline his status in rank. The family he had once dominated might be perilously close to moving downward in the world in this generation.

What did I know of the Gräfin—? That she was also the result of a morganatic union with the ruling house—but she had never mentioned the exact status of the female who had so introduced the very purple blood of royalty into her line. There were, I began to understand now that I was removed from the Gräfin's ever-present chatter, several facts which she had never touched upon. The Baron—by all the evidence I had seen and heard she certainly held him higher—and perhaps closer—than the Gräfin. Yet this morning she had suddenly been full of her husband's new station, his importance in the matter of awaiting upon the new Elector with perhaps the very welcome news that he had at last succeeded to rule in a state from which he had been exiled.

In the old days messengers bringing ill news sometimes paid for it with their heads—their lives. Was the reverse also true now—were the first to wait upon a newly ascended ruler apt to get rich picking in honors and offices? I could accept that.

What followed then concerning the favorites of the dead ruler? "The king is dead, long live the king!" The old cry of the monarchists came to mind. There would be new faces at court, sudden ascents to glory, sudden descents into oblivion. The Colonel—

I was staring at the nearest of those armorial beasts, a griffin I thought. Its fanged mouth was displayed open, as if to attack, its brightly enameled tongue curled and pointed. The creature became only a haze of color, my mind saw another face. It came to me again that in all the time I had known him, I had never seen Colonel Fenwick smile, show simple pleasure in something, be anything but a man either on guard or a soldier doing his sworn duty.

What was he like when neither duty nor wariness held him? Could he laugh, jest, lose that stiffness of back, that set line of jaw? He could not be as old as the Gräf, yet it would seem that he cultivated the airs of one who was gray and seamed with age. Was it the exile of his family, or his training in the Elector's service which had made him the man he now was?

I tried to imagine the Colonel relaxed, showing some warmth of heart and spirit, then shook my head at the impossibility of such a thing. Not even my imagination, were I to give it the fullest freedom, could change so much the face in my memory. Yet now that I had summoned that face into my thoughts I could not dismiss it—nor dismiss uneasy speculation concerning his future.

He had been the Elector's man, close to him. By the side of that bed his very manner had held a gentleness which I would not have believed he was capable of showing—had I not seen it. So, being who and what he was, he must have enemies in plenty. The Gräfin's spitefulness might be the lightest and least of the troubles he could now be facing. I dropped a cherry back on my small gold-edged plate. How many enemies did he have who would come now into the open?

I arose and the footman drew back, took a hurried stride to open the door for me. Why should the Colonel's trouble matter to me? Except, of course, that he was in a measure responsible for my presence here.

He had shown me no real kindness, no softness of manner, nothing which would make him a matter of anxiety—save again how it might affect my own plight. Yet— I was so a-sea in a wave-tossed rise of emotions I could not understand that I fairly fled back to the small sitting room where I found candles alight, the draperies pulled, and all done to suggest comfort and repose.

Except that there was no comfort in my thoughts, or repose for my nerves. I sat on one of the chairs and relived, in spite of myself, every moment of the night before. The secrecy of my visit to the Elector's death-bed—the perils that secrecy hinted at were now very plain. Though my grandfather had cowed his daughter, had still been able to enforce his will, dumb and dying as he was, did not mean that his wish would carry past the moment that the breath left his body.

I could no longer sit still. Instead I found myself up and pacing the room as a caged animal might pace, looking for freedom where there was no chance of it. Now I must pay for my folly—my blind plunge into a situation so unlike anything I knew that I was a blind woman lost in a maze.

Me—I— I must shut out everything else, bring my full mind to my own plight. The Colonel was a man, a man trained in court intrigues, or at least so used to them that he must have foreseen what would happen at the death of his master and made his own preparations before that event. He might well be over the first frontier already— A hireling who sold his sword— descendant of a Tory line—a man who was intelligent enough to look ahead— I summoned those thoughts to me. I was the one important to myself, and I was—

NO! I was not helpless! I had a good mind, and my

grandmother had trained me to think logically. What if my grandfather had made some future provisions for me legally? I need only say I would have none of those bequests, wanted nothing from Hesse-Dohna but to leave.

The difficulty now was that those tales of the courts with which Madam Manzell had favored those who learned German from her, and me the most of all, crowded into my mind in spite of everything I did to erase them. The utter and complete power of these petty princes and kings— What was a matter of astonishment at a distance became a source for fear if one was entrapped within it, as I was discovering now. Even the innocent might fear disaster—along with the guilty—as the Electress Ludovika had discovered. I wondered fleetingly if, in her fall, she had dragged down lesser members of the court, of whom no history now remained. That could be very possible.

But Kesterhof was not Wallenstein. I had yet to face any active threat against me. It was this sense of being alone which wore upon me. Where was the Colonel now?

My thoughts had made a circle, I was back once more concerned with that which I could in no way influence or perhaps even know. Unless Truda's frail contact might hold—

I found myself by the wall, tugging at the bellrope, before I had even thought coherently of what I might accomplish by questioning the maid. She had been evasive with me all day. If I forced her too far, she could retreat into complete silence and defeat me entirely. Still I could not set aside any chance—no matter how small.

It seemed to take a very long time before I heard the welcome scratching at the door. At my call Truda came in. Though my first glance showed me no change from her usual cast down eyes, mute waiting for orders, I was—

I was what? What was happening to me that I read into the slightest of things some momentous message?

116

This was new, and it frightened me. For I believed it to be loss of self-control, something I had dreaded above all else all my life—since my grandmother's image had impressed upon me the necessity for always keeping one's emotions under stout rein.

"Truda." I must take the plunge, or else I could not rest. "Truda, how much can I trust you?" I asked that boldly and would be, I thought dryly, well repaid for my efforts if she gave lip service only.

For the first time her eyes met mine. It was a faint echo, very faint, of that same searching I had faced from the dying man in the palace, though what quality did or could the Elector share with this young girl of a far different rank and background?

"Why do you ask me that?" For the first time she used no honorific title as she addressed me. Oddly enough I found that encouraging.

"Because we are alone here, Truda, you and I."

To my great relief she nodded. "That is so. These people, they are of the household as their kin were before them. Only to the Gräf are they answerable. They do not speak before me of anything but orders and what must be done."

I did not believe that she was lying. As she answered me she had glanced once over her shoulder, moved out farther into the room away from the door, even though that was firmly closed.

"What do they say of me—or have any spoken?"

Again she faced me squarely. "To me—nothing. But I heard—"

"Heard what?" I demanded as she paused. Perhaps the habit of years was very hard for her to break and we had but the most tenuous of bonds between us.

"That you are to stay—until another comes—with an important message. They have sent off also a man to Holstanhof—the village on the other side of the mountain. This was done after Frau Werfel read a letter the coachman gave her. They do not, I think, know that I heard of this, or that I saw the letter passed. But, gracious lady"—again she returned to the formal

117

speech—"I would be careful, very careful for what may come. The Gräfin is more than she seems and she has, I think, plans—many plans—"

Chapter 9

"And you, Truda, you are of the Gräfin's household—"
There was a change in her which I could not put name to, but it was there. Once more she glanced from me to the door and back again, so meaningfully that I thought I could guess what soundless message she so attempted to convey. As had the Colonel in the Axelburg house it would appear she hinted at some possible eavesdropper.

"It is as the gracious lady has said, I am of the Gräfin's household," she replied submissively, but her gaze once more upon me denied that allegiance. I could not accept that she was such an actress as to be playing some double game with me. After all, the Colonel had trusted her as his linkage in our secret visit to the palace.

"She has said that your father keeps an inn." I switched to another subject, seeking to approach my own need for knowledge in a more roundabout direction.

"That is true, gracious lady. He keeps the inn at Himmerfels, as did my grandfather, and his father also.

But our family are many and it is necessary that we earn for our dowries—"

"Your dowry? Are you then betrothed, Truda?"

She was again the embodiment of the perfect serving maid, eyes downcast, hands clasped at her middle above her embroidered apron.

"I am bespoken, yes, gracious lady. It is Kristopher Clingerman whose father is the miller. But Kristopher now does his years of service in the guard. So I will work also, that I may have a good setting out. It is so with many of the girls in Himmerfels. I am more fortunate, since my mother was able to speak for me to Madam Hummel who comes each year on her way to take the waters at Splitzen. She knew me from a child and got me the good place with the Gräfin. Yes, it all worked very fortunately for me."

Though her poise was still one of meek submission, Truda was indeed breaking out of the shell imposed upon her by class and training. However, one thing in her speech was of interest to me now—the inn. I had only the haziest idea of Hesse-Dohna, had never seen a map of the country. An inn so long established as Truda had reported this one to be must of necessity stand on some well-traveled road. The spas were often visited sites and, though I also had never heard of that of Splitzen, it in addition would be a goal for travelers.

Spa and inn to me argued roads, well traveled, in good use. In turn such roads meant coaches, perhaps for public transport. Who could give me better information concerning a possible way out of this land than Truda?

"Tell me about the inn, Truda. Is it far from Axelburg? Are there many travelers?" I tried to sort out in my mind the questions which would lead me to the knowledge I wanted most.

"Himmerfels is two leagues from the border with Hanover, it is on the great road, gracious lady. Since the wars are now over, there are many travelers, some who would go even on as far as Vienna in Austria.

They come often—like the English milords—with their coaches, some families altogether. I have seen the inn so full that it has been needful for my father to find places in the cottages for the servants of these milords. Himmerfels lies to the north and west of Axelburg, it is the town where meet two roads—one for those going on to Vienna in the east, and the other for those who would visit Bavaria in the south. It is a day's journey and then again half another from Axelburg, even when one has fresh horses ready at the posts."

"For the travelers who have not the money or servants as these milords you mention, Truda—are there public coaches they may take?"

She forgot her usual training enough to nod. "Twice a week that is so, gracious lady. But though such stop at the inn, few of them stay with us. Ours is an inn for the well born, you understand." Her chin was raised proudly. "Our cook came from Vienna. My mother has trained her servants very well. Many good things have been said about us by those who have stayed—one traveler tells another so we have messages sent ahead to hold rooms and prepare for those of the highborn!"

"So those who travel by the public coach are not welcome—"

Truda shrugged. "All are welcome if they conduct themselves properly. But they would not themselves be happy, nor would their purses be deep enough to pay for such lodgings. They are country people, or small tradesmen, students with pockets near always to let, people of no fortune nor consequence, you understand."

"I see." Only what I was assured of was that such a coach did exist. If I could—perhaps with Truda's aid—reach this very superior inn at Himmerfels, then even if I could not obtain a seat on such a coach, I could with my golden hoard hire other transportation. Which was heartening to know.

"There are many also who go to Splitzen for the waters," Truda was continuing. "People who do not want the more fashionable life such as is at Baden. They also my father can make very comfortable, and each year or so they stay with us. Madam Hummel has been coming so since I was a very small girl. She is a very fine lady, and very kind also. Her husband was killed in the wars and she is all alone as to family, so she travels much. To Vienna, to Rome, even to England she has been. I have often thought that it would be good to travel, to see new places one could then hold in memory."

"I would like to visit your inn, Truda—" I began cautiously.

For the first time I saw the girl actually smile. "Gracious lady, my father would be honored, we would be honored! But"—her smile faded—"it is far from here and—"

"And," I finished when she hesitated, "we may face trouble soon. Tell me, Truda, this Kristopher who is of the guard—is he the one who brought me to the Colonel?"

Her answer came as a whisper so low I could barely hear it, and her sudden agitation was plain.

"That is so, gracious lady. It was because of the Colonel that he entered the guard, you understand. The men for that are picked for their height, their fine bearing, their loyalty. It is an honor to so serve!" Again pride filled her tone.

"And you have a right to be proud of him," I returned. Privately I wondered if the Colonel were in trouble who else his fall from favor might encompass.

"They do not like the Colonel." Truda moved much closer to me and her whisper was even lower. "They would have done him harm if they could—"

I hazarded a guess as to whom she meant by "they." "The Gräf—the Gräfin—"

"They—and others. The men talked of it, Kristopher heard such tales. They said he was a foreigner, that the old Elector gave him too much power, favored him over those who had better claims. Kristopher always said that such talk was wrong—the Colonel is a man of duty, very loyal always to His Highness. Perhaps His Highness trusted him the more because he was not one of those others who were always reaching for more and more, greedy for all they could lay their hands upon. Now—now, gracious lady, there will be changes, maybe bad changes."

Her words followed all my own thoughts. What was happening in Axelburg now? I had made my choice, withdrawn from what I saw as a situation threatening me—now I almost felt a little ashamed. But I owed nothing to him—I did not! He was a virtual stranger, if he had not come into my life, I would be safe and comfortable half a continent and a sea away from this room and this tangle of intrigue and my own present impotence.

"We can do nothing yet." I was more voicing my own thoughts aloud than answering Truda. "Not until we know more."

"That is so, gracious lady." She nodded. "There is here nothing to be done—now."

If she might have said anything more, she did not have a chance, for there came scratching at the door and Truda turned swiftly to open it. Frau Werfel stood there, a lamp in one hand as if she had had so to light her way through the halls. Now I was aware that daylight had indeed gone and the dusk was deepening into night. Truda slipped quickly back into the shadows, leaving me to face the housekeeper.

"A message, gracious lady," she said, still no expression cracking the sour cast of her long narrow face. "The Gräfin will be coming. She will arrive in the morning."

I thanked her and she withdrew, though I saw her shoot a glance at Truda among the shadows. Perhaps she wanted to sweep the girl with her but had no good excuse for that, since I manifestly had not dismissed my maid. When she had gone Truda came once more into the light of the lamp on the table. There was a difference about her, she no longer kept her eyes cast down, nor her hands folded submissively. Instead she now raised one finger to lay across her lips, and nodded toward the door.

It was easy enough to decipher that—she did not trust Frau Werfel. However, I had already decided that I could not depend upon any now under this roof—except Truda.

Though the hour was early, I undressed and allowed Truda to put my hair in its nighttime braids. There were some books in a small case and while I did not find the Gräfin's reading matter to my taste (she, it would seem, had liking for the preposterously morbid romantic novels of a generation earlier—or perhaps the books were used only for ornamental purposes), I sat in my chamber robe and attempted to interest myself in the affairs of heroines who were eternally being abducted, imprisoned in haunted castles, menaced by ghosts of walled-up nuns, or vindictive monks, pursued through endless forests amid the crackle of threatening lightning and the roar of storms.

Unfortunately, silly though my selected tale was, in this time and place it came too close to my own situation. I could well envision, with my memory of that frowning fortress prison still fresh, that such things *had* once happened—to a lesser degree. Until, at last, I closed the book and slipped it back into place. Truda had pulled the drapery across the windows before she had left, now I went to the nearest one and held the heavy silken folds aside to look out.

There were lanterns set about the walls below, far enough apart so that each made but a small pool of light which encroached only little on the general dark. As I watched, seeking to see some stir of servant, some indication that I was not totally alone (for the house was so silent I could believe it was deserted), there was a clatter of hooves and the grate of carriage wheels on the pavement.

The Gräfin? But what would bring her here so quickly after my own arrival? I was startled at the number of possibilities which came to my mind. Still the equipage which drew into the lantern light and stopped just within range of vision was certainly not a coach with any luxury, rather a small gig, or so we could have termed it at home.

A single man stepped down, while the driver stayed in his seat. I watched the stranger, whose face was hidden from my view by a wide-brimmed, low-crowned hat, make his way out of sight, rounding the corner of the house toward the front door. Then the gig proceeded on stableward. So whoever had come was plainly to stay the night.

He was no visitor for me, I decided, as moments passed and no one came to my room. Finally, believing all my speculations a waste of time, I climbed into bed, but I left the lamp on the table by the door burning as I blew out the others. Never had I found it necessary to sleep with a light in my room, but this chamber, for all its modern furniture and soft luxury, did not make me feel welcome and I lay down with an uneasy mind.

It would seem that that was not a prelude to a sleepless night, however, for I did drift into sleep. If I dreamed, the dreams did not remain to haunt me when I awoke to find the sun bright on the flowered carpet, a morning so clear that all morbid fancies in the world could not trouble the most disturbed mind. Truda had drawn open the curtains, brought the tray with my morning chocolate, and set that by the window, was carefully proportioning hot and cold water from two cans into the waiting bath. I sat up and stretched, just to look about banished some of my worries.

Truda, however, had reverted to her earlier self and did not speak except in monosyllables when I attempted to talk. So that I finally had to accept that our short time of mutual misgivings was a temporary meeting only. I arose, bathed, dressed, drank my chocolate like an obedient child who was following the routine established in a nursery. Her taciturn mood took the glow from my own sense of well-being, brought back all the uneasiness of the day before. I was restless and, when I had finished the breakfast brought to my door by some unseen servant, laid out for me by Truda, I determined not to be kept indoors, but to see something
124

of the country about the Kesterhof—though I hardly expected that the lodge would have a garden for morning strolling.

I took up my plain straw bonnet, and a light shawl, for the woodlands I could see from my window gave the impression of chill. Truda had disappeared with my tray. As I came out into the hall there was no servant about. Again that impression which had been with me the night before returned, that I was alone in a place deserted by all. It added to my feeling of uneasiness that there was such a silence. Not a single sound save the ticking of a wall clock, which sounded unnaturally loud, was to be heard.

No Frau Werfel appeared at the door of the stairs today as I descended. The sunlight had not won in here, perhaps the struggle through the few high-placed, slit-like windows defeated it. Only those rows and rows of trophies, like monuments to the dead, loomed out of the shadows as I passed, my pace quickening as my dislike for the hall grew, to the front door.

That was a massive barrier, reinforced by great widths of iron, as if to defeat besiegers. The lock itself was so large that I imagined only a key perhaps the full length of my own hand might turn in it. However, at my tugging, it yielded, though grudgingly, and I stepped out into the morning as one might come out of some imprisoning cave.

The stable yard was to my left, and a drive of crushed stone curved from before the door in that direction. I turned my back on that and looked to the right. There had been indeed an attempt made to tame the forest-land into a more civilized vista. Underbrush had been cleared, though a number of well-grown trees so shaded the ground that there was no hope of inducing grass to grow as a well-tended lawn. Against one of these trees had been set a rustic bench and seated there was a man, a book in his hands, his eyes so intent upon the pages that he clearly was not interested in anything else.

He did not wear any livery, but was dressed in black,

his coat cut higher at the throat and buttoned down a longer length than any fashion I had seen before. Beside him on the bench lay a wide-brimmed hat which was also not in fashion. His hair was well salted with strands of gray-white, and his face was harshly cut, thin of cheek, sharp of chin and nose, his eyes small and set under very scanty brows. Not a pleasant face, nor could I ever imagine it wearing a smile.

His dress, his being in what was clearly the "garden" of the lodge taking his ease (if such a man could ever be thought to do that) argued that he was no servant, not even any upper one such as Frau Werfel, who clearly held the reins of the household in her competent hand. Nor did I think he was a bailiff or man of business. His clothing also was not new, though the linen folds of his cravat, which showed only a little, were cleanly white and evidently freshly laundered.

I stood where I was. Should I take the gravel path which led to my right, I would join him and I had no desire to do that. As I hesitated he looked up. Had my searching study in some way alerted him to my presence?

He arose, and now that I saw that one shoulder slanted higher than the other, while his head sloped forward so that he had to deliberately raise his chin to an uncomfortable angle in order to look directly at me. Still there was something about him which erased any pity—rather gave one a feeling of bitterness, or malice—

I nearly shook my head in counter to my own thoughts. Ever since I had come into Hesse-Dohna, it was as if my senses had been alerted to an unnatural degree, that I saw enmity and peril where none could possibly exist for any sensible person. I disliked these new feelings, yet they clung to me and I could not throw them off.

The man bowed, only it seemed that there was something of mockery in that bow, as if he did it as a piece of acting meant not even to impress me with any sincerity of good manners. He did not speak, and I had no idea of how to address him. A little flustered, I inclined my head in answer to his gesture of civility, and resolutely turned, not to walk the path into that half-garden, but rather down the carriage drive toward the woodlands. Nor would I allow myself to glance back.

I had gone only a very short distance when a second man emerged from under the trees. He wore a green livery jacket belted in, the belt supporting a long hunting knife, and he carried with the ease of one to whom the weapon was like another familiar limb, a shotgun. He touched the brim of his caplike headcovering, which was of leather, also bearing a crest set in the front, and spoke with an accent so pronounced I had trouble understanding him.

"The gracious lady wishes?"

Since he had planted himself in the middle of the drive, a barrier I could not avoid, nor proceed around without crowding him, I was forced to stop. That he would address me first at all, was, I knew, a breach of etiquette so marked that it could be deemed an insult. I had seen enough of the Gräfin's servants to understand that his attitude now was well out of the ordinary.

"You are?" My voice was peremptory enough to allow him to understand that I knew his manner was wrong.

"I am Gluck, Gluck the forester, gracious lady." He made no move to take himself out of my path. "May the gracious lady understand, this woodland has its dangers for those who do not know it—" He was finding words now, words in plenty. "It is not wise to walk without a guide or protection—"

I did not know whether he was offering himself as both. Instead I was now sure of something else. There were guardians set here—sentries one might almost say—who would make sure that I would not stray from the Kesterhof. In a sense I had expected this—but to be so confronted was still something of a shock. I hoped that I did not show my reaction.

His attitude was that of a man doing his duty. There was nothing now I could fault in his conduct or words.

So I must put the best face on my own actions as I could, not let anyone know of my realization that I probably was a prisoner.

"Thank you, Gluck." I did not add to that, only inclined my head slightly and turned back toward the house. Nor did I have any desire to join the stranger under the tree. Doubtless he also would gladly keep an eye on me for the benefit of the master of Kesterhof, though it was my suspicion that the Gräfin perhaps had more to do with any such orders than the Gräf.

But when I came again in sight of the garden the black-coated man had disappeared, while I had no more than set foot on the first of the steps leading up to the door of the Kesterhof when I heard sounds behind me heralding new arrivals. I faced around to see two coaches emerge from the wood-lined road. Unlike that in which I had been conveyed from Axelburg both of these were crested and the coachmen and footmen liveried, as if they were on a near-formal occasion.

The door opened and Frau Werfel, accompanied by a ranking of the indoor staff, filed out in stiff order. I withdrew a little to one side. The Gräfin Luise was handed out of the foremost coach by one who had traveled with her—the Baron von Werthern.

Her eyes lighted on me and she withdrew her hand from the arm of her companion and ran lightly up the steps, holding out both hands to me, her face expressing surprised delight.

"Amelia!" We might have been the oldest and dearest of friends the way she drew me swiftly into a highly scented embrace. Never liking such an exuberant manner, I stiffened, but she appeared to take no notice of my action. Instead she continued:

"The most wonderful news, my dear, you will not believe it! But it is the truth, the real truth! Come— we must talk—at once! There is so much to be done! Oh!" She released her hold on me and looked around in a rather surprised fashion, as if she had only this moment realized that we had an audience and that perhaps it would be better to contain whatever news had so excited her until we were more private.

Again her hand came out, this time to catch my arm and draw me with her up the next two steps, as she swept by the assembled servants, not even giving Frau Werfel either a word of greeting or a nod.

So we continued up the inner stair to the upper quarters of the house. Some of the excitement had faded from her face; instead she said no more; only looked as if she were thinking, planning something in detail. Hearing heavier steps behind, I glanced over my shoulder to see that we were being trailed by the Baron.

It was he who pushed a little past us when we reached the second hall, and, with the familiarity of one who knew this house very well, he opened for us the door into the sitting room of the suite in which Frau Werfel had installed me.

The Gräfin shed shawl and her gloves, pulled at the looped bow of her bonnet strings as she dropped upon the nearest chair. However, the Baron remained by the door, his eyes on her as if he awaited some clue as to further action which only she could give him. She looked to him now and nodded.

Without taking any leave or, in fact, saying a word since his arrival, he slipped out, leaving us together. Once more the Gräfin was smiling.

"Amelia—it is true! Even as we thought—it is the truth! How kind, how thoughtful he was—how just! What a pity that you did not have time to learn more of his kindness from his own lips! Oh, it is the truth, I assure you—there is no mistake in that!" Her words came in short blasts, as if she could hardly contain her high spirits. It would seem that some event she had longed for had at last come to pass.

"What is true?" I asked bluntly.

For a moment she again appeared startled, as if she could not understand some blatant stupidity on my part. Then she laughed again.

"Poor child, but of course you would have no way of

knowing—he did not tell you that, did he? The truth is that His Highness did indeed make provision for you. It is in his will—Konrad has actually seen it so written—" She nodded violently. "Oh, I cannot tell you how—but His Highness held Konrad in very high esteem, he meant that he should know at once—for your protection. His Highness knew that half of them would be down on you like wolves about one lamb when he was no longer here to protect you. He knew that so well that he made very good arrangements.

"How I would like to see the holy Abbess's face when she learns about the will. For all her claims of otherworld interests she will not take kindly to this. First His Highness does not allow her to pray him into the grave, and then he leaves this to torment her afterward—"

"Gräfin—Luise—" I could make so little of what she was saying that now I interrupted with a demand for enlightenment. "Please tell me—just *what* has happened."

She put her head on one side a little and looked at me with a coy smirk which I found at that moment highly irritating. Then she actually raised her hand and shook her finger at me as if she were the governess in some schoolroom and I was a very young, unruly charge.

"How naughty of you, Amelia, to go on secret errands in the night and say nothing to me. However, I can understand the reason." She lost her unseemly air of playfulness then, and quite a different expression, foreign to her plump face, showed for just a moment. One I did not like in the least, though it was gone before I could read its meaning. "You will not have to worry about interference from *that* quarter ever again, my dear. What has happened is what is important. His Highness, in his will, has left the whole of the treasure which was of his own collection to you! Think of it, Amelia—one of the most wonderful of all the collections in Europe—and yours—also he names you granddaughter and gives very firm safeguards for you—the
130

very firmest! You need not hide away here— By the end of this week all the court will know who you are and that you must be received with honor—the highest."

That she had discovered my night visit to the Elector's bedside was the first fact I sorted out of her river of words. The treasure—I thought of what we had seen on that one visit. That had no reality for me. But that my grandfather had acknowledged that he accepted me and made plain to everyone that it was a relationship to be honored—yes! That was what I had come for. For this moment I echoed the Gräfin's wish—that I had had a chance to know him better.

"But you did see him." The Gräfin had one of those quick flashes of insight which always surprised me. I wondered how she could catch my thoughts from time to time in that fashion.

"And—see—what I have brought you—these are yours—"

From the skirt pocket of her traveling dress she drew out a packet tied around with a bit of red cord, a roll so small it was hardly as thick as one of my fingers. I took it and smoothed the few sheets which made it. I was holding those painfully written words which my grandfather had set down as his welcome and only words with me.

Chapter 10

Four sheets over which that painfully made scrawl wan-
dered—I looked at them once more. Four sheets—but
here was a fifth! I had spread them fanwise in my hand
and now that extra one lay to the fore. Across it ran
the same wavering letters as made up those others.
Only this I had not seen before. Something my grandfather had written after I had been hurried out of his
sight?

"Must be safe—marry—arranged—he will make you
safe—"

Then came a last single word which was in so mutilated as scrawl that I could not be sure of what it was
meant to be.

"You see!" The Gräfin's voice was one of complete
triumph. "You hold there his wishes—that you marry
with Konrad, who will see you safe. Konrad is very
close to the new Elector, he has visited him many times
this past year. His Highness knew that, knew that he
could count on Konrad to see that you were safe, that
all which he wanted for you would be safe—"

"No!" My rejection of such an action was instant and
loud. I went to the nearest table and laid out those
creased slips of paper on its surface, looking carefully
from one to another. My grandfather's writing had been

of a necessity distorted by his illness, by the circumstances under which those messages had been written. And that last one had not been done under my own eyes as had the others.

"Amelia." The Gräfin had arisen hurriedly and now faced me across the table. "What doubt can you have that this is a good and right thing? You will have enemies, many enemies when the will is made public and it is known that the treasure is yours. His Highness knew this, he had planned for long that you should have a husband to stand between you and those who would drag you down." She leaned closer across the table, her eyes so fiercely on mine that she somehow compelled me to meet her gaze, and held me so fast.

"Do not doubt that you could be in deep trouble were it not you do have such friends as Konrad, yes, and as us! The Abbess, she is as spiteful as her mother, and has her party. There are others, too, greedy for power. Your claim will be questioned at once. Do you think that you, a stranger, a woman, of birth deemed doubtful—that *you* can face them?"

She laughed then and there was a malicious edge to her laughter.

"Poor Amelia, here the Elector's will is law. Do you even think that our new ruler would respect your rights had you not someone of power to speak for you? His Highness knew this well. Even before he sent for you your marriage was arranged; Konrad was made aware of what part he was to play. Was I not instructed to see that you had knowledge of him, know him? I had my orders—to keep you safe, to make sure that you had protection after His Highness's death, to see that the marriage—"

Her gaze had been so compelling, her voice so assured that I felt for a moment or two like a helpless bird under the paw of a hunting cat. Now the absurdity of what she babbled struck me. Did she really think I was so simple, so easily influenced that I would meekly agree to so preposterous a plan?

"There will be no marriage—" I interrupted her, raising my voice loud enough to cut through her flurry of words. "I have not the slightest idea of such a thing."

Her hand shot out and her fingers closed in a grip about my wrist that held more the strength of steel than the touch of flesh and bones.

"You will obey His Highness's wishes—why else were you here?"

I did not try to throw off that clutch. Instead I answered her steadily: "I came here for one reason only, Gräfin, because my grandmother wished for recognition, to have it made plain she was a lawful wife—as she was by the laws of my own country—"

"Your own country?" She flared back and there was no amiability now in her round face. "You are of the Family, of Hesse-Dohna, subject to the wishes of His Highness—"

I shook my head. "I am subject to no wishes but my own. What I came here for was not to be a part of any scheme set by others but for the one reason I have told you. As for the treasure—let it go to the Abbess, or the new Elector, if it will make either of them happy. I shall be glad to sign any deed of gift if such is necessary—"

She tugged at my wrist with a sharp jerk which, coming so suddenly, near pulled me off balance.

"You must obey his last wish—" With her other hand she stabbed down at that last bit of paper. "Have you not read it, foolish girl? Do you think that any of the court will believe such stupidity as you just voiced? They can do things. You have no rights here, understand? There is only the new Elector's wishes— And he is a man easily influenced—always by the last to gain his ear, so he blows this way and that from one day to another. Only if you have someone with strength and resolution to stand by you will you be out of danger.

"Konrad has been preparing for this day. He knew what he must do when His Highness sent him the necessary word. Why do you suppose he came here now? Because there is no time to be lost. You must be safe guarded, before the news is made public. Konrad has strong influences, he has many friends. No one can reach you when he stands on guard—"

On guard. The phrase stuck out of all her nonsense sharply. Guard—the Colonel! Was he a party to this wild scheme of my grandfather's—had he brought me to Hesse-Dohna knowing that I was to be married against my own will to a stranger I had disliked from the moment I saw him? Royal marriages were often made so—those most concerned in them sometimes not even seeing the prospective bride or groom until just before the ceremony. But I was not royal and neither was I going to be a party in such an affair. The Colonel—I could not believe that he knew of this. Yet I had wit enough now not to mention his name before the Gräfin, knowing her antipathy to the man.

"You have under your hand His Highness's last order to you." She again indicated the note. "It is for you to obey now."

Anger was rising in me. To burst in upon my life with what seemed to me an utterly outrageous plan for my future was beyond all one had to bear. Exerting my strength, I twisted free of her hold on my wrist, which she had somewhat relaxed, gathered the messages from the table, that last and most questionable one on top.

"We need discuss this no farther, Gräfin." Summoning all my power of composure, I again faced her squarely. "There is no need for argument. My existence will mean nothing to the new Elector—unless I claim what you say my grandfather left me. Thus he will have no reason to try to force me to anything. I need only let him know that I withdraw all claims I may have, either on family recognition, or upon any bequest left to me, and return quietly to my own land. It is a very simple and easy solution after all."

"Fool!" Now her face was contorted, truly ugly. "Why cannot make you understand? This *is* your country—you are subject to its ruler. You are in a position to make trouble for him. Do you think that he would let

you get beyond the boundaries—away where you migh
stir up trouble?"

"I would give my word—sign any agreement he re
quired of me—"

"Faugh!" Almost she spat that word in my face
"Words given can be easily broken, agreements repu
diated when one is beyond reach—"

Now my anger did flash out. "My word is not th
kind to be broken! Nor would any agreement I mad
go unhonored. I do not marry a man I do not know in
a foreign country at the whim of a dead man, who
until his dying hour, had no ties with me by his own
will. This is utter madness, Gräfin. Can you not se
that for yourself?"

Her face was flushed, her plump hands doubled int
fists now. That she was completely sure of herself I ha
to accept. What impression had I given that she coul
believe I would fall in easily with her wild suggestion
Still there was this, she had been bred up at court
under the complete domination of the custom which
made every whim of a ruler an unbreakable order. Per
haps she could not even accept that anyone would b
free of the fears and domination such a life would instil
in those who had accepted it as the proper way of life

Now she made a visible effort at control.

"Countess." She used my makeshift title formally
"I will leave you to think seriously of what I have said
Once more I must make it plain that you are vulnerabl
to whatever His Highness, the new Elector, may choos
to do with you. The consequences of obstinacy are neve
pleasant—they can be dangerous."

In quite a different mood from the exuberance sh
had shown when she had arrived in the room, she now
swept out of it, determined, I believed, to allow me tim
to think upon the error of my ways.

Think I did. It was true, I must face that fact, tha
in this country the ruler's word was law. The new
Elector could well resent the fact that his kinsman ha
dared to leave the treasure to a strange young female
one moreover whose very existence threatened to bring

to light an old scandal. That he would be ably seconded by the Princess Adelaide was a conclusion I must also accept. I was in a land foreign to me, one in which I might have no rights at all, and there was no one to whom I might appeal for assistance. Unless—the Colonel—

However, if he had also been a party to this marriage scheme, aware from the first that I was to be summarily disposed of to a man of my grandfather's choice, then he would not be any help either. I could see that there was danger here, I did not need the Gräfin's warnings to understand that. Also she certainly would not have brought me those scrawled bits of paper had not in some manner they passed out of the Colonel's hands into those whom I might well consider my enemies.

I smoothed out the last of those slips again—the one which I had not seen written. The disjointed words, as I compared them carefully to those on the other scraps of paper, were, as certain as I could be, in the same painful handwriting. I read them aloud—trying to think what had brought my grandfather to make this last urgent message such a one.

"Must be safe"—a wish for me? Yes, that I thought true.

"Marry—arranged—" Those bore out the Gräfin's story.

"He will make you safe—" A husband to stand between me and the wrath of those who would have good cause to anger. Then that last scrawl—the beginning of a name? It was only a loop of line, trailing downward to the very edge of the page—as if the pen had fallen from fingers too weak to hold them.

Had the Elector realized after we had gone that death was so close and so had made a last effort to speak to me so? Or—

I sat very still, the papers spread out on my lap, my mind busy with another speculation, one which might mean even more trouble ahead. Suppose in an intrigue-ridden court the first scraps of paper had somehow been gathered up, concealed for a space, then passed on to those who would pay the most for them in either gold—or coming influence? The Gräf had been one sent to apprise the new Elector of his ascension. Therefore the Von Zreibrukens might be thought people well worth cultivating by some ambitious underling.

So—with the papers to hand, the story of my night visit to the dying man made plain by the written evidence, someone else could have seized the chance to write that last one—for all its apparent resemblance to the others. The ambiguous "he" in that message—did that argue against the Gräfin's clever use of what she saw as an opportunity to advance the Baron? Would not the name have been the point to make? Or was her mind subtle enough not to mention the name, only hint and then enforce that hint with her protestation that this was all arranged before I ever left Maryland?

It was a very twisted skein they had looped about me. I was sure of only one fact, that I had no intention of marrying the Baron, and I determined to get out of Hesse-Dohna as soon and as best as I could. The treasure—that ill-fated inheritance—I wanted none of it. Could I ever make any of those so long bedazzled by it believe that anyone would deny ownership? The Gräfin had designed the new Elector as a weak man, easily led—

With one hand I crumpled together those bits of paper. What could I do? Just what resources did I have? There was the gold which weighed in my dress pocket. Foreign coins unfortunately, ones to be quickly traced, but still gold. The inn Truda had spoken of, on the road to a spa, to Vienna. Only, how could I even get out of Kesterhof? My actions would be even more under scrutiny since the arrival of the Gräfin.

Truda was my only hope. I went to ring for her, though I was not quite sure just how much of my present dilemma I might disclose to her. If it came to the point of actual escape, would her loyalty rest to my advantage or with those of her own people whose wrath might descend upon her if she gave me active aid? Never before in my life had I felt so alone and helpless as I did during those moments which seemed to strain into hours before the familiar scratching on the door heralded Truda's arrival.

She was once more wholly the subservient maid, awaiting orders. I beckoned her to me, standing as close to the balcony window as I might. If there were any eavesdroppers, this place was as safe as any I could find.

"Truda—" I still had not marshaled my thoughts, reached any decision of what I dared hope to plan. But I needed some one, so just to see her there gave me a small spring of comfort.

She glanced at me and then at the door. There was no mistaking the meaning of that gesture. Then speaking so softly that her lips barely moved and the faintest of whispers could reach me: "Scold me—I have not done something to your satisfaction—"

I caught her meaning. That Truda had been in any way taken into my confidence must not be suspected. I looked about me for inspiration, then demanded hurriedly why a fresh dress had not been laid out already— that I had chanced to brush against dew-laden bushes with the skirt of that I had on and must change. Into my voice I put what irritation I could summon, and that came easily enough since my interview with the Gräfin.

Truda made no answer, but her hand went out swiftly and she laid a small bit of much-folded paper on the bedside table. Then she went to the wardrobe and brought out another dress, laid it across the bed and moved behind me to unhook my bodice. I had the paper now, unfolded it. The message inside was short, and though I had expected something like it, this was still a blow.

"The Colonel F. has been arrested. No one knows where they have taken him."

So—I was alone! I did not realize until that very moment that I must have held in the back of my mind somewhere the hope that Fenwick would come to my aid somehow. Though how he could have managed that I had no idea. Very well, I must save myself.

I tore the bit of paper into very small pieces, then held those bits out to Truda, who took them from me and hid them again in her apron pocket, nodding her understanding. Once more hooked into a fresh dress, I went to my dressing table and studied my face in the mirror.

My reflection looked as always, I could read nothing in my expression to suggest that I had received any blow. Arrested was he? For what, by whom? No, that was no problem of mine; I must waste no time in speculating over the misfortune of the man who had in the beginning overpersuaded me into this whole affair.

Now—I could not remain in this room, hiding like a hunted creature waiting to be pulled out of meager safety. Would it profit me to seem for a while to fall in with the Gräfin's suggestions and play a pliable female, watching for their guard to relax? At present I believed that to be my only chance.

"Where is the Gräfin?"

"In the Green Parlor, gracious lady."

So the Gräfin kept to the upper story of the Kesterhof, shunning the dark antiquity of the lower rooms. The Green Parlor was across from my own sitting room and I headed for it briskly, trusting that my inner agitation would not show. If I could only at this moment display to the world that same imperturbable facade my grandmother used as armor in a moment of crisis, then I felt stronger. On sudden impulse I did not open the door immediately before me but went back to my own room, straight to the box which held my very modest array of ornaments and in which I had kept the butterfly necklace since I had worn it on my visit to the palace.

A decoration, the Gräfin had said, akin to those given for valor. Very well, no one needed more such a spur to courage at this moment than I did. With steady fingers I made safe the clasp, felt the cold iron settle about my throat. So armored, I returned to face my opponents.

For the Gräfin was not alone. Lounging beside her in a chair, his booted feet outstretched toward a fireplace which on this warm day held no shooting flames, was the Baron von Werthern. He arose at once, favoring me with a bow and a smile which was a stretch of his lips raising no farther than that. His watchful eyes fastened on the necklace. I thought I saw them widen then a fraction, but perhaps I was deceived.

"Amelia!" The Gräfin had regained, or resummoned, all her earlier affability, jumping up and coming quickly to catch up the hand hanging by my side to draw me farther in. I did not have to watch her to know that she was seeking to read my expression, eager to know how much I had been influenced by her arguments and half threats. Now I must play my game and I greatly feared that I was not fitted for such deceptions.

"I have been thinking." Such a beginning was the best I could summon. "As you have said, Luise, my position here is not without its difficulties. What we wish to do, and what we can do may be two different things." I sought words, wove them into sentences, at the present they were my only defense. "This has all come too suddenly, I cannot change my whole life so quickly. I must have more time—"

"Dear lady." The Baron was still smiling. "I fear our Luise, in concern for your welfare, may have been too abrupt in her disclosure of what you term 'difficulties.' But these do exist, and they are formidable. It is not my desire, you must understand, to frighten you, but you are a lady of intelligence, and you must be shown the facts, as unpleasant as they may seem.

"His Highness, due to his unfortunate ailment, could not make clear to those who did not know him well his full desires. It was his misfortune, also, that he had close to him certain advisers—or favorites—who had motives of their own for keeping him unaware of what might be happening. When he sent for you he was in better health, he fully intended to introduce you formally to the court, to make you secure in every way, and leave to you the legacy of that which had given him the greatest pleasure over the years.

"Then came the second and greater impairment of his senses. He was prisoner within his own palace. Those whose motives he had good reason to distrust were now able to surround him with such guards that his true friends could not reach him without great difficulty and then only under the eyes of his enemies. It was only with the greatest of efforts that I, who share in a small portion the same blood with him, was able to see him at all.

"His first concern in the latter days was your comfort and safety. Having been rendered nearly completely helpless, he was much burdened in his mind, yet he was determined to see you, to gain some feeling from you. His children had been little comfort to him—his son dead—one daughter also—the other much like her mother and in no sympathy with him. Though it may be hard for you to believe this, dear lady, he was a man of warm heart. Circumstances set upon him the duty of a loveless, a very unhappy marriage. So hurt was he by what he had been forced to do that thereafter he showed his real character to very few. I am honored"—the Baron paused, his smile gone now, his eyes steady on my face—"that I was one in his confidence. It is my consolation to know that I have never betrayed that confidence nor do I so now. For it was to me that he gave the very great honor of safeguarding the one person in the world he thought truly shared a memory and a background he had loved. Your grandmother was his only true wife—this I have heard from his own lips—"

For the first time I was impressed by the Baron. His words now meant more to me than any protestation or lure the Gräfin had delivered. He did not talk of "treasure" or inheritance, but of what I had glimpsed for myself during that one visit with the dying man—his concern for the past.

142

"Knowing well what intrigue and devious dangers you might have to face without his protection, he asked oath that I would protect you to the best of my ability. He did the only thing which would make you wholly safe, arranged for you a marriage—"

I had been lulled by his references to my grandfather's confidence. Now I was brought up short out of my drifting along with his soothing words.

"Sir," I said with all the emphasis I could muster, "having suffered himself from such an arranged match— as you have just finished telling me that he did—how could he so wish me to follow the same path? You have been most kind, but as I have already told Luise—there is another way out of this trouble, and one I am most willing to take. I do not want the inheritance my grandfather left—it means nothing to me. In my own country I have plenty to keep me in comfort all my life. With the Elector dead, and my grandmother also, there is no longer any reason for my ever appearing at court— of being in Hesse-Dohna at all. My presence here was supposed to be a well-kept secret. If it remains that— do you not see all that must be done is for me to assign to the new Elector that inheritance which seems to be such a lodestone for ill feeling, and to leave as quietly as I came, with no one—save those in the original escort—and perhaps the new Elector—aware of it."

"An ingenious plan." The Baron smiled again, a condescending smile which suggested that "ingenious" was not the real word in his mind—but one closer to "stupid." "But I fear it is one which cannot be followed. His Highness's will and all its terms are even now made public. Unfortunately the Princess Adelaide has already become aware of what was going on and discovered all. The Princess, my dear lady, has the unfortunate temper of her mother. She also has very powerful friends. Several of them have the ear of the new Elector. They would never believe you meant what you have just told me. It would be their contention that if you were allowed to leave Hesse-Dohna, you would repudiate any promises you had made, and there would
143

follow much scandal and trouble. It would be very easy for the Elector to take steps to see you remain here under his control. He need only write a single order and you might well be imprisoned for life! Would there be anyone powerful enough then to stand up to him and demand your release—have you any friend in what you term your own country to do this?"

I cannot deny that he shook me. The points he made were much the same as the Gräfin's, but the repetition of them sank more deeply into my mind and I could see the dreadful logic of his reasoning. It fitted well with those tales I had heard of the absolute power these German princes held. That the treasure meant nothing to me—how could any of these raised on the constant viewing and descriptions of its splendors believe that I was not greedy for it?

"If you are married, then you will have a husband, as well as a powerful court faction to protect you. No such summary action can ever be taken. Also—" He glanced from me for the first time to the Gräfin.

She looked a little uneasy. "What he wishes to tell you, dear Amelia—it is a matter of delicacy, but the time is so short that we cannot allow such refinements to confuse us. Such a marriage would be a matter of convenience only, your convenience, do you understand?"

I felt the warmth of color in my own face. Now the Gräfin plunged ahead a little more boldly.

"After a time, during which your difficulties are resolved, Konrad will take you abroad. Such a marriage can be easily dissolved—perhaps in your own country. You shall be free then to follow your own desire. And, since you swear you do not want the treasure, then I am sure all can be arranged—but only if—"

"I have a friend at court," I supplied. "This is a very difficult decision for me, Baron von Werthern. To say yes, even under the circumstances you offer, violates all that I have been raised to believe in. It merely follows a pattern which caused my family so much grief

in the past. I cannot easily nor quickly answer you—
I must have time."

"That is what is not left for us, dear lady." Perhaps
he thought that he had near won his point and, like
the men carved in those hunting scenes on the walls
of the hall below, need only now move in with short
sword to deliver the final blow to my hesitation.

"I repeat, I must have time." I held to that. That his
words added to the Gräfin's had shaken me inwardly,
I had to admit. While with the Colonel—but, no, there
was no reason for me to look in that direction any more.
Fenwick was clearly out of favor. Not only that, but in
dire trouble himself. I stood alone, but I still clung to
a very forlorn hope that if I were only given fraction
more time, I could break out of the web.

The Gräfin arose. "It is time for lunch," she said as
might any hostess. "Let us forget for an hour at least.
Worry does not let food taste the better."

Unfortunately the meal set out for us was in one of
the low, dark rooms on the lower floor. Warm as the
day was, the limited light, the gloom here, made one
shiver. I had little appetite and did no more than taste
the dishes offered, though the Gräfin urged me to try
a special omelet with such assiduity that I could not
refuse with any politeness. The dish was savory and
highly spiced. So that I had to turn to my wineglass
more often than I did at any meal. At least that part
of German heritage had never been mine, I had no
desire to drink deeply. My two companions ate and
drank their way through the courses. The Baron seemingly set himself the duty of being attentive and discussed the news of Axelburg, with speculations on the
coming of the new Elector, as he might in any company.

I had emptied my wineglass, and my thirst was not
assuaged. Just now I wanted water, for my mouth felt
parched, my tongue seeming to swell. There was more
wine in my glass, though I was sure I had not seen it
poured.

In fact the room was growing so dark that I wished

they would light the candles to dismiss the ever-encroaching shadows creeping out from the corners. So very dark—was there a storm brewing?

A sudden spasm of giddiness struck at me and I caught at the edge of the table, needing anchorage. I was falling— What? My last remembered sight was the half-emptied wineglass, and in my mind some warning struggled—far too late.

Chapter 11

It was more vivid than any dream, still I was a part and yet not a part of it. I stood unsteadily in a place so dark that the light of at least a dozen or more candles, some lamps which blurred when I turned, or tried to turn my head a fraction, blazed without making it all visible. That chill dark was a curtain, a wall, shutting me within one small space. I stood, yes, but only because of the support of an arm about me. When I strove to view who it was who held me, my dizziness became so intense I had to close my eyes quickly against a spinning whirl of lights.

In the past I had done many strange things in dreams, danced, run, ridden, crept, merely stood to watch a myriad of weird creatures pass. Yes, this was different. The standing so was more real, my dizziness was real. I tried to speak, yet all I could hear was a croak of sound.

Yes, I was not alone. I was aware of a second presence on my other side, though he or she did not touch me, help to hold me upright. Sickness was a sour taste in my mouth, a heaving in my middle.

There was a third figure outlined in the blaze of those lamps which assaulted my eyes, seemed to enhance my giddiness. He—she—it appeared as a patch of black with pale blur for a face, standing directly before me. I could hear a voice, very thin and far away, sometimes fading completely. It was as if I had been brought before some bar of justice to await a sentence. I—I was in danger!

Fear cut through the haze which enclosed me, made all clear for a moment or two. That stranger whom I had seen earlier in the garden, it was he who faced me, holding a book in his two hands, repeating a garble of words of which I could make no sense. I fought to move, to speak, and found that both actions were beyond me. The only answer to my efforts was such a wave of nausea that I would have fallen forward had not that hold on me tightened painfully, kept me still upright.

One of my limp hands was seized by whoever stood to my left. The grip was brutal, I felt a stab of pain even through the overriding cloud of sickness as one of my fingers was possessed and had jammed around it a cold band, ground down almost viciously clear to the knuckles. I fought for freedom again and once more retched weakly, swayed.

Surely in no dream could one feel so sick as this! Fear, yes, nightmares held the very core of fear, but not this illness of body. I closed my eyes, unable to bear the wavering of the lamps and candles. Then, for a period, I could not feel anything at all.

Once more I crawled out of whatever nightmare prison had held me. My nausea was so great that I could not control sour bile rising in my throat. I was leaning forward as someone steadied my head so I could spew forth that accumulation from my stomach, heaving weakly with one sharp spasm after another. Now I had no doubt that I was awake, nor that I was ill with such violence as I had never felt before.

Hands steadied me. A cloth wet and fresh smelling patted against my sweating face. For the third time I vomited, the retching now dry and without result, making my body sore with effort. I hung above the waiting basin prepared for another such attack. But the moments passed and it did not come.

Then I was gently eased back on a pile of pillows, the basin vanishing before someone stepped between me and the light. I found my vision was not so blurred.

"Truda—?" I whispered.

"Lie still, gracious lady." She brought once more that dampened towel, wiped my sweating hands, and then my face. I was propped high enough so that I could see where I was, though my mind seemed very slow and sluggish and it was hard to remember much.

I had been at the table—and now I was here, back in the room upstairs, lying on the bed in the chamber which had been assigned to me. Those two facts were very clear. But in between was—

"Truda, have I been ill?" I got out that question with little pauses between the words, for even to say that much was an effort. My body seemed utterly drained of any energy.

"It is indigestion, gracious lady—of no serious matter now that the poison is out—"

"Poison?" I echoed. There had been something—something very wrong—I had been a part of it, but to force myself to remember it now was a task beyond my efforts.

"Oh, not real poison." Truda's face appeared unnaturally pale, or was that another trick my eyes were playing on me, part of the acute attack I had suffered. "It is only that you ate something which was not good for you."

"Not good for me—" I seemed only able to repeat her words. I tried to remember better the table, those dishes which had been offered me in almost endless procession. What had I eaten? A few bits of fish, the very thought of recalling the sight of my plate made me nauseous again. My throat was sore, as if scalded from within. However, I fought against the lassitude which held me, for deep within my mind, hiding, from whence I could not seem to bring it to light, was that spark of fear. Something had happened, something worse than just this illness.

Fish, yes, some peas, and that portion of spicy omelet which the Gräfin had so firmly insisted that I eat. But the others, all of them had also helped themselves from those same plates.

"Others—sick—too?" I made the effort and got out the question as Truda came closer, her eyes watchful, her expression one of concern.

"Only you, gracious lady." There was a firm note in her instant reply. I saw her glance away as if there was someone else here to listen and she would so slyly warn me.

Listening—listening outside doors. The Colonel—he had made me first aware of that. The Colonel—where was he?

I sat up suddenly, setting the room whirling once more, gripping the bedclothes on either side of my body to maintain myself erect as best I could. The Colonel—

"He was arrested—" I had not realized that I spoke aloud that thought which memory capriciously supplied until I saw Truda's finger fly to her lips in warning.

My memory was flowing back, as if that single fact had unlocked the door behind which it had temporarily been barricaded. I recalled now my interview with the Gräfin, in the other room of this suite, of my second with the Baron. I allowed Truda to ease me back on my pillows, but I did not loose my hold on memory.

All they had urged upon me returned clearly now. To be ill just when I needed all my wits about me! That seemed a very wry blow of fortune. That my illness was not natural, of that I was sure. Perhaps those two had

149

taken steps to see that I would be in no way able to assert myself for a time.

I had been watching Truda but thinking my own thoughts, which, to my joy were now free and I had full command on them. My body was weak, yes, and I do not think I could have done more than totter feebly if I had tried to walk across the room—but my mind was clear and my sight no longer played tricks on me. It was my sudden realization that Truda was watching me oddly that shook off my preoccupation with myself.

"What has happened?" For I was sure that something had occurred, more than the fact that I had been obviously taken disastrously ill at the dining table. That dream—or was it a dream?

She did not answer me in words, instead she lifted my left hand from where it rested by my side and held it up before me. For a moment I could not understand what she was attempting to show me. Then the lamplight shone on that massive band about my third finger. I must have stared at it bemused, half thinking myself back in my dream again, when Truda spoke with great distinctness but in a half whisper.

"That is what happened, Baroness—"

Baroness? Konrad's proposal! But I had refused it—said I must have more time. I could not have married him!

"No!" I turned to Truda, demanding that she assure me that this could not be so.

She had the dampened towel in her hand once more, bent over me to wipe my forehead. As she drew that close she whispered again.

"They drugged your wine—they had a priest waiting. It is true, gracious lady, you are wedded. The household were told, they are celebrating it now—"

"But it is no true marriage! Surely the priest could have seen I was not myself, not competent to give any response—"

"Gracious lady, the priest is their man. All on this estate, in the village over the mountain also, for some leagues around are their people. They will keep you
150

here and when you go forth again—when they permit it—then you must, for the sake of your own honor, agree that the marriage was a true one."

My fingers were already working at that lying band, striving to loosen it, hurl it from me. It was too tight, it had been too firmly forced upon my finger. I thought that if I would rid myself of it, it would need cutting off!

So that confused picture of the man in black, of being held upright before him in spite of my illness—that was a marriage! My anger gave me strength. Did they believe that they could bend me to their will in this fashion—with a play of marriage? They might deem me utterly helpless, a tool in their hands to gain the inheritance, for I now had no doubt at all that that was what they strove to gain through this trickery. Yes, they might think that they had the game nearly won—but they did not know me!

They had been so careful to show me every difficulty and danger which might lie ahead. Still—my mind seemed wholly free of any drug-induced cloud now—and my thoughts fastened on one thing which I thought proved that they were not as sure of their plans as they would have me believe. To risk this mockery of a marriage meant that there was some reason why it must be hurried through, that time itself was a menace to their plans.

I must learn what they had to fear and whether that source of fear could be turned to my own account. So—

Settling back on my pillows, I ceased trying to worry off from my finger that band marking an infamous piece of trickery. Instead I looked directly at Truda.

"I feel most ill," I said in as faltering a voice as I could manage. "I cannot be disturbed—" Was she quick enough to catch my meaning? I had begun to believe that Truda indeed was sharp witted. There was no one else I had to depend upon, so trust was forced upon me now.

"You are indeed overcome, gracious lady. If you try
151

to rise from your bed, you will find yourself very faint—"

I was right! She had understood my pretense at once. I sighed, laying limply among the pillows, my hands at my sides, glad for a moment I need not look at that hateful ring which seemed to weigh so heavily.

"No one but you, Truda, I am too ill."

"That is understood, gracious lady. I shall send a message that you have been very ill and are now so weak that only a long sleep will bring you to strength again. Also I shall see that your food passes only through my hands—" She had anticipated me there and I was thankful for her quick wit. Whatever they had used to make me a puppet in their play wedding certainly had been near poison, as Truda had named it. I could not afford many more such bouts. But if they believed that I was left weakened, ill, I might not be for a while the target of any more attempts to bend me to their service.

"I shall not leave you, gracious lady, save when it is necessary. This I have already told Frau Werfel—"

"And the food?"

"Must I not eat? They will bring me at least bread and cheese if no other— Now it would be well for you to sleep—if you can now—for in truth you are not strong."

She was right. Any effort caused moisture to bead my forehead, left my hands shaking. Had they misjudged the dosage to leave me so reduced, or had it been a gamble? A wife safely dead even just after marriage might mean more success for their plans. Only I hardly could believe that that was so. Even though by European law upon marriage a wife became but another possession of her husband, her whole estate forfeited to his control, I did not think in this case they had gone so far as to wish me dead. That might have defeated them by bringing up too many questions from those such as the Princess Adelaide, who would have every desire to get to the bottom of an arrangement which removed the major part of the Elector's inheritance from her own grasping hands.

No, I thought I could shift this much truth from the Baron's and Gräfin's arguments—a marriage was necessary in order that the treasure pass into their hands. And a marriage would have to be proven before the world—therefore, a bride, willing, must be presented in due time to public notice. I thought that murder was not within the scope of their planning—not yet.

Lying there, my eyes closed, I did not sleep. My body was sore with the violence their potion had wreaked upon it, my mind was alert, trying to find this path or that out of Kesterhof to freedom. To appeal to the priest would, of course, avail me nothing. I had not seen anything in the man earlier to make me believe that he was one who fulfilled his office with honesty and honor. He would not have lent himself to the charade they had staged this night had he been an upright man of his calling.

Kesterhof and all those within it—even around it— if Truda's belief was to be accepted—would be stolidly loyal to the Gräfin's wishes. Was her lord also part of the plot? I thought I could accept that he was.

What could I marshal against all this? My own will and determination and such assistance as Truda could offer. It seemed that David might once more be pitted against Goliath. But my anger was hot, and in me those traits of character which must have been my heritage from my grandmother were ready to carry on a war, unequal though that might be.

I had been used ruthlessly, in such a manner that they appeared to think that I had no method of defending myself. Therefore, suppose I outwardly became the weakling they imagined me, perhaps to weep and pine, but show no will to fight? I did not know how good I was at playing this game, for never in my life had I been forced into such duplicity.

Truda moved softly about the room. My illness, which had begun about midday, must have lasted well into the night, for I could see that the curtains were drawn at the windows, lamps lighted. What were they doing below, or in the Gräfin's room—plotting, and planning—what?

I raised one hand as Truda came near the foot of my bed and beckoned to her. Again I saw her glance toward the door. It was there that she went first, to set her ear against its panel, listening. I waited for a long moment and another thought came to trouble me. For I remembered that secret way through which the Colonel and I had gone when we left the palace. In a place as old as this there could be such secrets also—how could I now be sure that I was not under observation from some hidden point?

So my eyes searched the walls where the very seeming innocence of those flowers and silken ribbons made a mockery of deceit. I shivered, knowing that I would never feel safe again, that I must use all my wits and determination, though I felt woefully weak in both.

Truda picked up another cloth, dipped it into a waiting basin and wrung it out. I caught the scent of herbs, strong enough to battle the odor left by the shame of my sickness. The refreshing towel in hand, she came to me.

As she bent over to wipe once more my face the towel formed a screen for my lips and I understood by her clever move that perhaps she also feared that we might be spied upon in some manner.

"Is there a way out—for us?" I whispered.

"Ah, gracious lady, let this lie across your poor head. The ache will lessen if you but rest," she answered aloud and then her lips added in a whisper as faint as mind. "I see none—yet—"

"I am so sick—" I actually achieved a moan to end my complaint. "Water—if I might have water—"

"At once, gracious lady!"

I lay against the pillows, my eyelids a little closed, but not enough that I could not view the room. As Truda went to fill a cup from a jug standing on a side table, there came a sound from the door. I willed myself not to stiffen, to show no sign of fear as the maid went to open it.

The Gräfin stood there. Her expression was one of deep concern. How much of that was feigned? I wondered as she brushed past Truda to approach my bed.

"Amelia!" I could smell her scent, thick and sickeningly sweet. She must be leaning very close to me. "Amelia—?"

I allowed my eyes to open fully, slowly, striving with any art I might possess to give the appearance of one dazed.

"Amelia, dear one, how do you feel?" She had taken up my left hand, the one bearing that repulsive sign of betrayal, was holding it clasped in both of hers. Though her flesh was warm, moist, to me it was like being touched by a snake and I had all I could do to subdue my instant desire to jerk away. That I did not was a triumph, small, yet still a triumph.

"So—sick—" I said weakly. "My head—it aches—"

"Yes, you are sick—but you shall be better soon. Lie still my dear, sleep if you can. Sleep—"

She put my hand back upon my breast gently. There was a small shadow of a smile about her full lips. In the light of the lamps—or was it because I was alerted to her—her face had a new look—she was a different person from the frivolous woman of fashion who had been my companion for what seemed now a long time. As she straightened up and turned away from the bed she spoke abruptly to Truda:

"Tend your mistress well, girl. She must be carefully watched. These sudden fevers can be of great danger— so do grave illnesses often begin. We have sent for the doctor from Grumlu, but he cannot possibly arrive before morning."

Truda curtsied, her eyes downcast. I watched her follow the Gräfin to the door. Her hands moved about the latch when that had closed and then she glanced back at me, a shadow of alarm upon her face. She stood for a moment, running one fingertip across her lower lip as if thinking deeply, and then returned quickly to my side, reaching to the pillows which supported me, moving them about with one arm as she drew me, as one too weak to shift herself, to lean forward against her own shoulder. As she did so her very soft words were spoken into my very ear.

"There is no lock upon the door, it cannot be in any way bolted."

As a last resource I supposed we could barricade it in some fashion with what furniture that could be moved. But the time for that was not yet, I was sure we were not yet reduced to such desperate straits.

"A map—" I whispered, "can you find me a map?"

To get out, of not only Kesterhof, but also the part of this damnable country where the Gräf was all powerful, was my first thought. We were two women alone and easy prey for any one else under this roof. I remembered with a sick horror Truda's suggestion that when I left here, *if* I left here, I would only be able to meekly accept the role they had forced upon me. The Baron's suggestion of a marriage of convenience might mean nothing at all. Such could be too easily annulled by either party.

"I do not know," was the answer she gave me.

I rested back once more against the pillows she had shaken up. She brought me the water I had asked for earlier and I drank, really as test to see if that might once more induce a drastic reaction. But the liquid went easily down my throat and no nausea followed.

Truda sat in a low chair near one of the lamps. She had opened a box, brought out sewing things, presenting a proper picture of a maid who was too well trained to sit with idle hands, even when at watch in a sick room. I was left to thoughts which went round and round, wearing ever deeper a path of helplessness in my mind, giving me no hope of clear action.

There was a small china clock on the mantel and the ticking of it seemed to fill the room like mocking, tittering laughter. I had time in plenty, but that was playing me false, if I could not use it to any advantage.

It is in the night that all the brave resolves one may

hold to by day are shaken, that our courage shrinks and grows the less. I made wild plans and saw their folly even as I did. Truda had laid her work, a square of white, out upon a tabletop and now I saw her bring out from her box a small tool with a leaden tip. Such I had used for myself—for the marking out of an embroidery pattern. Now and then she consulted, or seemed to consult, a small book which probably contained the pattern she would copy, so absorbed in what she did that I first wondered and then resented that such could hold her attention at such a time. Perhaps her help was all a sham—meant to entice me on in trust until I revealed myself utterly and then she could betray me—

"I am thirsty," I said at last, unable any longer to watch her unconcerned absorption in something so alien to what I was sure lay about me, if not about the both of us.

"At once, gracious lady!" She arose, but, as one who half forgets, she put within the pocket of her apron, so that it trailed a quarter out, the square of material on which she had been at work. Once more she filled the cup, brought it to me.

As she set it to my lips, her eyes met mine and then shifted to that which she carried. I took her meaning instantly, and set two fingers pinchwise to snag the edge of the square, so that when I had drunk my fill and she went to replace the cup, the square of cloth lay now under my hand.

I reached to draw the covers higher about me, and in so doing was able to spread out wider that bit of muslin, look down upon the lines marking it. This was truly no embroidery pattern. Rather it made little sense at all and until I saw that it was centered by a dot which had been so pressed in that it was very dark indeed and above that the letter "K" in a curl. Kesterhof? From it two roads—or so I deemed the lines to be. One I was sure was that which had brought us here—the other leading in near the opposite direction was that to the town over mountains where the Gräf's influence also held. All else was blank and I could imagine it a wilderness which I had no doubt was patrolled by just such men as the forester who had turned me back this afternoon.

To take to that woods without a knowledgeable guide was such folly that I did not even consider it. Both roads would be well watched. So much for my hopes of escape in that fashion. What remained to me?

I squeezed the bit of muslin tight within my hand. Bargain with those who held me? I could have laughed aloud my scorn at that. Nor was there a single person to whom I might try to get a message now that the Colonel had been swept aside from this playing board as a discarded piece.

Something the Gräfin had said on her visit to me now flashed into mind—that fever was the forerunner of serious illness. I must play that part as long as I was able. The dose they had put into my wine had made me violently ill. Could I now assume the guise of one whose constitution had been so disordered by the severity of whatever potion had been used that I was no longer a trouble to them, only a seriously ailing creature who could be disregarded as any threat? My thoughts had reached and clung to that when once more there came an imperative demand for entrance from the door and even before Truda could reach it, that was flung open.

The Gräfin again and a man—first I thought it was the doctor—and then I saw the Baron behind her. There was no triumph on Luise's round face now, rather I saw a grimace of fear. The Baron's hand was clutching her shoulder, left bare by the low cut of her gown, for she was dressed with the same formality she would have shown at a dinner in Axelburg.

He was propelling her forward toward the bed as if he held her prisoner. But there was no anger nor fear in his expression, rather a contemptuous complacency, as if he had full control of not only her, but also some situation which pleased him very much.

"You." He did not turn his head to even look at

Truda, but it was plain that he spoke now to her. "Bring pen, ink, from the desk—at once!"

He gave the Gräfin such a shove that she near tripped, having to catch at the foot of the bed to hold herself upright. Then he paid no more attention to her, instead he spoke over his shoulder with the same tone he had used to Truda:

"Grotzer—to me!"

The man who came in swiftly at the Baron's call did not wear a livery coat, rather the plain black of a city man. His face was narrow, his mouth pinched, as if speaking a word was to lose something precious. Steel-bowed spectacles perched on his bony nose. Behind those his eyes blinked as if they were so weak that even the lamplight hurt him.

In his hands he carried a portfolio and lying on it was a sheet of paper. He scuttled around the other side of the bed and pushed that forward as if he meant to hold it ready within reach of my hands. Truda had appeared on the other side with an enameled inkwell, a pen.

The Baron took both from her, not quite elbowing her away, but he was not yet through with her.

"Can you write your name, girl?"

"It is so, gracious lord," she admitted.

The Baron nodded. "Well, enough—two witnesses— that is all that are needed, is that not the law then, Grotzer?"

"It is so, your lordship." The man's voice was as dry as a rustle of one old sheet of paper against another.

"Then, Baroness." Now his master turned upon me. "We need only finish our business. You will sign!"

At a gesture from him Grotzer did drop the portfolio and the paper it supported upon my knees, while the Baron pushed the pen down with a determined jab into the inkwell and then spoke again.

He had thrust the inkwell itself back toward Truda, not even waiting to see if she took it or whether it and its contents would land upon the bed. Now he reached over, took up my right hand in a punishing grip and

159

set the pen between my fingers. With his other hand he indicated the bottom of the paper which had been so summarily presented to me.

"Sign!" he commanded in the tone of one who would brook no refusal.

Chapter 12

So assured and brutal was his manner that fear itself brought me out of the role of half-conscious invalid I had hoped to play. There was that in his haste to get this done which was a strong warning. He had forced the pen into my fingers well enough, but he could not make me trace a single letter.

"What is this?" I managed to get out the question, refusing to be overpowered by his force.

The Baron's face flushed, it was plain that he was prepared to allow no counter to his own will. His hand raised to strike, open palmed, against my face, bruising my lips against my teeth, sending a sharp lash of pain through my head. I was so startled at his blow that I gasped for breath. Never in all my life had I met with such usage as this.

He loomed over me until his anger-reddened face was only inches away from mine and the wine stench of his breath was strong. The hand which had thrust that pen into my fingers tightened its grip now about my fingers. Spatters of ink flew across the coverlet as he deliberately brought his strength to bear in a white-hot circle of pain about my flesh.

"Damn you!" There was a fleck of white spittle at one corner of his mouth. "If it is necessary to teach you who is master—then that I shall be very pleased to do—"

There was something in his eyes then from which, in spite of my attempt to hold courage about me as a cloak, I shrank. He must have guessed my fear, for he laughed coarsely.

My hand prisoner in his hold was brought up again to the paper.

"Sign—!"

There was no help against his forceful cruelty. I did not expect that Truda would dare stand up to him, and the other two were his allies. I looked down at the paper as he still loomed over me, his will a tangible weight on me.

The document was in legal terms, that much I saw. What did its words bind me to? Yet I knew that I had no chance at all against him. He applied more pressure to my wrist until tears of pain came into my eyes.

"If you break my bones"—again I found a small rag of courage left—"then I shall not be able to do what you will."

He grunted, but his grasp loosened. Even through his mastery of me, the sense of that must have made him think again. That I had gained anything was false. So, because there was no other way out, I scrawled my name near illegibly at the foot of the paper. The Baron dropped his hold upon my half-numb hand and jerked up the document to near eye level, holding it so close his face that I wondered if he had some weakness of sight.

Then he gave a sharp exclamation and rounded on me. His eyes were more than cruel—they could have looked out of the face of some medieval torturer who enjoyed his work. Once more one hand raised as if to give me such a punishing blow as would have rocked my head on my shoulders or driven me unconscious.

"What is this foolishness?" he demanded, his voice the roar of an enraged animal. "This is not your name!" He waved the paper before my eyes. "You make mock of me—*me!* It shall not be so, you slut, you nameless whore of a whoring line!"

"That is my name. I have signed it with my name—"

His fingers bit into my shoulder, cutting into my flesh, and he dragged me forward and up, having thrown the paper toward the man in black. I saw the fist coming at me and could not dodge it. There was an instant of shock, of such pain as I never knew could exist, and then nothing.

My head hurt, there was a dull pressure there, as if someone had inserted my poor aching skull into an iron band which was slowly being tightened, ever tightened. Also there came sharp jolts of other pain, so intense and sharp-set that I strove to flee back into that place where there was no feeling at all. Yet I was not to have such comfort.

I did not think, I could only feel, and this torment went on and on. Slowly I became aware of the fact that my body was moving—that is, what I rested upon could not be a stable bed, rather a support which swayed and shook. It was that movement which brought to me those sharper stabs of agony. I tried to beg for rest, that I be left alone. Whether I uttered any sound at all I do not know.

It would seem that I was of tough stock, I was not to be allowed to once more slip away. In spite of the pain the outside world began also to return once again. Not only was I being carried in a moving support, but there was a wind, or at least puffs of air now and then which touched my aching face. Perhaps it was those touches which were restoring me to fuller consciousness.

The pain was there, that I could not elude. Only now I was more just bruised and aching flesh. My mind began to awake. I had been on the bed in the Kesterho nd then— Piece by piece the details of that last scene rept back to me. The paper which the Baron had rought. Sign! His voice seemed to ring again in my ars, heighten the ache in my head.

I had signed—why, then—? I remembered his fist oming at me. His anger—why—? I had done as I had een ordered. It was now as if my cramped fingers gain traced that name—

"Amelia Harrach—" My name—I *had* signed my ame. Why, then—?

There was a jolt which snapped my head half around. he following pain was such I was once again merciully released into darkness.

Cold, it was so very cold! I must be lying in the snow. ad I fallen somewhere along the path up from the iver landing? I remembered that the snow sometimes rifted there. They would find me—they must find ne—I was so cold—and the pain in my head—as if ice ad thrust its way into my very brain. Cold—

But I no longer swung from side to side. I was lying till—it was a blessed thing to be still—even in the now. James would be here soon—he would call Rafe, 'eter, they would take me back to the manor house. etty would come with blankets, and the stone jar filled vith hot water to set at my icy feet. I had been having uch queer, queer dreams. But I need not remember hose now! I would be safe soon—out of the cold, back n my own safe bed at the manor.

For how long I drifted in and out of that dream I hall never know. Did I call for James—for Letty—for thers who had watched over me from childhood? If I id, I am sure there was no one in those hours who vould have understood, or cared if they had. There was o warmth brought me, no attention paid to my hurts.

I awoke out of that half-life slowly, opening my eyes pon gloom from time to time. Twice someone pulled ne up, sending pain flaring through my head. The hard dge of a cup was pushed against my lips causing more ain, and liquid slopped into my mouth when I opened t to cry out in protest until I was half choked.

163

Only I discovered that the liquid allayed the parch ing of my mouth and my throat and I drank eagerly I opened my eyes, but that made me dizzy and I coul not see truly, nor know who fed me so.

"Truda—?" I croaked once, hardly knowing from which recess within memory I drew that name "Letty—?" But no one answered and I was droppe back, to lie in my swing between one world and th next.

I was awakened more completely once by voices— one was angry in tone, though I could not make out th words—they were very strange. Only after that seemed to be fed more often and I was no longer quit so cold. I think that my sleep became normal and n longer was the stupor of the very ill.

When I aroused next the pain in my head was onl a low ache and I found I could open my eyes withou feeling so ill. I was not at home in the manor—thos light walls and many windows to let in the sun had n place here. Painfully I began once more to patch on piece of near elusive memory to the next.

The manor—but I had left the manor—how lon ago?—a long, long time—numbers of days, weeks months meant nothing now. Then there had been an other room—one with a great bed, curtained, strange— and beyond that another room in which—

So I might have turned a key to open the door whicl prisoned much of my mind. For now I remembered— the Kesterhof—the visit of the Baron! Only this wa not that room either! Where was I?

I tried to rise a little in my bed, to discover that tha attempt now only left me sickly dizzy, but started onc again a tormenting throb in my head. To even drav my hand upwards was a lengthy and exhausting busi ness. At last I brought my fingers to my cheek, th touch of their tips made me flinch away. My jaw wa swollen, painful.

Even as I tried to explore my hurts, so did I also lool about at what I could see without attempting to tur my head. I was in bed, yes. But the covers over me wer threadbare, old. There was a musty smell of dust here. Straight ahead was a stark stone wall which had a single break in it, a solid door crossed with bands of what looked like half-rusted metal.

What light was here came from no lamp or candle but was pale and grayish, like the daylight of a storm-ridden day. The room was dim and grim, also. I could see nothing but the foot of the bed, which seemed hardly more than a rough cot, the wall, and the door, while a chill appeared to spread from the walls—reaching out to cover me far more firmly than did the patched linen and musty upper spread lying over my body.

Where I might be I could not guess, but the more I stared at the wall, the closed door, and my thoughts grew clearer, the more I began to guess what might have happened. This was no room for a guest no matter how unwelcome—it was far more the cell of a prison! Did I lie somewhere in the underrooms of the Kester-hof, perhaps one which Frau Werfel had not been em-powered to show a curious visitor? The belief that this must be the truth I faced and accepted. Also I under-stood what might have brought me here. That name I had signed—in truth it was my own and the only one I would ever acknowledge. Only as Baron von Werth-ern's wife, no matter how much of a mockery that mar-riage had been and was, my name might not be con-sidered here my legal one—Amelia Harrach. Whatever they had attempted to win from me with that docu-ment, their plan had failed, though I had lost by it also—or I would not lie here.

There remained one small hope I could hold to—since I had not signed as Konrad wished—then it was to their advantage to keep me alive. While I still lived, I could hope—

Once more I moved my hand, this time making a difficult thing of raising it so that I could see if that tying band was still upon my finger. It was. So weak was I that I must let my hand fall on my breast. At the same time there was a sound from the door, I was about to have a visitor.

165

I could not believe that it was Truda. For a moment I hoped that she had come to no harm. It might well be that the Baron and the Gräfin would want no witnesses to their treatment of me. However, there was nothing I could do now for any but myself. I watched the door, curious to see just who my gaoler was—sure that the Gräfin herself would not have taken such a job.

The woman who stalked through, bearing a tray, was certainly no one I had ever seen before. She was tall and thin, but stooped forward, and had a face which awakened no thoughts of friendship. Time must have taken a wide toll from her score of teeth, for her chin, on which grew a bristle of gray hair, rose to meet the hook of her nose. She seemed to have no hair on her head at all, for she wore a bonnet such as a hairless baby might have, the strings of it tied directly under her upward-pointing chin.

Her dress was of no style, rather a voluminous robe of gray, girdled with a leather strap, the free end of which bobbed back and forth as she strode toward the bed. Still holding the tray in her hands, she put out a foot to a length I would not have thought possible and raked into view a stool near high enough to be termed a table, on which she set the tray.

Dipping a coarse towel into a basin of water, she came purposefu'' to me and set about bathing my swollen face with little care for any pain she caused, taking up one of my hands after another and subjecting them to the same act of cleaning. She did not speak and I would not break the silence between us, not yet. Better play the game, I had decided upon in Kesterhof (though I had had little success with it then) of appearing less conscious than I was. Having made me tidy after her own rough fashion, she produced next a vessel with a spout, not quite a teapot in design, but having some of its features. Bracing my head against her bony shoulder, she put that spout to my lips as an inducement to drink.

The stuff was near cold and greasy tasting, but I

discovered that I was hungry and even this slop brought some satisfaction. I finished the contents of the strange feeder and she slammed that back on the tray before she set about straightening my bed.

Her rough handling made my head ache, so I found that it needed very little acting on my part to lapse back into an apparent stupor once again, though I tried to sort out what little I could gather from her general appearance and actions.

I slept, waked, was tended always by the silent woman in the queer garb. She never spoke to me, nor did I, trying to find my own way through the bewilderment which clouded my mind, attempt to ask any questions. It was very plain I was a prisoner, but where my cell might be I had no idea, save I suspected that it perhaps lay within the walls of the Kesterhof.

Why I did not have another visit from the Baron was also a puzzle. I had spoiled whatever plan that sheet of paper represented, while his brutal treatment of me hereafter had made plain how little he valued my welfare— So—why had he not appeared again to enforce his will, as, with his strength against mine, I had no doubt he could eventually do?

The ache in my head grew less. I allowed myself to move cautiously about in my bed, striving so to bring back strength to my body. Now I could brace myself up, look around the barren cell in which I was imprisoned.

Cell it certainly was. There were only the plain stone walls—one broken by the iron-barred door, that directly opposite it by a slit of window so narrow and deep-set that if the sun ever shone outside, none of its rays struck into this dank place—only a gray light which faded into deep dark when night came. The only furnishings were the rude bed-cot on which I lay, a stool which also served as a side table when my wardress had need of some support which could be moved closer to my bed, and a flap of time-darkened, splintered wood supported against the wall to my left by two rusty chains the ends of which were embedded in the stones. There was no mistake that this cell was intended for a prisoner.

I still wore the garments in which I had been dressed on that day—now how long in the past—when I had gone to that fatal meal with the Gräfin and the Baron. The dress was creased, spotted with stiff patches which I thought might be blood, perhaps from my cut lip which healed slowly. The swelling along my jaw also subsided, though it still hurt me to open my mouth widely, and the teeth along that side of my face ached.

My hair had lost the pins which had held my braids in place and wisps of it were matted about my forehead and neck. I must be a grotesque scarecrow in comparison with that neat young lady, but there was no sliver of glass mirror here to tell me so. The dank chill of the narrow chamber brought me to edge the upper cover of my bed around my body to serve as a shawl.

In the wane light of that room, for want of better employment, I had examined that spread, for it had not the coarse feel of the other coverings of the cot. In fact I discovered it must have once been equal to such as were used on a state bed—such as that which had been mine in Axelburg. In spite of the grease and grime now ground into the fabric it was of heavy velvet, interlined with brocade now so dirty one could only guess it had once blazed with color.

There had been a design embroidered across the center of the heavy square. However, as I studied that, I thought that the threads had been deliberately loosened and picked out, some pulled with such force as to leave spreading tears in the cloth. I believed that I could dimly make out that some coat of arms, though so mangled, was the general pattern that was only a guess.

I had counted four comings of the dark that I believed meant nights before I had gained the strength to attempt to stand upon my own feet. Under my wrinkled stockings the chill stone struck as cold as if there was nothing between the stone floor and my flesh, while I had to hold on to the bed and then the wall to steady myself.

Perhaps I was under observation, though I could see no break in the door to suggest a peephole for a guard, nor any crevice between the stones of the walls. However, for that I did not care. My objective was the window and a chance to see where this prison might lie.

One hand against the wall supported me as I began a very slow and giddy journey toward the slit, only the lowermost portion of which could be on a level with my eyes. The air blew strongly and I held my coverlet as a shawl closer about me.

However, all I could sight from this position was just open sky—not even a treetop, or the green of a bush was visible. Which was a puzzle, knowing the forest setting of the Kesterhof. I leaned against the wall, breathing deeply of that fresher air, drawing upon my strength. It was plain that if I were to gain any further knowledge, I must stand higher. Which meant bringing hither the stool and climbing up upon it. A feat I was not sure that I could accomplish in my present state of weakness. My determination was now such an obstinacy that I was driven to do what moments before I might have deemed impossible. Back I shuffled, and I moved that stool toward the window and the wall, by pushing it, first with one knee and then the other, before me. At last the wood struck full and solid against the stones.

Dropping the cumbersome cover from me, I reached up with both hands to catch the sides of the window slit where the stone of its casing protruded like a sill all the way about the edge. I lingered so for a moment, again gathering my strength, and then made the last effort, stepping up and at the same time pulling on the stone while my fingers were bruised by its roughness and my nails broke.

I tottered and half threw myself outward, against the slit so that the wall itself could support me, my hands locked on the frame. Once more I looked out.

No trees—nothing—but empty sky!

Where was I? This was not the Kesterhof, set as it had been in the valley with the remains of the old forest enclosing it. Slowly, with the utmost care, lest I become dizzy again and fall from my perch, I lowered my head so I could look down. I almost fainted then.

For I was gazing down from some great height, and never have I had a head to look so. I clutched at my window support, closed my eyes instantly against that swoop of descent, of the feeling that there was nothing to save me from toppling over to fall and fall, forever and ever—

I *must* know. There was a sharp stab of pain from my swollen lip as my teeth struck into it and I fought my battle, eyes still closed. I *MUST* know! What I did then was far harder for me than it would have been to face Konrad von Werthern at the height of his rage. I made myself open my eyes, and not only look down, but steadily, with a need for finding somewhere, on those plunging slopes, a clue to my prison.

I could see nothing that I recognized. There was forestland, yes, but far below me. With my bad head for heights I could not judge how far. So they had taken me out of Kesterhof, brought me to some place they probably considered far more safe and hidden. It could be anywhere within the boundaries of Hesse-Dohna and I would be none the wiser.

Having made myself stand through that survey, I at last slumped down upon the stool which had served me as a ladder. Burying my face in my hands, I tried to think coherently, but for some moments my mind was in a daze. How had I been brought here—and when—

Truda! My own situation had filled my mind so completely that my memory of the girl came as sharp as a blow. Me they might have good reason for keeping safe prisoned, but would Truda's life mean anything when she would be able to disclose their plans? I did not place murder beyond the Baron if that would further what he wanted most. Of his desire I was entirely sure—the treasure—that mass of gold and gems which had been my curse instead of any inheritance.

Almost, my thoughts became bitter, it would seem that that dying man in the palace had willfully arranged this to end once and for all any chance of his past arising to shame him! I could, after what had chanced to me, believe any diabolic intrigue.

I had drawn Truda into the coils about me. It did not matter that I had been unaware that my enemies would have used me as ill as they did—I should have been far more wary. Never should I have asked Truda to accompany me to Kesterhof. At this dark moment I could well believe her dead and already buried in some secret forest spot by just such a man as that Gluck, a hireling of the Gräf, who had first proven to me that I was entirely in their power.

What did I have now that I could use in my own defense? There was nothinq that I could do for Truda—unless by some miracle I could indeed win out of here and appeal to the law—

The law? What law?—the Elector's will was the law and the new ruler would have no reason to favor any tale of mine. I rocked back and forth, the misery of my case flooding through me like another and even more deadly illness.

No! I raised my head, my hands became fists as I stared at the door. I was still alive, I had regained a measure of my strength. While I lived I still could—must—do something!

The coverlet which had fallen from my shoulders lay in a coil on the floor. I gathered it up and threw the bundle toward my bed. Perhaps it was the heat of despairing anger which brought new strength into my body, for, when I got to my feet this time, I did not totter but stood firmly, in spite of the cold under my feet.

Then I began to take inventory of what I still possessed. Who ever had bundled me away to this cell had not bothered to search my person. I had sought the seam in my shirt slitted to allow a hand through to the

171

pocket in my under shirt. The packet was still there. I slipped that out, felt it carefully without unwrapping it, for I did not know when my silent wardress might make one of her appearances. The gold was still in it. Could that woman be bribed? I decided instantly that it would be folly to try, she need only take it all from me and give nothing in return. Good will or honesty were the last qualities I could hope to find in this place. Around my throat—yes, I still wore the iron necklace. Fingering it I thought it a pity that the workmanship was so delicate a thing, it offered no tool or weapon worth the considering now.

Since the door was plainly beyond my opening, I began to think of the walls. My experience in the palace had planted romantical ideas of hidden passages. Now I laughed at that idea, and then, hushed in an instant, for my laughter sounded so near crazed that it frightened me.

The cell was growing steadily darker. Still I went to that bench table—or whatever purpose it was meant to serve—hanging by the rusty chains. The wood of its upper surface was not smooth. There were many scratches and indentations. As my fingers swept the dust from those I realized that they had meaning. There were letters put together—forming names! Meaningless, save it made only more certain that this cell had been used before, perhaps for long years. I was not the first to be so imprisoned.

I pulled at one of the chains. Rust flacked off in my hand, but there was only a surface dusting of that, the chain itself was as immovable as the stone which held its upper end. There a last glimmer of light caught one line of letters, so deeply graven that even dust could not hide them. A line of letters with beneath them a symbol cut deep, very deep.

"Ludovika—" I had not known I read that name aloud until the sound echoed hollowly through the small room.

Ludovika! The evil Electress—who had vanished

into Wallenstein never to be seen again! Wallenstein—!

I swayed, caught at one of those chains to steady myself. I knew now where I must be—in that fortress-castle of such dark history that the very land around it was considered cursed.

My mouth was dry, I stepped back, staggered, fell once more on my bed. Wallenstein—!

All my courage of moments earlier fled. I shuddered and held my arms about me. Though I could no longer see that name so deeply scratched into the wood, it repeated itself over and over again in my mind.

I did not faint, though I would have welcomed that release from thought and fear. I was still conscious when the door opened and a very dim light shone in. The wardress was coming with her tray.

She looked for the stool where she generally set her burden before turning her attention to me. That it was gone for the first time seemed to make her aware that I was not as always, lying weakly at her mercy. She raised her eyes directly to me. There was no expression on her dour hag's face. I might have been no more than the stool which had removed itself from its customary place.

She did not approach me, rather went on to the chained bench and there sat down her burden. Then, taking up the candle she carried, she turned away to the door. I broke—

"The light! Leave the light!" I begged her.

She neither halted nor turned, but was gone. The door closed behind her with a sullen thud.

Chapter 13

I crouched in the swiftly fading light, my eyes still on that door. Wild thoughts of lying in wait somehow when next I was visited, of attacking my wardress came and as swiftly were banished from my mind. I had no faith in my own strength against the woman, who, old and bent as she was, still gave the impression of the ability to hold her own with any captive. Nor could I be sure that she came alone—that there was not someone awaiting in the corridor without. Still I refused to believe that I could not discover some small weakness which I might not turn to my advantage.

In the meantime, for the first time in what might be days, I felt hunger. At least they still supplied me with food. I went to the chained bench and inspected what lay on the tray. There were two plates, wooden ones such as might have been found, I believe, in the hut of some very destitute peasant. The wood was old, and, even in this dim light, showed stains. But in my hunger I did not care. One was curved enough to be termed a basin and in it was a portion of what looked like thick soup or stew, congealing now so that gobs of grease rode on its surface. On the other there were two rounds of dark, thick bread. A battered mug held something which smelled like country beer. A horn spoon as old appearing as the plates was the only eating utensil. I dipped that into the stew and ate, crumbling the hard bread bit by bit into the liquid, since it made my sore jaw ache even to consider chewing it unsoftened.

The serving was very far from the dainties of the Gräfin's tables. However, it was generous enough to satisfy my hunger and I gulped it down. Though I found the beer—if beer it was—so distasteful that I could not finish that portion.

Though I sat waiting as the darkness grew thicker and thicker (so that at least even my eyes, adjusted to this gloom, could not make out anything inches away), the woman did not return for the tray. I guessed that perhaps her visits were over for this day.

I had never been afraid of the dark, but in this present sent thick black I felt smothered, as if I were already buried, dead or not. Also the chill of the cell became stronger and I huddled back into the bed, pulling about me the coverlet. As my hands ran over the unevenness of that old embroidery I remembered again the name so deep set in the wood of the bench—Ludovika. Had this old velvet rag been hers? One bit of her old luxury somehow transported with her into this grim exile?

That beautiful disdainful creature, whose ennui and power the dead artist had so well caught in that fabulous scene of the Electress's birthday, had she come to this? I recalled the Gräfin's words in the carriage—how long had she been able to exist in such a prison, reft of everything which had been her life, which she had taken as her right and not just a privilege?

I found myself moving, hardly aware of what impulse set me on my feet, back toward the bench, one hand outstretched before me. There was the palest glimmer of light which must mark the window slit, but none of that seeped beyond the sill. My wrist struck painfully against the edge of the bench, then my fingers swept back and forth, seeking, I could not say why, the letters of that fateful name, so deeply scored into the battered wood that I believed no passage of time would ever erase them.

How long had it taken her to cut that self-set memorial? What tool had she found to use as her pen. Rage must have filled her—certainly it was rage, hot, consuming—never despair. I was as sure of that as if I had heard her outburst of hate in my ear now. My fingers slipped away from the grooves of that deep driven line of letters, moved, as if my wrist had been caught in near as strong a grip as that the Baron had used to force me to his will. What I touched now was that circled device which lay below the name.

Though my forefinger followed the lines of it about and about, I could not at first make any sense of its design. I tried to think of a coat of arms. No, this, even though I could no longer see it, held no seeming of armorial bearings.

Again my conviction was sure, even as I had been so certain that rage had been the emotion which had driven the prisoner to inscribe her name. Also— I brought my hand back with a jerk. Was I again drugged in some fashion, given in that unappetizing food some mind-destroying poison? I thrust the hand which had explored back under the folds of my improvised shawl, retreating until my legs struck against the cot bed, and I fell rather than seated myself upon it.

Surely I had not felt that—a heat, a fast growing heat from the lines of the device, as if they shaped a basket in which coals smoldered? To believe that was to accept that my wits were indeed disordered. I was not—I had not—lost my hold on sanity no matter what lay behind me!

Feverishly I half whispered:

"I am Amelia Harrach! I have been imprisoned here—for a reason I do not know. I am me—myself—"

The hand which had felt—which had NOT felt—that change pressed now against the pendant of the butterfly necklace where it lay upon my breast. As if there were some saving amulet or charm, my fear left me.

Only to lift again as my thoughts repeated "amulet," "charm"? Such things were the follies found only in old tales.

Still, nothing now would have brought me to my feet again, sent me across the room to touch that device carven in the wood. Though I tried to berate myself for my cowardice. This was superstition, the refuge of the untutored mind when confronted by that for which there seems to be no rational explanation.

What had the Gräfin said of the Electress—that one of her familiars, her trusted servants—had been a hexenmeister—a dealer in knowledge not of this world? But that was also a belief dismissed by modern rational thinking. This land had once been drenched in the blood of the innocent, denounced by enemies, by those ridden by hysterical fears, as being the servants of the devil. It would not be strange that with so demon ridden a history such beliefs could still find rooting—or had a hundred years ago.

Be as it might I could not sleep. I did not even want to lie back on the muddle of my bed. Instead I sat there in the dark, finding myself straining to hear—what?

Once there did come a cry which startled me into a choked answer. Only that sounded from beyond the slit of the window. Some night hunter, winged and seeking its prey, I told myself. All else was silence, which was so abiding I fancied soon I could hear the beating of my own heart.

No, I must put my mind to other things, to thinking about what I could do. I must refuse to let myself be cowed by the past, even by my present helplessness. I was alive—I was gaining again my strength. Tomorrow I must try to learn what I could from my wardress—I must demand that I be heard by whoever commanded this place.

Truda—the Gräfin—both had said there was a garison here. Very well, the commander of that must be my gaoler. If I created enough disturbance, might not that reach his ears? I could do no less than try—I must—

The sound this time was not any cry of a night bird—no! I tightened my grip on the coverlet around me as I turned my head in the dark—first to the slit of window just barely visible still—but in a moment or two I was sure it did not come from there.

Rather it—it was out of the wall—that very wall from which hung the bench bearing the Electress's ill-fated name! As if, through the very solid stone, the sounds managed to seep like a trickle of water. Singing? If so faint, and perhaps faraway, that no words could be distinguished. Only, I was sure, it bore a rhythm which suggested singing—or a chant.

I strained so hard to hear, and at last I was sure I was right. That rise and fall of song was coming closer or growing louder, though still there were no true words within it.

The sound was thin, I thought that only one voice was raised. Now it grew so loud that I could distinguish the breaks between words. It was a chant rather than a true song. But the words were in a foreign tongue oddly accented, the tones running up and down the scale—sometimes so high they were like the cry of a small bird, other times descending near to a guttural mumbling.

To my ears it would seem to be just on the other side of the wall now. I threw aside the covering and did what I would not, could not, have done earlier, crossed the room, leaned far enough across the table shelf to lay one palm against the cold stone. With my right hand I dragged up the battered tankard, splashing the lees of the bitter beer wide cast, and used that vessel to pound on the wall.

That I could expect any help from the singer or chanter, I did not even stop to think of the possibility of that. However this was sound, produced by a human voice. I was not completely alone and forgotten in the dark, and I longed for some acknowledgement of my being.

The chant ended sharply at the first clang of the metal against the stone. Another prisoner on the other side of the wall? That was my first guess. There followed utter silence, to my vast disappointment, though I was not sure what I expected. Then—words—not in any chant now—but uttered in a weird moaning:

"Death—death—"

A warning? Yet there was something strange about that cry. Firmly I raised the tankard and once more rapped sharply.

"Death—" the wail once more answered me.

"Who are you?!" I raised my own voice, hoping that it would carry through the barrier wall. "Where are you?"

"Fear death—"

Not fear, but a kind of irritation, gave me force to rap for the third time. I had begun to suspect that perhaps this voice was another device of my gaolers, meant to keep me unsure of my own sanity. Devious to be sure, but who could tell what refinements of torment the Baron might have designed to keep me under control?

"Who are you?" I demanded again.

There was only silence for an answer and at last I put down the battered tankard, feeling that I was going to get nothing more out of that frustrating wall this night.

I returned to the cot, but I felt more at ease, in a manner, than I had since I had come to my clear senses here. If they were playing such childish tricks on me, then that argued that I was still of such importance to them that they must take care in my handling. That gave me a little satisfaction, so that at last I huddled down among my covers and slept.

Nor did I dream. It seemed that within me there had risen a new confidence. Perhaps because I had not been thrown into a panic by the wailing voice I had defeated that earlier shock my imagination had bestowed when I had thought that device on the table had glowed under my touch. I had conquered my morbid fears and stood confidently against the attempt to terrify me. At least my nerves were so quiet that I woke from that sleep feeling far stronger in mind and

179

body than I had since that last clearly remembered morning in the Kesterhof.

The light of day lay across the cell in a shaft from the slit of the window. Sight of that added to my confidence, made firmer my resolve that this time I would not play the cowed captive. My chance to make good that resolve came soon after I awoke. For once more the grate of the massive door sounded through the cell. This time I stood up, away from any support, ready to face my wardress.

She entered as usual, this time her burden being a can of water, while over her other arm were folds of what looked like clothing. This she dumped without ceremony on the foot of my tumbled cot, setting down the can with a force which slopped its contents of water over the brim.

"Who are you?" I asked clearly, placing myself in her way as she turned to collect the dishes she had brought the night before. She looked at me as if I were no more than the stool, the chained table. Nor did she utter a sound.

I put out my hand and caught her arm under the tight gray stuff of her sleeve. With a surprising show of strength she gave a single twist which loosened my grip, then with a push of her flattened palm sent me near off balance, back against the cot. Pointing to me and then to the contents of the can, the pile of clothing she made emphatic gestures that I was to wash, to dress in what she had brought. But she uttered no sound, and I wondered if she were indeed mute, or merely obeying some command that she was not to communicate with any prisoner.

Taking up her tray, and giving me no more notice she went out.

I found two towels among the clothing, a bone comb and a piece of strong-smelling yellow soap wrapped in a bit of cloth undoubtedly meant to serve also for washing. The clothing was coarse—a smock of heavy material, a petticoat, and last of all a dress of the same drab color and shape as that worn by the wardress herself. All were clean and I was glad to be rid of my own soiled and crumpled clothing, even to put on what I was sure was prison garb. I washed, though the soap made my skin smart, and I could only dab lightly at my cut and bruised face. There was no mirror, but I unbraided my straggling hair, combed it well and re-braided it by touch, having to leave the braids hanging loose over my shoulders.

My toilet was hardly finished before the wardress returned. This time she had a tray in her hands, and, folded over one of her stooping shoulders some cover-ings for the bed. Slapping the tray down on the table, she dragged the present sheets off my cot, dumped the fresh ones in a heap in its middle, making plain that the task of spreading them out was to be left to me.

The food was gruel of some grain, gritty and without flavoring, but warm. There was also another tankard, this time holding thin and bluish milk. But that was all. She waited at the door, her witch face impassive until I had finished, then took the dishes with her and left.

My new garments, though clean, were clearly old and fashioned for someone shorter and of much fuller body than my own. The baggy folds hung about me. They had a musty smell, as if they had lain in close packing for a long time, while the skirts ended well above my ankles and the sleeves left both wrists and a goodly part of the forearm uncovered. I shook out the rough sheets and made up the cot bed, drawing out the process as long as I could for the need of something to occupy myself. Then I began a much more careful sur-vey of the cell itself.

Yesterday I had climbed the stool by the window and realized that, even though I could in some way force my body through that narrow way, nothing lay beyond but a frightening drop down into a depth I could not even measure. There was the cot, the stool, the table edge—and in one corner a place for other bodily ne-cessities, which was merely a hole in a three sided ridge, leading far down into darkness.

181

For want of any better employment I moved the stool to the side of the ledge table and started to trace those marks which must have been left by those who had proceeded me here in imprisonment. There were names—mainly, I noted, of women. None were as deeply scored as that I had found the night before by chance. That lay directly at the end of one of the supporting chains where the rusty metal was embedded in the wood. For a second time I traced the letters with a finger tip.

I had no doubt that the "Ludovika" who must have spent much time and no little energy in setting those letters there was the same woman whose story had been used as an object lesson thereafter to all unfaithful wives. Perhaps she had richly deserved what had happened to her—yet—

It was the device under that name which fascinated me more. Now that the light from the window was better, I could see the lines of indentation. There was a circle, and it contained a five-pointed star—the lines of that surprisingly straight for being drawn freehand. I could have covered it all well with my flattened palm, thought I had no desire to touch the wood anywhere near it.

Peering even more closely now, I could see that in each point of the star there were smaller lines which were much dimmer than those which enclosed them, merely squiggles, though I believed that each differed from the other. It was certainly not any crest or part of an armorial bearing.

Glancing along the table I noted that beneath or above some of those other names were also symbols. But the majority of those were rudely scratched crosses or other religious designs, none having been done with the exact precision of that which lay to mark Ludovika's despair.

Despair? No, somehow I could not couple that deadening expression with the woman of the Gräfin's tale. Rage, bursting, unappeasable rage might better express what she must have felt to be so entrapped after

182

her years of freedom to do just as she pleased. I was as sure of that as if the long-vanished Electress still paced up and down the narrow space here between door and window, her hands doubled into fists, her mind dealing only with the vengeance she would wreak—if she could.

So vividly did that picture of her come into my mind that I found it, a fraction of a second later, startling. It was as if there was some link between past and present, that she reached out with her hatred and found something in me which bound us together.

I shivered, steadying myself with both hands on the edge of the shelf table. Yes, I had reason enough to want justice for myself, but surely I had a right to that! My present plight was none of my own contrivance, save I had been foolish when I should have been wise. But to my mind I had never harmed any other soul to gain my way. Unless—

Truda! What if she had been disposed of merely because she knew too much? That fear was back with me again. Perhaps I would never know.

I sat staring at that star within the circle, the symbol which—which— I made myself now loosen the grip on the table, advance my left hand, the one which still wore that branding ring. With the tip of my forefinger I touched the middle point of the star. Though those subordinate lines were so faintly etched in connection with the others, I could feel the one there against my flesh. Was I waiting for warmth to rise? But that was folly! I had only imagined that!

Still it was without my conscious willing that now my fingertip traveled about the points of the star, counterclockwise, lingering for the period of several breaths on each of those symbols I could feel so well, see so little. This was as if I were following some ritual, some necessary pattern as one might unseal a secret lock—

Nor at this moment did I regain that sensation of fear which had sent me back in such a hurry in the night. Rather there was something sensuous, pleasant, almost comforting in the feel of the lined wood under my questing finger. In my mind that oddly vivid picture of the raging woman faded. Something else was growing, a confidence, a belief that, though every possible fact appeared against me now, there was hope and more than hope ahead.

Having traced the pattern to the end, I sat back on the stool, my hands now folded in my lap, my eyes on the wall, on the chains set there to support that ledge. Rusty they were on the surface, still I did not doubt that the metal beneath them was still core strong. I saw that they were not set into any blocks, but rather wedged between the stones. There was no hope of freeing either, I was sure. If I did—then what good would a short length of chain do me. Such certainly would not give me a ladder to climb down the side of the cliff on which this fortress had been erected.

That chanting—the wailing— I had dismissed that as an attempt to prey upon my nerves—the wailing at least. Though the chanting now seemed to be a different matter. One thought of chanting in relation to a church. This was a fortress, a prison. My thought flashed off to my single look at the Princess Adelaide, the formidable Abbess. Perhaps I had been wrong about my wardress. She was, instead of a gaolkeeper, rather a member of some religious order—housed here at Wallenstein—strange as that might be. Some vow of silence could make her mute.

Then the chanting in the night might well be a part of worship. I knew little of the formal church here in Hesse-Dohna, of what rites they followed. But that any order under the command of, direct or merely influenced by, the Princess Adelaide would look upon me with favor was too much to be expected. If, however, I were here by not the Baron's orders but by those of another, there might be a new bargaining. Perhaps I could make clear my own desire to have nothing the late Elector had seen fit to bestow on me—beginning with a husband. Again I found my fingers on that ring, striving to twist it off—with no better result than I had met before.

The day was very long and I found it maddening at times to be pent in this cell, tormented by my thoughts, with nothing to do. I made myself relive from the beginning the whole of the decision which had brought me here, seeing now how very great had been my folly. The Colonel—I had been (I decided now, bitterly) far too influenced in a strange way by the very personality of the man: He had, in some manner, exuded confidence to the point that I had accepted him as a guarantee of safety. I should have been warned at how slight that protection was when he had avoided me so persistently during the voyage, the trip to Hesse-Dohna, left me to the company of the Gräfin—disappeared utterly once he reached Axelburg.

Our wild adventure in the night, when I had at last made the acquaintance of my grandfather, had once more made me feel that, in his company, all would go well, that danger was kept at bay. But he could not even protect himself. Arrested, the Gräfin had reported. Perhaps already dead—

Dead—the wailing behind the wall lashed out from memory. We find it hard to think of dying when we are strong and young. It is an end which comes to others, but not us. I could not accept death even now.

I made myself lie down on the cot after I had eaten from the food brought by my silent wardress at what might have been, judging by the light outside, mid-afternoon. It was again a stew-soup, with the hard bread, the tankard of beer. But that I pushed aside and boldly demanded water.

She took no notice of my words, only standing by the door to wait for me to eat. However I learned then that my supposition that she was a religious must be right, for she looped between her age-crooked fingers as she waited a cord which was knotted, her touch resting for a long moment on each knot, though her lips did not move in any prayer that I could perceive.

When I had done she came to the bench table, but she lifted the tankard from the tray and put it down with some force on the board, leaving it behind. The door closed. I surveyed the tankard suspiciously—the drugged wine I remembered only too well. Could this drink have been doctored as well—leading to all I had heard, or thought I heard, in the night? That could well be—the stuff was bitter enough to cover the taste of any dose. I was thirsty, but the liquid of the stew would have to serve for tonight. Taking up the tankard I went and emptied its contents down the convenience in the corner. Perhaps they might believe I had drunk it.

As the light from the window faded, I drew about me again that velvet covering which I had used as a shawl, and which the wardress had not taken with her when she gathered up the used bed linen. I hated the touch of the stuff, it was spattered in places by what seemed old greasy stains. I wondered if it were indeed a remnant of the days when Ludovika had been pent here.

I think I dozed off at last. There were no more visits and I decided that two meals a day was to be my due. However, I was much stronger, and certainly far more clear headed than I had been the night before. A queer expectancy awoke me into the dark. I had no way of telling the hour save that the night was very black and it took me some time before I could even make out the windowsill.

Then it came—that same distant chanting growing ever stronger beyond the wall. I imagined a procession of women, perhaps only a handful of ancient, forgotten sisters of an order also now unknown to the world outside these walls, passing through the night on their way to some chapel. But that way must lie in part just beyond my wall.

Listening so intently as I did now, I began to believe that what I could hear was a single voice, not the well-blended chorus of a number. My wardress alone, finding her tongue to mark out a ritual which made her days here meaningful?

I was off the cot, close to the wall. This time I did not reach for the tankard to signal. That was of no use. I would only get mockery in return. Still I would not

186

leave this post, that sound, as unintelligible as it was, meant I was not alone in a place where the only voice ever to be heard would be my own.

The chant broke off, not as sharply as it had at my rapping the night before, but rather as if the ritual it signified had now been completed. There was silence, the thick silence of the night, not even any sound of wind from beyond the window.

Then—a sound from within the very room where I stood. I threw out my hands, caught at the edge of the ledge table. That was moving! Again a clank. And—

Light—thin, wavering, yet to my eyes dazzling, through the dark. It formed a line above the ledge table, high enough so that I had to tilt back my head to view it. The line became wider—the size of my palm, wider still. Stones were moving away, leaving an opening, not the size of a full door, but a hole large enough through which I could see—like a window—a window much wider than that of my cell.

Chapter 14

The source of the light was beyond my line of vision.
What I did see, half light, half shadow, was a face
framed with a filmy veil, a portion of which fell forward
to half mask the features. Even through that gauzy
covering I could make out wide, dark eyes, a half-open
mouth. But this was no hag such as played my keeper.
Rather I was sure that the face was very young, hardly
more than that of a child.

As we stared at one another through that wall opening she raised higher the source of the light, a two-
branched candlestick of dull black in a strange twisted
design, while the tapers set into it gave off an aromatic
scent, not as heavy as church incense, yet pleasing
when it fought the dank odor of the cell.

"Death—" Her lips shaped the whisper which hissed
in to me.

I did not know her purpose here, but, because I was
certain she was so young, and unlike the wardress, I
answered briskly:

"Nonsense!" Why I chose that particular word of refusal to be overawed by my strange visitor I could not
have said. Its effect upon her was surprising. She stood
as one completely startled herself, uncertain as to what
she must now do.

"I do not know why you are trying to frighten me—"
I continued in the same tone. "Who are you and what
are you doing here?"

Beneath the shadow of the veil on her face I saw her
tongue tip move across her lips.

"Death—" That one word I could understand before
she lapsed into pure gibberish and I drew back a fraction. The idea that I was confronting a madwoman—
or girl—could not be dismissed.

"I don't know what you are talking about," I endeav-
ored to keep my voice as calm as possible. One should
not, some remnant of recall told me, excite the insane.

Both her hands were in sight now. The one which
did not hold the candle moved in a series of slow gestures, as if her fingers plucked something out of the
air, balled the invisible together, and then tossed it at
me. What she thought she was doing I could not understand. But, mad or not, she and her secret wall-
opening might be my only key to escape and I would
humor her if I could learn anything from her.

"What is your name—?"

Her head went up in a proud toss. "Ludovika!" She
proclaimed as one who had recited some title which put
her far above any common person.

That I was being visited by any spirit of a long-dead
woman I refused to accept. On the other hand, to play
her game might well be the only way to keep her attention, to discover if, through her, there was any form
of escape.

She was staring at me searchingly. Then, suddenly,
she put aside that air of arrogant assurance; there came
over her face a look of warmer humanity.

"You do not believe, you are not afraid, are you?"
The note in her voice was indeed high and young, that
of one still close to childhood.

I must take the chance, I decided. "You play Ludovika, yes—that I believe—" I said with caution.

She laughed, almost maliciously. "It is a good game.
The rest—they believe. They have to—I have the

power!" She nodded confidently "*She* had the power—she could hex—kill even. I know— They shut her in there—right where you are—but they couldn't keep her—not for long. She could make them do what she wanted—she got away— Only they think the devil took her—and lets her come back. But that's me—I do as she would do—I make them afraid. I'm learning—a lot—when I know enough—then they will be afraid of *me,* just as they were of her. But—" She held her head slightly to one side surveying me, not with any sign of malice, rather curiosity. "You're not afraid. Don't you believe me?"

"I believe what I see," I returned. "If you have Ludovika's power and she was able to get out of this cell—then use it and get me out."

I saw her lips stretch into a smile. The hint of malice was back in her face. Now she made an impatient gesture with her free hand to sweep the veil back off her features. Yes, she was very young.

"Why are you here?" she countered. "Are you like Ludovika—one whom they fear? Do you know the hexing?"

"I am one somebody fears," I agreed. "As to hexing—" I shrugged. There was no reason to admit to yes or no on that. I was sure that her help might be better engaged if I left that question unanswered.

"Like Ludovika!" She nodded. "I thought maybe it was so when I saw them bring you here. They set Sister Armgrada on you—she cannot talk, you know. So they think she cannot carry any tales. What will you do if you get out—hex them—those who sent you here?"

"I will do what I can to make things difficult for them," I assured her. Magic would not enter into that, but just let me be free and I could perhaps make some disturbance in Hesse-Dohna which would both keep me safe and return at least in small measure what had been done to me.

My visitor laughed again. "Good! I like you. *She* would have liked you too. You are not afraid, and you want to strike back! That is what one should always
190

want to do—fight!" She uttered the last word fiercely as if she, also, faced some battle she was determined would go her way. "All right. I shall help you. I cannot open this wider—can you climb through?"

The window space was not too wide, but if I slipped off the bulky dress my wardress had left me, and perhaps even the heavy petticoat beneath that, I thought I could make it. I was unfastening the clumsy hooking as I asked: "What is beyond?"

"One of the passages. It is narrow," she warned. "But you can make it—I think."

I bundled off the dress, the petticoat, and rolled them together. Then I knelt upon the scarred table ledge. The girl drew back to one side. She was out of my sight until I put my head and shoulders through the window. The passage in which she stood was indeed narrow. I would not have to reach out my arms very far before my fingers struck the stone of the other wall. I wriggled through with difficulty, then reached down and picked up the clothing I had shed.

My visitor sniffed disdainfully. "Sister Armgrada's castoffs! Phu, they stink! You'd better not put on the dress. There is a place where you"—she was measuring me with her eyes critically—"will have to turn sideways to get through."

Her own dress must have been a trouble in those narrow ways she spoke of. The gauzy veil fell a little below her waist, but the gown she had on was of another time. In the limited light of the scented candles it was pale, without any color save a glint of metallic thread running in an elaborate pattern over its folds. The bodice was cut very low, near slipping off her thin, adolescent shoulders, perhaps only the sharply nipped-in waist held it on her at all, while the skirts were very wide.

She wore a necklace of what seemed to be pearls, and more were in drops from her ears. There was a faded magnificence about the garment, as if it were a shadow of a court dress of an earlier time. Yes—of Ludovika's time. So much had this girl entered into the
191

role of the Electress that she had somehow found this faded glory. Her body had none of the roundness of maturity, her breasts were small and not plumply cushioned above the low circle of the neckline, her bare arms were bony and her skin looked slightly grubby. Her hair, under the veiling, had been bundled up in a loose fashion, a crude imitation of the precise curls of a court coiffuer, the ends straggling down over her shoulders. Having seen me through the window, she now held the candle a little higher and toward the wall. I saw the projection there even as her fingers closed about it, dragging it down. Once more sounded the grating, then that opening in the wall came together, so that from this side also I would have guessed it had never been, had I not seen it open.

She looked over her shoulder as she turned away from the wall and smiled again, her free hand now flicking at the wide skirt of her gown.

"Do I not make a proper ghost?" she demanded. "The good sisters—there are three of them, you know—all old frights who look more like the witch they pray against then *she* ever did—they had Father Homan in twice to lay me—praying and waving holy water and the rest of it. Now they try to pretend I am not here at all. They shut their eyes and pray so loud you would think they would rock the very stones off the walls! Just let them wait a little longer. If I can just find out what *she* knew—then they would have something to pray about!"

She raised her candlestick the higher now and moved along the narrow way. It was necessary for her to turn slightly sideways and bunch together her skirts in one hand, in order to pass. I had pulled on the petticoat, made very sure that my packet of gold was well fastened about my waist, and pulled the coarse dress about me as a shawl. For my guide was right, slender as I was, I found the path none too wide.

The passage ran straight for a space, inward and away from the outer wall. There was another place where it was narrow again and I wondered how the girl ahead had managed to get by the projecting stone so lightly—perhaps it was by long practice in clambering around through these ways.

Who was she? Another prisoner who had somehow found the secret of the fortress and made forays out of her cell at night? I was not sure of that—her youth, the dress she wore, argued that she had access to parts of this castle which would not be hers if she were a captive.

It was plain from her steady progress that she did know where she was going. Nor did she ever glance back to see if I still followed. Finally she came to a halt so suddenly that I nearly ran upon her. Once more she faced what looked to me a solid wall, but she put her face close to it, and from her mouth came that wailing which I had heard the night before.

"Death—death—!" The words trailed off into a sound which was more the cry of a demented person. She was silent then, as if she listened, and I saw her face alive with a look of malicious mischief. If she awaited some sound from the other side of that barrier, she was disappointed. After a moment she shrugged and started on. However, as I passed, I examined the wall with such care as the glimmering withdrawal of her candles allowed me. There was to be seen a similar projection as that she had moved to open the window-door. Another cell—another prisoner? Who? Why was that unfortunate also here?

I had to hurry to catch up, for the passage widened a little here and she was holding her skirts higher and hurrying. Then we were upon a flight of steps leading up and these were so steep that I fell behind, not trusting to my balance, though the girl did not slacken her pace by much.

We came out on a second narrow way, this time slanting off in a different direction. She had halted halfway down then and was again close to the stone. As I came up behind her I saw a slit there and a bit of light. She watched only for a moment then stepped aside and motioned me to take her place.

I was looking down from some height into a much larger room than any cell, and one which did not present such a picture of the past. There was a long table there with benches on either side. Some men in uniform lounged on those, drank from tankards, one or two were actually reading newspapers! I saw racks of muskets against the walls, and other things which I thought might be part of a barracks guardroom. There was talk among those below, but some trick of the walls or the distance reduced that to only a dull rumble of sound.

My guide was again moving ahead and I hastened to catch up with her. It appeared that she wished to play no more tricks. Then one wall of the way we followed became wood paneling as if we had reached a portion of the fortress which was intended for comfortable living. The end of the passage came and once more the girl peered through a peephole, waited some time.

Then she blew out the candles, leaving us in thick dark. I heard small movement before a panel slid aside and she slipped through, gesturing for me to follow.

The room into which we had come was as unlike the cell in which I had been as that was to the bedroom in which I had fallen unconscious before my awakening here. In its appointments and furnishings it was not unlike the state bedroom I had occupied in Axelburg. Here also was a curtained, dais-bed, massive chairs, tapestried walls. But there were no signs of occupancy.

My guide moved quickly to a wardrobe which stood like a menacing cage in one dark corner, for there was only a single candle burning on a nearby table. As I followed her I saw that across the door, there was a massive bar pushed into place, as if this was a fortress within a fortress and my guide must so make sure of her privacy.

She paid no attention to me now as she brought out the wardrobe clothing which she tossed onto a nearby chair and began to twist and turn to reach the hooks and ties of the dress she wore. With the speed of one who has done the same many times before, she soon shed her ancient dress and donned a high-collared, full-sleeved white muslin which was perhaps not of the latest fashion such as favored in Axelburg, but as close to that as might be found in a more provincial setting. Her hair she combed into a loose fall becoming to a young girl, though not particularly enhancing the lines of her thin face, smoothing it into the semblance of order with a broad ribbon. When she had finished she looked no more than into her teens, though her face lacked that bland innocence which was thought fitting to such an age.

The dress she had discarded she handled with far more care, seeing that it was hung, then a veil lovingly folded about it, within the wardrobe. Having made the exchange, she at last swung around to face me. In the meantime, I had also put on the coarse outer garment my wardress had left me.

Young as she was, my guide still held command of the situation. She pointed to the chair over which her garments had been so lately spread and seated herself in turn on a footstool pulled near to one of the throne-like seats, flanking the wardrobe on the other side.

"Who are you?" She asked that with the snap of one who was seldom, if ever, had her wishes crossed. "They said you were mad, you know." Her eyes, which were her best feature, so large and lustrous, narrowed a little. "I don't think I believe them. I did not last night when you struck the wall. You weren't frightened— But who are you—and why are you really here?"

"I am Amelia Harrach. But as to why I am here— that I have no true idea at all."

"Harrach." She repeated the name slowly. "But"— there was real surprise in her face now—"that is the name of the Elector—his own name. And you are certainly not the Princess—I have seen her—fat old thing!" Her nose wrinkled disdainfully. "You are important, you know, or they would not send you here— This is a place where they keep those who must not be allowed to talk. What don't they want *you* to talk about?"

195

"Who are you?" I countered. That she was free to roam about as she had this night argued that she was no prisoner. Now she pursed her mouth slightly, her head a little on one side, watching me with a certain slyness.

"I am Lisolette von Rensch. My father is commandant here. And this"—she flung out her hands in a gesture to indicate the dusky formal chamber in which we sat—"is the room of the Prince Franzel, who *was* mad, or so they said when they would have his younger brother for Elector a long time ago." It was plain she was watching me avidly to see how I would accept that particular bit of ancient history. *"He* did not have the *power,* you see—so he died over there—in that very bed. They say he was poisoned. But they gave him a great funeral after all—and then his brother was safe on the throne and no one cared—or, if they did, they knew enough not to say so. But why are you here? Are you a princess to be locked up because you are a trouble to the new Elector?" She did not give me any pause in which to answer but swept swiftly on:

"They do not tell me things, you understand. But I learn, yes, I learn!" Her head nodded vigorously up and down. "I learned long ago that if one seems to be interested only in the dull things, the tasks one is set, people forget and sometimes speak clearly. Also—after I began to dream—" She stopped short and her hand flew to cover her mouth. For a moment she looked frightened and uneasy. Then her chin arose a fraction and she assumed again some of the air of complete confidence she had shown during our passage through the wall ways.

"I have my own ways of finding out things. They brought you here secretly—by night—and they said that you were ill—mad—so that the sisters have charge of you. But if what they said were true, you would have rather been taken to the house at Speakenhoch, where they keep those who have really lost their wits. There was a guardsman here who did that. He tried to kill a bear he said was loose in the long gallery, but of course there was no bear at all. I think that perhaps she made him see that. *She* wanted to know how much power she had—" Again she was suddenly silent.

"But you are not mad—and you are called Harrach. So why are you here? You will tell me, you know." Her confidence was not that of a young girl, rather that of one who has tested her control over others and learned successfully just how and when to use it. I did not, however, find it binding on me. What my thoughts were concerned with was how much of the truth I dared share with her—and to what extent I must trust her with any of my story. She was frowning and, though her gaze was still on me, I had a strange idea that her mind was fast locked upon some other problem which was of pressing interest to her.

"*She* must have sent me to you, that I know," she said then, as if she were speaking her thoughts aloud. "But you are a Harrach and *she* had good reason not to wish any of you well—"

"Is your *she* the Electress Ludovika?" That this girl spoke of a woman long dead as if she had connection with the affairs of this day hinted certainly at disorder in Lisolette's own mind.

"But of course! It is by her— No, there is no reason to tell you that! Are you not pleased to be out of that box? If *she* has a use for you, then we must discover what it is. So—why did they bring you here?"

"I do not know—except there is something which the old Elector left me—something which they want. I think they will want to keep me hidden until they can obtain it."

"And who are your enemies?"

I could think of at least two, but that the Gräfin and the Baron had the power to send me into a royal fortress as a hidden prisoner, that puzzled me. What part could Lisolette's father have in this game? Was he some friend or ally of the Baron, ready to lend his assistance? If I said as much as I suspected, what would be the girl's reaction?

"Those I know of are two," I answered slowly, deciding to voice no suspicions. "One is the Gräfin von Zreibruken, the other the Baron von Werthern."

Lisolette's expression did not change. "Of them," she waved a hand, "I have never heard. Because the Elector is dead there will be many changes. I have heard my father, his senior officers talk. The new Elector—few men know him well. He has been away for so long. They are uneasy over what he may do. But orders have come and my father knows it is best to obey them for now. When they sent the man—he obeyed that one. It is always so, I think, when one ruler dies and another comes—people are afraid and some lose everything. *Her* friends lost much—their lives!"

A rage which was not childlike or young suddenly contorted her features. "Yes, those who had served her best—they were killed! And *she* was shut from all which could help them—or herself. *She* had to wait a long time—*she* had to wait for me!"

That look of rage was gone, in its place was such an expression as might transfigure the face of a worshipper. "Yes," she continued, "*she* has a use for you. Even though you are a Harrach. That must be true, or I would not have been sent to bring you here. Now." She got to her feet with brisk decision. "Here you must stay. You need have no fear of surprisal." Her smile was sly again. "This part of the fortress has no visitors. There are too many dark tales about what has happened. Also I shall show you—if any do chance to come—for it may be when they find you gone they will bestir themselves to search farther than usual. Now attend carefully!"

With the air of a governess instructing a none-to-bright pupil, she picked up the single candle and beckoned me back to that section of the wall through which we had come. The panels were carved with a series of heraldic animals, grotesque and unpleasant.

With her thumb Lisolette pressed hard on the bulbous eye of a griffin and the response was the back swing of the next panel.

"It is easy enough, as you see. I must go. But you

stay here—and I shall see you again—when it is the time. Leave the door unbarred."

"And a candle?" I asked even as she turned to cross the room.

She frowned. Then dipped the one she held, holding its flaming wick against that of another which stood, hardly higher than a stub, on a nearby table. Without another word she slid the bar from its hold at the door and slipped out into a hall, which I could see did hold some light, leaving me alone in what she had made certain I would understand was an ill-omened chamber.

I waited for a long moment, listening for any sound. The silence itself seemed strangely to hold some quality of apprehension. I made a careful circle of the room with that stub of a candle. By the massive, ornate furniture this chamber, many times the size of my former cell, had either been meant to house a visiting lord, or else a prisoner of such rank that he must be given some of the treatment of an honored guest.

However, it must have been long abandoned. Though the floor had been swept, there was a thick deposit of dust on the bed itself and the smell of mold and decay was strong. I discovered two windows behind drapery heavy with grit. Both were wider than the slit which had been my only opening on the world, but they were well covered with a cross-hatching of bars set very firmly into the stone. I could see little in the dark without.

I opened the wardrobe and looked at what it held. The dress in which Lisolette had played her ghostly role that night was not the only one. Another of the same archaic fashion, but of a deep crimson shade, also hung there. While on the floor were set several pairs of slippers, each having high heels. I touched the red dress and found it to be of a damask far heavier than any fabric used in this modern time and I wondered if it could be possible that both gowns were in truth once worn by the vanished Ludovika.

There was something else in the wardrobe, standing

on the floor beside the frayed satin slippers—a box which had the appearance of a book—such as those massive wood-bound Bibles which are sometimes found in ancient churches. But that this was a box was evident by the fact that there were hinges at one side of the upper cover, and a small lock at the other. The top was carved to resemble the tooling on the cover of the book one could so readily compare it to. But there was no engraven cross. Instead that same symbol of an encircled star was picked out in a red which either had been recently renewed, or which time had not dulled. For the book-box certainly possessed the look of age.

I had pulled it out on the floor to see it the better. Now I tried to raise the lid. However the lock held tight and I had no luck in that. Setting aside the candle, I picked it up. It was heavy and it was certainly not empty, for as it shifted, loose contents moved from one side to the other. Another possession of Ludovika—perhaps one which held that which so engrossed the mind of Lisolette?

Baffled, I returned it to its place and closed the wardrobe, going once more to sit on the chair where I had perched earlier and try to make some coherent sense of what had happened to me. It was true I had been freed from the cell. Not only that, but I had been introduced to the passageways within the walls where I might play a successful hide and seek if any searchers were aroused in the morning to hunt me down.

On the other hand my freedom depended largely on the whim of a girl, who, if she were not mad, had thoughts and beliefs which bordered on that state. How did I know that at that very moment she was not denouncing me to her father? Still what purpose would she have had then in bringing me out of my cell at all? And her own night activities—for she plainly had been playing ghost in the fortress—would be revealed.

No, I believed I was safe—for now—from any betrayal from Lisolette. Slowly I went over in my mind, as best I could, everything she had said to me. I thought it apparent that she believed she was in some way
200

acting under the guidance, or by the wishes, of that woman so long dead. In other words, she was, by the old beliefs, possessed. But as long as she thought she had been led to free me for some purpose, I could perhaps prevail on her to believe that I should not only be free of my cell but the fortress itself.

I was tired, the sleep I had earlier fought now half drugged me. Sleep—dared I try to sleep? Yet I could not continue without rest. I eyed the dusty bed and at last gave in to the demands of my body and stretched myself out on its surface.

Chapter 15

I awoke into a dull grayness, lighter than the night which had closed me in when in the cell. Yet it was still not day. I sat up on the bed and swallowed once, and again. My throat and mouth felt as if the chamber's dust had seeped in to coat them both. I would have given much at that moment for even the bitter beer which had been offered me in the cell.

Now that I could better look about me I noted that the gray light came from the other side of the room, running in lines along ancient curtains which must not have been drawn for years. My stocking-covered feet felt the grit on the floor carpet and, though I could not see it in this light, I was sure that dust puffed up with every step I took. However, I continued until I reached that drapery-covered wall and drew back the edge of an ancient fabric which slit and tore under my hands. Then light did burst in upon me with a near-dazzling glare.

This was day and the windows here were wider than those through which I had tried to see earlier. Also I was not looking out into open space, rather down into a court completely surrounded by the bulk of the fortress. There was no entrance into this inner space save two doors, one in the wing on my left, one cutting the section immediately opposite me. Both were closed, nor could I note any signs of life at any of the blank-seeming windows within my range of vision.

I was careful, once I had discovered the disintegrating state of the curtains, not to pull them back too far. It was not necessary to do so in order to be aware that I had merely moved from one prison into another. For the window before me was also latticed by bars. However, to see the day—and a portion of sun which filtered down into the courtyard—was invigorating to the spirit. I arranged the draperies carefully that some of that blessed light could enter the room.

Though the door was unbarred, I knew better than to venture out. But I was both hungry and thirsty, and I could not be sure that Lisolette would have any desire, or perhaps even any chance, to supply me with food or drink.

I could not judge by the degree of light just how late was the hour. The time could be near midday for all I knew. To be pent here was hardly better than to be celled below. Had they discovered my absence from there? They must have by now. If so, certainly a search was up. Lisolette might not have believed they would come in this direction, but I had little faith in her confidence. So I turned back to survey the room itself once more.

I could, of course, retreat into the passage, as she had showed me. Only the candle she had left was burned away, and to enter that dark warren within the walls with no light was something I would do only as a last extreme. The cumbersome pieces of archaic furniture in the room must have stood there two hundred years, perhaps even more. I thought if anyone tried to draw the curtains on the bed those might simply fall into shreds, so cobwebbed were they by age. The wardrobe did not promise any shelter. No, it would have to be the passage, without a light.

In spite of myself I kept creeping back to my vantage point at the window. Surely if a search were in progress throughout Wallenstein, there must be some evidence of it. Sooner or later I would see someone move beyond one of those windows, even open a door and venture out into the silent courtyard. Yet at the moment I might be standing in a long deserted ruin where not even a bird crossed the sky.

Finally I dragged a stool near to the window where the light gave me a measure of confidence and sat there, once more attempting to marshal my thoughts into some helpful order. I must eat, more than that I must drink. The needs of my body kept breaking in upon my poor attempts to plan what I could do. Only, to find either food or water, I would have to leave this hiding place, venture out into ways I knew nothing about, where I could be easily recognized for what I was by the first inhabitant of this pile who I was unlucky enough to meet.

Or I could go back to my cell, perhaps confounding my wardress by appearing—but I did not know any way out save that which would be hidden from me once the wall window closed. If I only had a candle and could go exploring farther!

There might be other passages to be found besides those giving upon the cells— The cells! I recalled then Lisolette's second play-acting the night before. How she had crooned her "Death—death—" before that other patch of wall. Had that marked another cell, the abiding place of a second prisoner? If so—who was she—or he? What other enemies to the state (if that was what I was considered) had been immured here?

Suppose I could do for that unknown what Lisolette

had done for me. Thus find a companion in distress who would—or could—aid—

I tensed, swung around. So silent had been that room that the silent sound seemed to reverberate as strongly as had the bells which had signaled the Elector's passing back in Axelburg. I could not at first locate its source—a scrape—a ring of metal against metal—a—

The time it took to cross the room, lay hand on the eye of the beast who guarded the tunnel way could be measured by my quickened breaths. Once there, I still hesitated, determined not to enter until I knew that I must.

That sound, louder—familiar—!

I choked down a gasp. That I had heard before—a servant's scratching on a door as a plea to admit an inferior—far different from a demanding knock. However, though I faced the door, I remained where I was, watching. Nor did I call out any permission to enter.

The heavy barrier swung inward. At the sight of the slight figure it now framed I relaxed. Lisolette swung through the crack, shut the door quickly, and stood with her back against it, peering about until she saw me.

She was carrying a small basket and this she put down on the floor, leaving it behind as she crossed the room, light as the wraith she played by night, coming to stand before me and look searchingly into my face. Seemingly having made sure of me so, she gave a brisk nod and gestured to the basket she had left.

"Food, drink—" She kept her voice to a low thread of whisper. Then she laughed silently, the sly, malicious quirk back about her mouth. "The sisters are praying—they think the evil one took you! They have not yet told my father—or any of the men. It is good that their rule keeps them to their part of the castle. I think that they are afraid—afraid of having to report you are gone. They are so sure that *she* was of the devil—they pray against her all the time, you know. That is why their kind first came here long ago. They were sent to watch her, to make sure that the devil could not get past their relics and their prayers to help her. Only—*she* was too strong for them.

"When they found *her* gone they said she was dead. Dead!" Lisolette tossed her head. "They were all fools! How could they even know what *she* could do when she wished. They said she was dead, yes, but they *knew*—that is why they always stayed—why they were commanded to stay—to keep *her* bound by their eternal praying. Now they will say you are dead, too."

Once more she laughed. "Is it not fitting? They will send soon, I think, some message to my father saying the prisoner died of the fever, and that they will bury her in their crypt. My father will be relieved, because this is a secret matter, and one who becomes too knowing of secrets comes also into trouble. So you need have no fear—"

"Lisolette!" This girl was far lost from reality, I thought with a shiver, for I have a horror I cannot control, of the unnormal, the mind-broken. She lived in another world of the night and her own acting. "Lisolette!"

Something in the sharpness of my tone must have broken through her absorption in her own beliefs and concerns, for now she looked at me with more of a natural consciousness in her face.

"It is good that they are not hunting me yet." I drew that much out of her garbled talk and hoped that what she said *was* the truth. There was a kind of sense to it. A reason that my absence had not been reported as yet—either through some fear on the part of my wardress or else because of superstition. If I had that much on my side— Only, how long would their covering of my escape continue? I could not accept Lisolette's blithe assurance that they would continue it long. Also, what if those who had sent me here should come seeking what they wanted of me? I could not see either the Gräfin or the Baron calmly accepting any account of my death without definite proof.

"They will not be hunting you," she nodded again. "You should hear them! They are praying until the very walls of that cursed chapel of theirs rings! How *she* laughed when they tried to pray *her* into nothingness!"

She was sliding off again into her fantasy world.

"Am I the only prisoner? Last night—you called 'death' outside that other wall." I must get her away from her belief that Ludovika had something to do with our present when that unfortunate was long since dead.

"He is there. But *she* does not care about him. Why should she? She has me—and a use for you. She does not need him—"

"Who is he?"

"The soldier—the one they brought from Axelburg—the friend of the Elector—the old Elector—" Her impatience was growing stronger. "*She* has no wish for any friends like that! He is like those who made trouble for her in the days when she was a great lady—before she passed beyond to her own power. She has no use for him—"

A soldier from Axelburg who had been a friend of the old Elector—Colonel Fenwick? I could not be sure. There was apparently no chance to enlist Lisolette in his favor, I guessed, not now. But if it were he—and he could be freed the same way—! I must play Lisolette's game—until I could move on my own.

"You are sure she wants me to do something for her?" I must humor her for now.

Lisolette nodded vigorously. "I must go—Frau Spansfert will be looking for me. She is afraid that my father will send her away if she does not know everywhere I am. But also she is afraid to tell him that she does not for much of the time. However, he is anxious about his own affairs, so forgets all but those now. He has the men out drilling and has called for the accounts to be explained to him. Already he has inspected the cell of the soldier three times today. I think he is very unsure who his new master may be, and he does not want to lose his place here—it suits him well."

The tone she used in speaking of her father was one of lofty contempt. However, the information that the commander of Wallenstein was so uneasy was not too promising. His daughter might not find that menacing. I did—not being enmeshed in her own private world.

"I need some candles." I spoke abruptly, my thoughts looking ahead to plans of my own.

"They are in the basket. I shall bring you more food tonight. We must go together to *her* place. *She* will want to speak to you—tell you what you must do."

Abruptly the girl turned then and was at the door before I could put out a hand or raise my voice to stop her. I was uneasy enough to follow her and slide into place the bar she had used the night before to seal off this ill-omened room. Making sure that was in place, I turned to inspect the contents of the basket.

I found a plentiful supply of bread and cheese, as well as a bottle of water. For which I was thankful, having no desire for wine or the sour and bitter beer. There was in addition, four candles, the thick kind usually meant for carriage lanterns, rolled in a piece of newspaper. The latter I smoothed out and found that it was undoubtedly several days old, for it carried an account of the soon-to-be-expected arrival of the new Elector and the plans for the interring of his predecessor, upon his arrival, in the crypt of the cathedral built by their far distant ancestor, the redoubtable Axel.

Hunger and thirst appeased, my next thought was the passageway and the need to discover whether the prisoner Lisolette spoke of was Colonel Fenwick. If he was under such constant inspection by his guard—to bring him into the passages might be highly risky. On the other hand, I wanted not to be drawn any farther into Lisolette's mad world as she had suggested just before leaving. There was no telling when the girl might turn on me if I failed to humor her belief in the dead Electress's "power." With Colonel Fenwick beside me I felt that I might face anything—even confrontation with all the might of Hesse-Dohna at their strongest—and that of the devil, who appeared to be thought present here, into the bargain.

I discovered that one of the thick candles could be

wedged into an old iron holder, tall and clumsy, but still sturdy under its coating of rust. There was an old fashioned tinderbox beside that on the table which perhaps Lisolette used for her own midnight lighting. With the aid of that I put flame to my candle and prepared to reenter the hidden ways within the walls, having shed my cumbersome gown, and pulled its folds once more about me for a shawl. Pressure on the eye of the beast was followed by a faint sound and the panel opened to let me through.

For a moment after the panel had shut once more behind me I knew a thrust of panic as sharp as any pain. However, as I swung my candle about, I could see that inner latch on the wall which marked the opening on this side. I was not sealed in, though to venture these dark ways alone drew upon my fortitude to an extent I had not foreseen.

Back I went along the same path Lisolette had used the night before. Again I paused to look into that hall which was also a guardroom. There were men there, but fewer than there had been when we had spied upon them earlier. Among them stood an officer. Apparently he was inspecting a group of four about to go on some guard duty. He was a stout man, red faced, with a brush of coarse mustache which was pied black and gray, though his thick brows were wholly black, as was the bristle of hair which showed below his high-crowned helmet. He strode back and forth before his very small company with an impatient stamp of the feet and his whole attitude suggested irritation, or perhaps some worry with which he battled within to more purpose than he busied himself with the outward defense of this sprawling fortress.

The commandant? I wondered. Though I certainly could see little resemblance between this bulky and stolid man and Lisolette's thin face, large eyes, and general air of one who could well assume a wraithlike state when necessary.

Again I could catch a murmur of voices, perhaps the officer exhorting his followers. But the sense of the words did not reach me. Then they turned and marched off with the stiff-legged precision of mechanical toys behind their stamping leader, and the room was left vacant.

My lookout hole was well above the level of the floor and on this side of the wall there were none of those projecting handles. Certainly there was no way out here, not that one would dare to try it at such point. The hall itself had certainly been more than a guard-room in the past, for the arches between the pillars supporting the vaulted roof were carved, surmounted with shields bearing arms now shadow-concealed.

The racks of weapons were at present installed on a dais, and though the stone was bare, there was only the most clumsy and solid of furniture remaining (such as might be found in an inn where peasants gathered). I believed that perhaps at one time a semblance of court might have been held here.

I came to the flight of stairs and descended those one at a time as does a child who is uncertain of her footing. They appeared even steeper than they had the night before, and I longed for some kind of a rail I could grasp to steady myself.

Now I was in that lower passage and I held the candle out before me, watching the wall avidly for that projection which would mark the other cell where Lisolette had stopped to play her ghostly game. It was there, and my hand fell upon it. If I only knew who lay beyond!

Lisolette's account of her father's frequent visiting to make sure his prisoner was secure kept me now from bearing my weight upon the hidden spring. Suppose my guess was wrong and it was not Fenwick who lay beyond that wall, but rather some stranger who might even be ready to use me as a bargaining point with his captors—turning me over to them in return for favors for himself? Wallenstein soon bred within one mistrust of all one's fellows. I had been surprisingly lucky in that I had somehow caught that girl's twisted fancy.

Could I hope that any such good fortune would continue?

I should have waited until night. Only then Lisolette would have returned. In what was close to true agony of indecision I pressed as close to the wall by that lever as I could get, near grinding my ear against the stone in an effort to hear what might be beyond. I had heard Lisolette's wailing from my own cell, she in turn had heard my hammering with the tankard.

Now I fairly held my breath to listen. Perhaps there were some cracks between those seemingly so solidly set stones which would allow sound to pass, even if there were no spyholes. For now I could hear a regular beat—a noise my hopes suggested was caused by the ring of boot heels against stone, the measure of someone pacing back and forth.

No voices—nothing but that marching sound like a sentry at his post. A sentry—? Had this prisoner one *within* his cell, had the commandant's uneasiness led him to *that* precaution?

What must I do? If I could only be sure—!

I turned the heavy metal candlestick around and around in my two sweating hands. The dress I had huddled about my shoulders as a shawl slipped to the pavement. I could not continue here so indecisive.

Sheer anger at my own lack of courage led me to a move which might well be fatal. I raised the candlestick and struck against the stone of the wall inches away from the lever. Twice I struck, forcing myself to action.

The pacing sound had instantly stopped. I waited, breathing very slowly, listening—

There came nothing but silence. My imagination sped to show me the worst which might be beyond the wall, a sentry facing the stone, alert to the sound, looking for its source, ready to raise a call for help in tracing out—

Then I near cried out. For almost at the same point where my ear touched the rough, damp stone there came a click of sound and then another. I was heard and, unless the sentry I had imagined was unusually resourceful and cunning, that answer must have come from the prisoner. I wished wildly that there was some sort of code known to us both, a pattern of rapping which might make me sure I had nothing to find beyond but another prisoner. However, that was denied me.

I could only experiment. This time I tapped three times, with the space of two slow breaths between each blow. My answer came in the same pattern. It must be the truth—that it was the prisoner. And he *was* alone or he could not have risked answer.

There was only the final action left. I put the candlestick on the floor and bore down with both hands and all my strength on the lever. For a long moment I feared that whatever lock held was so time-set into place I had not the strength to move it. Then, grudgingly, with a grating which near frightened me into quick retreat, there opened a line between the stones I faced.

I bore down harder, dragging at the lever, and the crack grew wider. Finally it became an opening the width of my palm. Midway along, it showed part of a face, eyes peering into the passage.

Eyes—and there was no mistaking for me even that small fragment of a face. I knew that slightly lifted eyebrow, the old seam of scar causing it. It was the Colonel. I saw his gaze in turn widen as he looked up to see me in turn.

I stopped to snatch up the candle, hold it high.

"Are you alone?" My foremost fear made me demand that.

"For a time, yes. They have been checking on me as if they fear I might melt into the stones. But how—and why—?"

"No questions. Listen, I shall do what I can to get this open, but I may not have the strength—it has been shut for a long time, I think—"

"Do what you can." His voice held the old note of command. "There may be also some way I can aid." His fingers appeared, gripping the stone. "How does this go?"

"Upward—" I had returned the candle to the floor and was once again bearing down on the lever.

"Upward it is!" His fingers closed on the upper edge of that narrow opening and I knew that he was straining as best he could against the same stubborn stone. Inch by inch it gave, though sometimes I thought it would never move another fraction of the way. Then the same amount of space was open that had shown in my own cell. I had gotten through there, but could he? Eyeing that, I greatly doubted it, and leaned limply back against the wall facing the despair of having gained only so little.

"It will not go farther, I think," I told him. "Can you come through?"

"We shall see." There was no despair in his answer, just a note considering, as if he were weighing one chance against another. I heard movement on the other side, but he was now out of my sight, for I did not have the energy at that moment to move away from my wall support, save to gather up the candle so that it might be out of his way should he make the effort to scrape passage to me.

It was not his body which was thrown in to me, rather a bundle of clothing, weighted by boots. I understood that, just as I had had to strip off much of my clothing to try that door, he was doing likewise. I reached out and caught that bundle, dragging it to one side.

His head, arms, bared shoulders, came into view, those shoulders scored and in some places showing welling blood in deep scratches. He fought, and, I, regaining my wits, put down the candle and the bundle of clothing and went to give what aid I could.

My pulling may have helped, but his battle against the stone was a cruel one, leaving his near naked body scratched and abraded, blood oozing in many places. It was only due to his courage and determination that he made it, to half lie at last against the wall, his breath coming in deep gasps. All which covered him was the remains—the scanty remains of torn drawers, but this was no time to think of any proprieties.

I was already back at the lever, fighting its stiffness until the slit closed, with a little more speed than it had opened. Near as exhausted as he looked, I crouched on the floor also, the candle between us. He was breathing more normally now and I saw him shiver. Quietly I opened the bundle he had thrown and hunted his shirt.

I drew him slightly away from the wall and wrapped the shirt about his shoulders, noting that the patches of blood now welling on his skin were not the only hurts recorded on his body. There was a puckered scar along his ribs and another seam on his upper shoulder.

My hands on him appeared to arouse him at once, and I saw he was looking straight at me. Then, for the first time during our acquaintance, I saw Colonel Fenwick smile—not only smile—but he laughed softly! For a moment I wondered if he were as mind-turned as Lisolette. Then he raised one of his bruised and bleeding hands to push away from my face a strand of hair which kept looping itself down over my eyes.

"We are a pretty pair," he said softly. "Where do we go now, my lady? It seems that you have learned something here which is to the advantage of any prisoner. But why and how?—"

My only thought now was that we must get away. If one of those periodic visits should be made to his cell soon—then indeed the whole of castle would be aroused—even if my own escape had been kept a secret.

"We must go—up—" I pointed in the direction of the passage.

He pulled himself away from the wall and dragged his bundle of clothing toward him.

"Give me time to get on my boots," he said. His lips were still quirked in that smile, which began to irritate me. I was honestly afraid, and I saw nothing in the least amusing concerning our present predicament.

I waited for him to draw on breeches and then boots,

213

but he left his shirt loose about his shoulders, and carried his coat over his arm.

"I'm a little too sore for this. Now—if we go up—then we must."

He turned back to give one more keen glance at the wall and I guessed that he was trying to make certain that the aperture was entirely closed. I scuttled ahead, wanting nothing more now than to gain that chamber where I could bar the door, be sure of a breathing space before I was goaded again into some perilous action. Such good fortune could not continue, of that I was dismally sure. I could hardly believe, as I edged up the steps, and heard the sounds of his passage behind me, that all had gone well even this far.

This time I did not pause at the peephole on the guardroom, but kept on, the candle ahead of me like a banner, until the welcome sight of the wood paneling told me we were near our refuge. I found the latch and stepped through, he pushing his way with greater difficulty behind me.

The panel snapped shut and we stood together in the very dim light as I hastened to blow out the candle.

"Now." His voice no longer held that amused note, but it rang with all the old note of command which had ever aroused antagonism within me. "How did you come here, my lady? What has happened?"

Chapter 16

I hurried to the basket and that flask of water which had been so refreshing to me earlier. Surely there was
214

enough left to tend his wounds, for I feared that if they went uncared for, they might be the worse for the dust and ancient filth of this forsaken room.

"Sir." I gestured him forward, pointing to the stool by the window where I had spent those earlier hours. "Let me see to those cuts and scrapes."

He shrugged and I saw that even so slight a movement of his abraded shoulders brought a wince in answer. As he dropped his jacket to the floor I went about the end of the bed and pulled on the shapeless dress. Then I jerked at the covers across the massive width. The upper ones tore in my hands, ancient satin and velvet yielding quickly to the strain of my efforts. Underneath those was linen, frail and thin, to be sure, but still clean of dust and the only thing hereabouts to serve my purposes.

With strips and wads of this in my hands I went back to where my patient waited. He had seated himself on the stool, but was now leaning forward, peering through my own watchhole between the drapes. There was something so tense in his pose that I feared Wallenstein must have at last come to life, that we were indeed to be the hunted.

Yet when I came close enough, the flask with the remaining water in one hand, my bundle of old linen in the other, to look past him—I could see nothing but the same emptiness I had watched for so long.

"Your shirt—" I swept the garment from his shoulders and dropped it beside his jacket. At the manor I had learned nursing of a sort—the care of minor hurts, fevers. My grandmother had kept her own herb garden and had made a study of such things, since the aid of a physician might often be several days away. No false delicacy had kept her from seeing that I also learned what was to be done for our people should some emergency or accident occur.

Still now, as I moistened my pad of linen with care, keeping in mind that none of the precious water must be wasted, I found it oddly disturbing to set about the business of doctoring. It was a kind of shyness I had never experienced before as I made myself matter-of-factly swab at those bloody smears along his upper arms, across his chest and his shoulders. Because I felt that discomfort at such employment, I launched into speech with a quick desire to turn his mind, if not mine, away from my embarrassment.

"Sir, why were you sent here?"

"That is easy enough to answer." He sat quite still under my ministrations. I longed for some healing salve, for more water—there were gouges in his skin which seemed to me dangerously deep as I washed them, very close to open wounds. "I was—am—loyal to a past which a great many now wish forgotten. I know too much to make them comfortable. But the greater question—why are you here, my lady? Wearing such a dress." He reached out to flick with a finger that voluminous and musty skirt. "What happened to you?"

I glanced at that infamous ring on my finger. Above the band the flesh looked swollen, so hard I had worked to try and rid myself of it. Answering, I strove to make my voice as level as I could, to keep my hands steady as I tried to ease his hurts and give an account of myself.

The beginning was easy enough, my journey from Axelburg to the Kesterhof. Then I chose my words with more care, trying not to allow my horror and disgust at what had happened to me break through to color my account of the drugging, of Konrad's visit to my bedroom, and his demand that I sign the papers he presented.

I was not prepared for the sudden clutch upon my wrist, for being jerked around so that I faced my patient in the small light from the window. His eyes—I had seen them cold, measuring, marking his aloofness from anything but his duty. Once—down in the passage—I had seen them soften for the first time, perhaps with exuberance brought about by his release from the cell. Now I saw them filled with near devilish fires. So grim was his countenance at that moment I would have shrunk away had it been possible, but he held me fast.

"This is the truth?"

My old antagonism stirred. "Why should I lie? Look you!" I brought up my other hand, held it out into the full light so he could see the ring. "Would I wear that—not that I wish to—but it sticks so tightly I cannot rid myself of it—either actually or figuratively? How I came here afterward—" I shook my head. "They drugged me again, I believe—" Hurriedly I told him of my final awakening in the cell below. "I think they still hope to get something from me—or I would not be alive."

That first fire had faded a little from his gaze. He loosed my wrist.

"Your pardon. You have indeed been badly used." His eyes were hooded now, I thought that even his apology was a little absent, as if he were thinking deeply. "Only, I cannot see— No." Now he shook his head with some decision. "I would not have believed that Von Werthern had the influence to have you sent here—even secretly. Von Zreibruken has always been a disappointed man, yes. He felt that taking a wife (one whom he deemed of mixed blood) from a close connection with the Harrach line should have given him a higher place in the Elector's council. Only, that he would concern himself with this—no. I do not think you have more than guesses—

"However, if you were imprisoned—then how did you get free? How could you have learned of their ways within the walls?"

"That is all by the courtesy of the Electress Ludovika. Please—lift your arm a little—there is a bad scratch here—" For the moment I was not inclined to play at guessing games as to why I was here, it was more important that I discover some method of getting elsewhere as soon as possible. While I could not deny that, irritating as the Colonel could be even in his present seemingly helpless state, he inspired one with confidence.

"Ludovika?" he repeated.

So, as I finished such attention as I could give his

hurts, I told him the story of Lisolette and her obsession with the dead Electress, of how she had freed and also shown me the secrets which lay within the walls.

"I would say this is beyond belief," he commented when I had finished, "yet the fact we are both here proves it true. This is an ill-omened place, and superstition is strong in this part of the country. Your young 'ghost' could well have become so fascinated by the story that she began as a game to play such a part, and now has thought herself into believing it. The legends about Ludovika are not pleasant ones. It is very true that the commoners—and the court (even the Elector of that time, himself, if accounts are to be credited—and I have seen those set down with the exactitude of legal documents)—believed her to have access to unnatural powers. Certainly her closest adviser was executed as a follower and servant of the devil." He picked up his shirt and slipped it on, drawing it carefully about him.

"I wish I had salve." I was sure those careful movements told more of pain that he would ever admit. "Perhaps when Lisolette comes again I can persuade her—"

"I do not think from what you have said she may take kindly to giving me any aid." He arose to his feet and was once more peering out of the window. "When she comes it would be better for me to stay out of sight. Have you any idea how far those wall passages extend? In the other direction, I mean? Such ways often have an exit to the outside—used in times of siege or storming of a fortress. I wonder how that girl chanced on them at all—"

"When she opened the way into my cell I did not look in the other direction, I just followed her. But my cell was on the outer wall—and there seemed to be nothing below but a deep cliff." I described all I had been able to see through the slit window.

"However, there could be some turn, some linkage." He was frowning a little. "The commandant here is in two minds over what game to play. It can be true that these sisters would conceal your escape—if they are as Lisolette reports them. But there will be no such covering my vanishing. It could be that the entrance in the wall cannot be detected from that side. Certainly I had no idea of it. It may also be true that the commandant has no idea concerning the games his daughter plays. That does not mean, however, that a strict search would not uncover something, or that the girl, weak minded as she appears to be, cannot be startled or frightened into revealing what she has been doing. Even to bar that door"—he nodded to the one leading to the outer hall—"would arouse suspicion if a room-to-room search was made."

His words so followed my earlier speculations that I believed there was a necessity of once more retracing the way through the walls to discover whether, somewhere beyond my own cell, might lie just such a hidden exit as he suggested. Only when I spoke that thought aloud, he shook his head.

"Not now—not yet. It would be better if you play Lisolette's game a little longer, learn more. What lies in here? This seemed to be built against the wall very tightly." He had gone to the wardrobe and was running his hands along its side toward the wall. "Such sometimes have secrets also."

"She keeps her ghost dress—and another in there." I opened the door and let him see the hanging garments.

He touched the wide, stiff skirt of the one she had worn with the fingertip veil. "This is old right enough. It could well have been one of Ludovika's. What's this?" He stooped and picked up the book-box, holding it closer into the candle flame.

I pointed to the design deep graven on the cover and told of its fellow which had been carved on the shelf table in the cell.

"Hex," he said. "You can see such on doors, even on the walls of barns. The countrymen believe some designs mean protection. Others are symbols to draw power when used according to secret doctrines. This is
219

very old also—" He had been striving to open it, but the lock resisted even as it had for me.

Now, box in one hand, he took the candle from me with the other and prowled around the room, looking at the two tables, one of which had a second candlestick on it. Instead of a cup ready to hold a candle, this possessed a sharp-pointed spike on which the wax could be impaled. He caught that up, having set down the box with the light, and began to lever the edge of that point beneath the edge of the box lid.

I could see that he worked delicately and with caution, as if he had no wish to mar the ancient wood. Whether he could have solved the problem so, we had no chance to learn, for we were startled into frozen silence by a sound at the door.

For once I thought quickly and took from him the box, heading for the wardrobe, with my heart pounding. I had it back and the door closed and then I turned—to see an empty room. Where my companion had taken refuge I did not know. Only there lay his jacket, and that I sprang to collect, having just time enough to throw it, with the mass of torn and wet, now bloodstained linen, under the edge of the window draperies, trusting to the luck which had not failed me so far that those would conceal it all.

Lisolette came in, appearing almost as ghostlike in her cambric dress, her pale hair floating loosely about her shoulders, as she had worn it in her disguise. To my surprise she was giggling as might any schoolgirl who had managed some mischief in a way successful to herself and confounding to those she had some reason to dislike.

Clasped in her arms was a bundle of some size. This she dropped on the floor as if she had found its contents both heavy and cumbersome. She smiled slyly up at me.

"They are so angry—and I think that my father is also frightened. Yes, I do believe he is frightened!" She had dropped down on the dusty floor beside her package and now she again looked up at me, plainly highly amused.

"Something has gone wrong—with his prisoner— I could not hear much—the lieutenant was there and so I could not listen at the door. It is good—now they will not be thinking about us! We have so much to do. It is the right time of the moon, you know—perhaps you could not see that when you were down there. But the phases of the moon are of the greatest importance— the power rises with it, and weakens with it. We are lucky in that this is the right time and we do not have to wait. But of course *she* knew that and it is why she sent me to you. Only I did not understand then how important it all was.

"Now—" The girl stood up and stood back a step or two looking me up and down critically as if such an inspection was of the utmost importance. "Yes, I am sure it will fit—it must. And I have brought under-garments. You could not wear those clumsy things you have—not under what she has for you."

She stooped again and twitched her bundle open. There was another basket—this without a handle— also a number of folded garments, which certainly looked far finer than the coarse chemise and petticoats my wardress had supplied.

"Wait—" Lisolette sped back to the door and reached outside to drag in a can of water and a basin.

"I had to made two trips," she said, as one pointing out the fulfillment of a distasteful duty. "Now you can wash and be ready. I cannot stay—but I shall be back. There is more food there— And—"

She went to the wardrobe to open the door. Her hand stroked the skirt of the red dress.

"This is for you. It was *hers*. You are to wear it."

With that she was gone, leaving me still more mys-tified at the meaning of the game she played, and in which she now proposed to include me. The bed curtains moved and Colonel Fenwick emerged from hiding.

"Do you see?" I demanded of him. He was looking,

not at me, but to the door through which Lisolette had vanished.

"Tell me," he ordered, "everything you can remember that she has said concerning this *she,* whom I take to be Ludovika—"

Though I could not see what such imaginings would mean, his authority was such that I did struggle to recall all the disjointed and superstitious nonsense, or so it seemed to me, Lisolette had said at one time or another. He listened gravely, as if every word I called to mind was a portion of a puzzle which it was very necessary to fit together.

"It seems that she believes Ludovika escaped—"

"If she did, it was through death. But Lisolette apparently believes that she is still alive—in some manner."

He again wore the look of one thinking out a complicated plan of action.

"Show me the trick of the panels." He spoke with even greater sharpness, and took up the candle. "I must learn where the other end of that passage may be."

"We can—"

Now he shook his head. "No, I go alone. Do as the girl has said." He pointed to the clothing she had brought, the waiting water. "It may be that only through her we can hope to get out. But I must make sure."

Though I was ready to protest hotly, I could see by his expression that it would do no good. He added as he took up the candlestick:

"Be very sure, I will take no chances. And I shall return as quickly as I can."

I made him free of the secret of the eye hinge and watched him vanish into the wall runs. Reluctantly I returned to follow Lisolette's instruction, though it was good to wash the dust and grime from my body, put on again the soft, clean linen she had brought me. To wear the red dress was another matter. The skirt went on easily enough, though I had to draw in my breath to fasten it. But the bodice, so extremely low cut, was another matter.

Certainly I filled it better than Lisolette did the other dress, but the bareness of my shoulders was something I could not get used to, while the bones of the sewed in stiffening pushed my breasts up and out in what I considered a most indecent display, though I could not view the results in any mirror. The iron necklace was the only covering I could cling to—I neither had shawl nor scarf.

I had to comb my hair and braid it, but there were no pins left to establish my customary style of coiffure, so those braids spilled down across my shoulders, giving me some manner of concealment. The wide, stiff skirts were difficult to manage and brushed the floor. I had tried to cram my feet into a pair of the slippers, but all those were too small and I had to remain content with my heavy wool stockings, those already thickened with dust, as my only foot covering.

Beneath my new dress I still slung the bag of gold and that parchment which now meant so little. Suppose we did get free, how could I go across any countryside in this dress—fashioned for appearance at court a hundred years ago or more?

The small basket contained more food; also, something else which I caught up with a surge of excitement. For a weapon it was not very formidable, being a knife with a blade long enough to deal with the round of smoked sausage beside which it lay, but it was the closest thing to a weapon that I had seen for days. I used it to carve off a section of the meat, delighting in its keenness as it slid through the hard brown roll. I ate only a small portion of the food, putting the rest aside for the Colonel.

Then I gathered up the torn linen I had used to tend his hurts and brought his jacket out of hiding. The linen I spread out flat on the bed and drew over all the disintegrating covers, arranging the scene as best I could as it had first appeared, while the jacket I laid

223

in the shadow of the hangings. Lisolette had not appeared to notice the disheveled condition of the bed earlier—I hoped that if she came again, she would not see anything amiss.

I could not sit still, but paced back and forth, from the place I could look out the window, to the panel behind which Fenwick had gone, looking out from one to try to see any sign of search, listening at the other for some sound to herald his return. The silence of the room weighed upon me. Can one *hear* quiet? In those long, long moments I felt that it did have some substance of its own which *could* be heard—that the absence of sound itself was a weighty thing to listen to.

It was almost a relief at last to catch sight of movement in the courtyard. One of the doors that set in the wall opposite the window from which I spied was thrown open abruptly. A squad of soldiers issued forth, spreading out fanwise as they came. They held muskets and had the air of men about to engage in some deadly skirmish.

I could not see what lay a floor below my own window. Was there another door there through which they must now enter? Three of the men had gone to that other door and passed within, but the rest were heading straight for the wall of the wing in which I sheltered. I turned so swiftly my skirts swept around the stool and I nearly lost my balance. To bar the door—that would make any searcher suspicious.

If I could erase from this room any sign of my occupancy— I must! There were the garments I had thrown off, the basin now full of soapy water in which I had washed—the empty can—the baskets of food— What could I do with them? Transport all into the passage?

The dress in the wardrobe, that which Lisolette wore in her night wanderings—a single glance at that might well betray her secret for all time. I must do the best I could to hide all signs of occupancy.

It took me only a moment to open the panel and brace it so. Then to speed back and forth with all the things I had noted, taking at the last the dress and veil of Lisolette's wearing, together with the coat Fenwick had left.

To edge through the narrow door of the panel in my own present bulky wear was a problem. I had had no time to bring with me a lighted candle! I retreated so into utter darkness, letting the panel close, waiting to hear the tramp of feet as the searchers must be making their way from room to room.

I dared not move in this thick dark, for I had so bundled in all the things I must hide that they were in a chaotic mass about my feet. From the dress and veil I held pressed tightly to me arose a faint scent—cloying—sweet—yet unpleasant. That seemed to grow stronger until I felt dizzy as it choked my nostrils, filled the air. It was like no perfume I had ever scented before—sickly—perhaps rising from flowers cut only to quickly die—

No! I shook my head vigorously. I must concentrate on listening—be sure, if the room *was* entered, that nothing could reveal our presence. The dark was so heavy it was like being locked within a tomb—no! I must not allow my thoughts to stray so morbidly.

A sound! I had guessed rightly! That had been the room door flung open. There came the tramp of feet, heavy on the floor. Could they track me? The thought just occurred to me. With all that dust—how could we not have left tracks.

"Phuh—!" An exclamation of disgust. "Three spiders here if the sergeant asks."

"This is a strange room—" Another voice, younger, not so coarse.

"Strange it is, Florian—Prince Franzel was murdered here if the story is right. All this wing is unlucky. Come—there is nothing but dust, and how could he have gotten into this wing anyhow? The outer door below was locked, you saw how hard it was for the sergeant to turn the key. Unless he went through walls—"

It was as if a hand, large and brutal, had closed upon

225

my throat. Go through walls! That searcher had lit upon the truth. They need only follow such a suggestion and—

Those steps were retreating. I heard the door thud shut. However, I continued to stand where I was, my arms filled with dress and jacket, my heart pounding so hard I wished I dared lean against the wall for support. I counted slowly to a hundred, hoping thus, in a little, to measure time. Then I slid open the panel.

The chamber was just as I had left. Their search had not been thorough, though the curtains had been dragged farther back and torn even more. We must, I made note, be careful to avoid passing near that window, keep well back in the room.

I moved out of hiding and once more transferred all that I had hidden. When I opened the door of the wardrobe to rehang the dress, I was startled. There stood the rows of shoes, and beside them the book-box. If the searchers had sighted those, why had they not said anything, or taken such evidence? Maybe they had not noticed, the wardrobe did stand in such a shadowed corner. They had been looking for a man in hiding, they could well have thought that both shoes and box were left here in the long ago.

Suddenly, weak with relief, I sat down on a chair to wait.

I had no way of telling time. It seemed that the Colonel had been gone far longer than it would have taken him to make the trip even down as far as my cell. Did the passage run much farther, perhaps being cut into the raw stone of the outcrop of mountain on which Wallenstein had been erected? In my mind I could picture a flight of uncounted stairs winding down and down into the depth of the rock—to come out—where?

As time passed I grew so overwrought that it was all I could do to sit still. However, I knew that I must not move around lest some searcher either catch a glimpse of me through that now uncurtained window, or, passing perhaps in the corridor, hear me. When one is prevented from doing something, then that becomes the very thing each nerve in one's body strains to do.

There was a sound! I looked quickly and eagerly to the panel, but that did not herald the return of the Colonel, rather it was Lisolette who came through from the secret way. But how—?

At the edge of the room she hesitated, giving a quick glance around. Then she blew out the candle she had carried and walked around the foot of the bed, avoiding the window. Standing there, she gave me a measuring survey and then nodded.

"They did not find you. You used the passage to hide, did you not? *She* will be pleased at your understanding. They are gone. Such as they never see what is before them unless they are tweaked by the nose. We have much to do—"

"Where did you come from?" Had she met with the Colonel in those hidden ways? If so—why had she not said anything concerning him? I had to keep tight rein on my tongue to hold back such questions.

Lisolette giggled. "Oh, there are many entrances. Some I found for myself, some she showed me because it was necessary to know how to reach the place—*the place.*"

She had gone to the wardrobe and now lifted out the box which she carried to the table. Taking up that same spike-pointed candlestick the Colonel had tried to use to force the lock of the box, she impaled one of the fat candles on it. Then she glanced at the half-uncurtained window.

"See if you can draw that closer," she ordered. "Set a chair to hold it. They are still roaming the halls and we must not provide light in an empty room. But light we must have now."

I sidled along the wall beside the drapes and drew the tattered one as best I could. Following her instructions I then lugged and pulled at one of the massive chairs, getting it into place so that its back, high as that was, covered most of the slits in the fabric.

Lisolette was chanting, in a voice which was hardly
227

more than a whisper, using a language I could not understand. She had set the candle very near the box and now she drew from beneath the folds of her dress at the collar line a chain from which swung a key. Still chanting, she set the key in the lock and opened the box.

With the care of one engaged in an important task she began to take out objects and set them in precise order within the circled light. There was a bowl so small I could have cupped it within the palm of one of my hands, looking so old its surface was covered with greenish encrustations. Into this she sifted carefully a little powder from a leather bag which she then returned to the box. After that came a knife or dagger, its blade and hilt both black, though the latter was wound around by a scarlet cord. Last of all she had a cylinder, also of metal looking very ancient. This she twisted until it came apart, when from it she drew a piece of what looked to be much-creased and handled parchment.

Flattening that sheet out on the table, she looked over her shoulder at me.

"Come!" she ordered. "We must be about *her* business. But we do not go unprepared. *She* is with us, watching, making sure. Do you not feel this? You must!"

Chapter 17

I was uneasy, yes. How else should I feel in this place? But that there was anything hinting of superstition in my emotion I forced myself to deny fiercely. Lisolette picked up the burning candle, held its flame down into the bowl to meet the power she had shaken there. She leaned over to blow gently and was answered, a few moments later, by a thin curl of pearl-gray smoke which arose first in twists, and then straightened out into a rod of vapor soaring into the dusk of the room.

Into this she thrust both her hands, twisting and turning the fingers in and out as one does while washing, so that the column of smoke was broken and edged out in puffs. I could smell it now—cloying—sweet—too sweet, like some flower already touched by the blight of decay. Again her hands moved, catching at the vapor as if it had substance, then drawing those hands to her head, smoothing her hair between the scented palms. It was as if she bathed in that trickle of smoke.

While she did this her eyes were fixed, not upon the smoke itself, but straight before her. Words I could not understand fell, rose, and fell again in the cadence of a chant.

The smoke died, the last wisp of it she caught at jealously, held to her until I thought to see that it was actually a ball she rolled so now between her palms. Then she raised her cupped closed hands to the level of her nose, leaned a little forward to inhale deeply of what she held, or seemed to hold.

I had drawn back from the table, for there was something noisome in the thick odor of that smoke, thin and tenuous as vapor, which made me feel ill, giddy. Grasping the back of one of the chairs, I held on so, keeping my feet, fighting against a weakness which came in surges to attack both my physical strength—and my courage. I had never before, even in the days just past, in that time when I had confronted Konrad's rage and brutal usage, experienced the same kind of fear which arose and pressed in upon me now. This was not of any normal world, even of a world in which casual cruelty was a common thing.

Lisolette turned away, but not before she had taken up the knife. Her eyes were wide, unblinking, still that stare was not turned on me. What she saw, or believed she saw, lay elsewhere, beyond the boundaries of my vision. With the concentrated absorption of a sleep-walker she went to the wardrobe and reached for the gown she wore during her night-haunting of the secret ways.

She dressed herself in it, adjusted her veil with practiced hands, while her eyes fixed on something else. Now she no longer chanted, but still she spoke, while the manner of her speaking was so eerie and unnatural that I found myself clinging even more closely to the chair which was my support. For it was as if she were talking with another—an unseen companion, uttering those sounds, then waiting for some reply, before speaking once again. I found myself searching the dusky room for that other. So strong was the impression the girl created that I could almost believe there was a third with us in the chamber. I fought then, fought my own imagination, against that strange certainty which Lisolette raised.

Perhaps the smoke was of some herb or substance which could cause hallucinations because, for all my battling to retain a barrier against illusion, I could indeed accept now that there was some presence with us—a personality, if you will—growing stronger, more compelling—demanding—

Deliberately I used the nails of one hand against the other that still grasped the back of the chair, digging them deep into my own flesh, even as a cat or some other clawed creature would defend itself. The pain was sharp, but I enforced it—as an anchorage against I know not what danger.

The dagger Lisolette had set into the bodice of her dress, so its crimson-wrapped hilt showed against her pale skin. She did not cover her face with the veil this time. Rather she went purposefully back to the table, silent now, as if her conversation with the other was done, that she had received some instructions. There her hand closed about the roll of ancient parchment which she had taken from the tube. With the fingers of her left hand she picked up the candle and for the first time she looked directly at me, that glassy stare gone, clearly she was alert and knowing once again.

"It is time to go—" She gestured me toward the hidden door in the paneling, plainly giving so an order that I open the secret way.

The skirts of the court dress I wore dragged about me. They carried the sickly sweet scent of the smoke as I gathered as much of their fullness into one hand as I could. I felt unpleasantly exposed with this very low bodice, while the iron necklace about my throat was cold against my skin. Unfortunately I did not remember to pick up that knife which had so pleased me earlier.

We made our way into the passage, but went very slowly, for the skirts of our dresses were hard to manage here. Twice I felt the old stuff of mine tear against some projection of the wall; though Lisolette was more deft in control of hers, the roll of parchment having joined with the knife in the forepart of her bodice.

Down we went once more, I ever alert to some sound heralding the return of the Colonel. What we might do—or Lisolette might—if we met here, I could not guess. That I would have to leave to the fortunes of chance alone. However there was no sound, save that whisper of our own passing.

The stairs, the Colonel's cell—then mine— Two or three paces beyond that our way took a sudden turn to the right. We must now be very close to the wall of the outer cliff. Once more we faced steps, so steep and narrow I was glad that I wore no high-heeled shoes, though the chill which struck upward through the damp woolen stockings I wore as my only foot covering numbed my feet.

Down we went, slowly, Lisolette taking care here and advancing a single step at a time. My fingers slid along the walls on either side, until the flesh was rasped near raw, striving to find some hold which would be a support should I slip. I have never had a good head for heights, and the passage, so little revealed by the candle ahead of me, seemed to plunge forward with a slope steep enough to make my giddiness of the upper chamber return.

I found myself counting under my breath those steps, so very narrow—fifty of them! We must be below the foundations of the fortress, edging into the very stuff of the cliff on which it perched. Lisolette said nothing and the only sounds came from the rasping of our skirts against the walls.

On the sixtieth step I was barely holding onto the rags of my courage. The one wane hope which supported me was the Colonel's suggestion that one of the hidden ways might provide a secret exit from Wallenstein, fashioned to be used in a time when the fortress might fall to some foe.

That he had come this way I had no doubts. I longed to hear some sound to suggest that he was returning. More and more I clung to the hope that he would have the strength to deal properly with Lisolette, and that on him would rest our escape from this nightmare.

Ten more of these hellish steps—for to me this descent had become a passage into those infernal regions of which older generations had made so black a warning. Then there came an end in another passage. Here, though the candlelight picked out now and then the traces of tools which had been used to make the way more passable, there was also evidence that we were traveling through some natural cleft in the rock. There was no masonry to be seen.

The way was cold, so cold that I shivered continuously, my bare shoulders pimpled with raised flesh. I would have given anything for a shawl, even that rough garment I had left behind. Lisolette walked more briskly, I was certain that she knew exactly where she was and had a definite goal. The passage widened out and her pace became swifter, until she was nearly running and I must hasten to keep up with her and that precious candle.

We emerged in a burst of speed, as if she were so eager to gain her desire that she could no longer wait,

nto a chamber cut in the rock. It might have been a
ave, but there was much evidence that it had been
dapted by the will of man to another purpose.

By the thin candlelight I could only make out some
tanding objects here and there along the walls, and,
t the far end, a raised platform. Lisolette was busy,
urrying along one wall and raising her candle high
o hold its flame to a series of rusty iron baskets, each
f which must have been crammed with tinder and
urnable wood, for they caught fire quickly. That done
he turned and sped to light a similar line on the op-
osite wall.

I could see clearly now and what I saw was enough
o root me in sheer astonishment, as if the stone had
ripped my feet and held me completely prisoner. Those
gures I had only half glimpsed were now plain. Pillars
f rock stood in two rows, forming a guard. There had
een no attempt to chisel any form into the rough stone
elow the shoulder line, but each was topped by a man-
est representation of a human head, while each of
hose heads was that of a dead man. The mouths gaped
oosely, the eyes were blank. Some had been vilely
vorked upon to suggest the heads of those so long dead
hat the bones of the skull showed through rotting
esh.

Lisolette, having completed her circle of the wall
askets and finished their lighting, now made her way
o the platform at the far end. There was a last basket
here, set upon the stone at floor level, and into that
he thrust her candle and left it. The figure on the
latform was not one of the pillar-heads, but had been
ashioned to show the whole of a squatting form. So
bscene was that thing that I gasped, unable to believe
hat mankind had ever worshipped such, for that this
vas a temple, a very old temple, I had no doubt now.

The thing was more than life-size and it was fe-
nale—obscenely female, with vast bags of breasts lying
pon a huge mound of an obviously pregnant body.
Vhile the legs were stretched well apart to expose the
nost private parts of my sex. Huge as that swollen

body was, the head was small in comparison, only a round ball which bore but two indentations for eyes and no other features.

Lisolette was on her knees before that horror, reaching up her hands to it. I shuddered. Its very grossness was an insult, a degradation of my sex, and still it was plain that this child worshipped before it.

The place was old, old and filled with something which pressed in on me. I could feel a kind of tugging to drag me forward. Lisolette—I had no feeling for her but no one, no one must pay homage to *that!* It held in itself all the most bestial of the past—

I found myself beside the girl and I caught at her shoulders, trying to drag her back and up, away from that thing squatting there. Without even looking at me, her eyes only for the image, she twisted in my hold with astounding strength. Her hand went to the front of her bodice and she brought forth both the knife and the roll of parchment. As I tightened my hold on her she turned a little. Her expression was vicious, her lips drew back from her teeth as might those of a striking wolf, and she slashed at me with the knife.

I flinched away, aware that in her present state she could well kill. There was a dribble of froth at the corners of her mouth.

"*She* comes! You are for *her!*"

Swinging around, with her back now to the image, the girl lunged at me, knife ready. There was no doubt that she meant to kill me. I flung myself out of her reach, dodged, as she moved with a wolf's speed to follow me. There was no weapon—the candle with its heavy stick! But that was several feet away—

I dodged again, striving to get within reaching distance to seize upon that. All which was sane and human had vanished from the girl's face.

"*She* wants you," she panted. "Then she can live again—she must live again! The Old One has promised it. You have her clothing upon you, you are of the blood she wants—she will have you!"

She sprang at me with such a fury then that I tried

once more to elude her, but my unwieldy skirts tripped me up. I fell half on my side, while that knife descended straight toward my body, and I could only fling up one arm feebly as a shield against the blow.

The steel never reached me. Lisolette screamed. Dazed, I looked up to see that both her hands were caught in a strong grip, one determined enough to be able to hold the insane girl. The knife fell to the floor, and I threw myself on it, while the Colonel held my attacker, and her screams made a deafening, hideous din in this evil place.

She had that strength which often comes upon those of broken minds, and he had difficulty in restraining her, slight and young as she was. I thrust the knife into my own bodice and stumbled to my feet, drawing myself up with a hold on one of those skull-headed pillars, just in time to see the Colonel raise his hand and strike Lisolette on the jaw as she clawed and bit and kicked with frenzy. Her head snapped back as she crumpled in his arms, so that he laid her down at the very foot of that obscene image and then came quickly to me.

"You are not harmed?"

I shook my head, trying to catch my breath. "Lisolette?" The question I made of her name came forth in a creak.

He knelt beside the unconscious girl, touching the pulse at her throat.

"Only unconscious. I had no other way of handling her."

"I know." Some might have deemed his blow a brutal one, but I understood the necessity for it. I felt as if I had been running past my strength. There was a sharp pain in my side, hurting so that I looked down to see if the knife had really gone home into my flesh and I had not been aware of it during those moments of deadly fear. But the red stuff was unspotted, though it was much frayed and tearing apart at the seams.

"What do we do—?" Somehow I found breath again in spite of that pain.

I no longer stood alone, or rather swayed weakly. There was a strong arm about my shoulder as I was drawn close to the warmth and support of a body which felt as unmovable, as impregnable as the walls of rock about us.

"We go on. I have found the door. It is a hard way—"

I looked up into his face. There was resolution there and more than hope—a promise.

"This place—" Once more that pain came in my side. I felt the pulling. I will swear all my life there was another presence in the light of those basket torches than just the three of us, the girl curled in a ball like a sleeping child at the feet of that horror carven centuries beyond time, the man in the tattered and blood stained clothing—I in the slitting dress of a forgotten—and damned—court. There was an—identity hovering there. Rage—hot as the flames in the basket—a helpless rage all the more searing because it *was* helpless.

Yet, when I looked at the lumpish squatting thing I knew that the feeling did not center in it. Those who had worshipped here were long gone. Perhaps the forces they had recognized and symbolized in the image had lingered—until something else had drawn upon that residue, brought it to feed another way of power.

Once more I looked to Pryor Fenwick, welcoming the warmth of his body close to mine, the protection of his arms about me.

"It is not the place—alone—" I voiced what I felt. Almost I expected him to treat my strange emotions as I would have earlier—vagaries of overwrought mind, the result of hysteria.

Instead I saw him nod.

"This is very old, but there were those who came later, who turned to old beliefs, twisted them. Come—" His arm still about my shoulders, he drew me to the platform, up on it, though I went reluctantly.

"Lisolette." I dragged against his hold for a moment and looked to the girl.

She stirred, gave a small whimper.

"We cannot take her. She is not badly hurt and she

must know these ways well. This is not the first time she has been here."

"Please—!" I pulled free from him then, but he followed me and stooped to help me stretch the girl out on the stone. Her eyes opened and she looked up at me. A wide smile stretched the lips above her bruised jaw.

"You—have come!" She clutched at my skirts. "As you promised! My lady—at last!"

"She has come—and now she must go—" the Colonel said in an even voice, much like a priest reciting some ritual. "She must go—again into the way—"

To my surprise Lisolette did not look at him at all, but she nodded eagerly.

"Yes, go free, my lady. Just as you did before when they thought they could shut you forever into the darkness! They were fools! Such great fools. Go—go quickly. And when you are on your throne again you will send for me—promise!" She clutched so tightly that the cloth of my skirts shredded even more into strips of disintegrating cloth.

"I promise—" There was nothing else I could say. She seemed unaware that the Colonel was with us. But she watched me get to my feet as she loosed her hold on me, and her eyes followed, as my companion, again with his supporting arm around me, led me around the image into the shadows where the flames from the baskets did not reach.

"She is out of her mind," I said. "Should we leave her here—alone?"

"She is safe. Come—!" His pull on me was insistent enough to bear me along. I went, knowing that what he said was true, Lisolette knew these secret ways, had probably explored them many times over.

We faced another opening in the wall, this one behind the looming, ugly shadow cast by the squatting image. Through it, in the distance, I saw a spark of light, enough to make that open mouth of the narrow tunnel, if tunnel it was, less terrifying. The Colonel did not loose his hold on me. Perhaps he felt that, once free, I might return to the temple. Now he quickened

pace, drawing me along as I had to gather up the bil
lows of my tattered skirts so that their disintegrating
folds might not trip me up.

My feet had worn through part of the thick woolen
stockings and the rough stone was making me flinch
and limp, but I managed to match step with him after
a fashion. Now I saw that the light ahead was the
candle he had taken, sitting on the floor in the midst
of the way.

This had been a natural cleft in the rock and not so
much had been done to smooth or convert it from that
state. The Colonel let go of me at last as he stooped to
pick up the candle, which, I saw to my dismay, was
now hardly more than a stub.

"We must hurry," he said imperatively, "while this
lasts. There is a difficult place ahead—"

Hurry we did, his boots clicking loudly, or so the
sound reached my ears, across the stone. Then he
halted abruptly and threw out one arm as a barrier to
bring me to a stop against it, swinging the candle out
so that I could see what trap lay before us.

Whether it was of man's devising, to hide the ancient
infamous sacred place, or from subsidence of nature
we could not tell, but there was a break in the way, a
gulf across which there was no bridge.

"Where do we go now?" I asked, having no wish to
go closer to peer down into that dark pit opening at our
feet.

"Down." He turned and surveyed me, put out one
hand and jerked almost savagely at the rotting stuff
of my skirt. It tore easily, fell away from me in long
frayed streamers. I gasped as I stood there now less
than half clad.

"You could not climb in that," he said impatiently.
"Now." He set the candle back on the floor of the crevice
and caught at me again. "Over—there are holds for
feet and hands—"

I wanted to scream that I dared not, that it was
impossible for me to even try. But there was something
in this man which allowed me no escape, I knew that
238

what he ordered, that I would do—if my body could obey at all.

"I will go first, then I can guide you." He made the candlestick fast to his belt at the back, anchoring it there with tugs to make sure of its safety, by rags torn from his shirt. Then he swung over the edge of the drop. Against my will, against every quivering nerve in my body, I made myself creep to that same lip of rock and watch him descend. He went only a little way and looked up to me.

"Turn around," he ordered. "Slip over, I shall guide your feet to the first holds. Come!"

I did as he commanded, that which moments earlier I would have sworn I could never have faced. His fingers clasped my ankle, drew my foot down until it fitted into a hole in the stone, then the same with the other foot. Flylike, and for what seemed like hours of giddy torment, we descended in that slow fashion, always his grasp finding the places for my feet, while I gained a little courage and was able to free my frozen hold on one set of supports and allow him to guide me to the next.

Yet when we reached the bottom of what seemed to me a gulf without end, and I leaned weakly against the wall, gasping and wet with sweat so that my chemise and the torn bodice were plastered to my body, I was not even sure that I had done this at all, that it was not some kind of a nightmare.

I looked around half-dazed. He was holding the candle once again in a firm grip, half-shielded by one hand, for there was a current of air moving here which we had not felt in those stagnant ways above. There was something else, too—something that that light caught upon.

With a choked cry I pushed back against the rock which grated against my bared shoulders. A skull lay almost at my feet. Its black, blank eyeholes stared straight at me. And it was part of a huddle of bones, small bones, slender. The candlelight, dim as it was, caught a glint of metal and my companion stooped again, reaching out for what lay there.

He had held the light so close that I could see it—or did it, by some strange and eerie chance, take on for one instant some burning life of its own, making itself so known to us, enticing us to take it up? It was a medallion, set, I think, with gems, only jewels could have so sent up those points of glitter. It I had seen before—or the symbol of it—the sign Ludovika had carved below her name in the cell she had known.

"Don't!" My cry echoed from the walls about us. I found the strength to lean forward, to clutch at his bruised and scratched shoulder, dragging back his hand when he would have picked that up.

"It's hers, Ludovika's." My voice sounded hysterical in my own ears. "It's—it's evil! Leave it—please leave it!"

He arose, to stand for a long moment gazing down at the huddle of delicate bones. "So—this is where she ended," he said slowly, "to become a legend— She must have tried to escape. Rumor was always strong that she had followers in strange places, and that which we left above was surely no shrine for good."

"Can we go? Oh, please, let us get away from here!" I edged along the wall, away from the bones, but more truthfully away from that which lay among them. My hand, I had caught my left hand with my right, held it tight against my breast. It seemed that my own flesh fought against me, that a compulsion to pick up that unholy symbol was so great that I must dig my nails punishingly into my flesh to prevent my taking it. I knew then there did lie some queer spell upon this place and that I must summon all the strength of will I had to stand against it.

My companion seemed unmoved. He turned away from the tumble of bones with apparently no great effort. Only now he came to me and once more put his arm, strong and warm, about my shrinking body, drawing me on to the left, leaving that strange tomb of a woman who had known too much about things better left alone.

We did not have far to go before the air about us was fresh. Our candle flickered and went out, but I suddenly did not care. I was not alone and the wind which touched us carried the scent of growing things, the cleanness of the outer world, driving away the musty dankness of Wallenstein.

Together we scraped a way between two great rocks which masked the entrance to the cleft, fought a painful path among bushes which scratched and tore at our already rent clothing, until I feared that I would finally emerge totally bare of body.

"There is a forester's hut." My companion's voice was a whisper out of the dark, but the warmth of his body was still beside me. "We must reach there—it is unoccupied now."

He must have carried his earlier explorations for some distance before returning just in time to save my life. For, that he had done so as Lisolette's mad obsession had overwhelmed her, I could not deny. Now he moved easily through the dark as if he had known this path, if path it was, for a long time.

I found the dark bewildering, for the night was clouded, and though Lisolette had spoken of a moon, there was certainly none to be seen. However, I was able to sight the rise of a darker bulk before us. The Colonel loosened his hold on me for a moment or two. I heard the creaking of some door, and then once more his hand reached out and I was drawn inside into greater darkness.

"Stand where you are. Let me close the door and then we shall have a light."

I was very willing. That we had come safely out of Wallenstein seemed at that moment to be such a great and unbelievable venture that I felt dazed and queer, even stupid. I could hear movements in the dark and then the candle, or a candle, blazed from a spark.

"Here, my lady." The candle was on a rude table,

but he had left it there to catch up from somewhere a coarse cloak which he flung about me. For the first time I felt the heat of my own flush as I realized what a figure I must present. However, the folds of the cloak covered me and my rags and now I was able to look about me with some equanimity.

Chapter 18

Dawn made gray what sky I could see through the small crack where I had dared loose the inner shutter and peer out. The tainted wood which came so close to the base of that rock supporting Wallenstein formed a forbidding wall before me. I could not sight a single promising path or opening.

I pulled the cloak, which was nearly my only covering, closer about me. Fatigue and the wear upon my nerves of the night's work had struck me down earlier. I could remember only dimly of lying upon a shelflike bed. Still there had been a warmth which was not born of any fire, the warmth of knowing that there was indeed one I could trust and who cared what happened to me. We had spoken together very little. That last struggle which had brought us out of immediate danger had reduced us to just accepting the fact that so far we were indeed free.

Now anxiety awoke in me again. So close to Wal-

lenstein—and with only a demented girl a barrier between us and the knowledge of our enemies as to where
we could be found. I had already clutched tightly many
times over that bag of gold which was my strongest
hope of future help for us both.

There was a stir in the dusky room of the shelter.
I turned swiftly, having made fast once again the shutter. In the more than half dark my companion was only
a dull white figure rising from a pallet which had faced
mine across the room. I heard him grunt and utter
some heated words under his breath and knew that his
bruises and scrapes were not easy to bear.

However, he moved alertly, as a man who is trained
in the instant response of a soldier under danger, coming to the table to light once more the candle. The
tatters of his shirt were gone and on his wide shoulders
and chest the marks of his hurts showed dark. Those
must have given him pain and I wished that I had to
hand some remedy to soothe them. Now I had not even
water.

Water—! The sudden thought of it made me thirsty.
Just as I also knew hunger.

"No sign of trouble?" He broke the silence between
us as if I were a junior officer he was asking for a report.

"I saw nothing but the woods."

He had gone to a cupboard fastened to the wall and
now jerked open the door of that. "Bare," he commented, "at least of any food. But we may be in luck
otherwise—" With a long arm he swept out a bundle
and brought it to the table. What he shook out there
was clothing.

"Changes for bad weather perhaps," he commented
as he shook out and held up in the light some pieces
of what looked to me the coarse stuff a peasant might
wear. There were several shirts, a leather vest, and a
pair of breeches, the latter spotted with dark patches.
The smell of them, mildewed and worse, reached me
clear across the room. "Not pretty, no." He must have
seen my wrinkled nose. "But when the devil drives,

one does not pick one's way. And we cannot wander on in our present state."

I was blushing again, and I squirmed a little under the protection of the cloak. Clothes had suddenly become important. While his state was little better, his breeches, in spite of showing many smears and smudges, were not torn. However he had a more villainous look, for the sprouting of a beard added a great deal to the general grim cast of his face, and his hair was an untidy thatch grayed with dust and standing very much on end.

"Where do we go?" I tried to be as matter-of-fact as he.

"Now, that"—he had seated himself on one edge of the table, swinging one foot, covered by a much scratched and battered boot, back and forth—"is an excellent question. The chase will be up—is up, of course, right now. This is largely deserted country. Any we would find hereabouts would be of the sort better avoided. They would turn us in for a copper."

"I have money—" I brought forth the bag I had carried in secret for so long, and went to the table to empty it out.

He whistled as I brushed aside as worthless the parchment which had been one of the things to draw me into this tangle, and pushed forward the gold.

"This also—" I parted the cloak at my throat enough to indicate the necklace, which seemed to me now a collar of slavery and which I would willingly have dropped back there beside that unholy medallion of the Electress Ludovika.

"Hide that!" His command came instantly. "Such could well betray you— Its existence is known to those who you have the most reason to fear."

He frowned down at the gold, not as if he saw the money, but rather was mulling over some thoughts of his own. "We need food, shelter—"

"And a way to get out of this cursed country!" My resentment of all which had happened to me boiled over that moment.

244

"And a way out," he agreed. "Which is not going to be easily found. Oh, if we can reach the border we may be able to slip across by some smugglers' route. If we can move fast enough—or you can— When they find me gone I shall be their first quarry. Your presence there may still be a guarded secret and they will not dare to hunt you too openly."

I made my choice, only it was no choice at all, I realized, even as I spoke. "We go together. I am your charge—" That was an admission I had never thought to make, one which earlier would have outraged all the belief in myself which my grandmother had fostered. Still it was the truth—this escape must be our common venture to the last. What would the last be? I wondered fleetingly, and straightway sealed any such thought away.

"Truda told me that her family has an inn near the border, there are coaches passing there on their way to some spa." But would we dare approach that? And what of Truda? Was she, too, a prisoner in the same dark pile from which we had managed to escape? If so—how could I leave her there? She had been drawn into this affair only through me. "Truda—"—I spoke my thoughts aloud—"was she there?"

"Truda." Again it was as if he had dropped into his own thoughts. "I wonder— Yes." He did not give me any easy hope. "She may well have been so silenced. However, we cannot remain here."

Once more he set turning over the clothing he had found. A shirt and a pair of breeches were pushed in my direction.

"Luckily this is not thickly settled land. These are the best to be offered to you, my lady."

I eyed the musty garments with disfavor, knowing that he was right—I had to have something to cover my present near-naked body. Modesty in these circumstances was all a matter of degree. But I limped as I went to pick up what he had sorted out. My feet were bare now and sore from the rocky ways, though during

our escape I had not been so aware of that small difficulty among such larger ones.

He gave a quick exclamation, and, before I knew
what he was about or could elude him, I found myself
swung up to sit on the table while he brought my feet,
still ringed about with the worn-through stockings,
into the full light of the candle. I flinched at his touch
and saw that old grim look settle about his mouth.

"Shoes—boots—" He turned back to burrow once
more in the cupboard but apparently could find nothing. "Wrappings will have to do, my lady. But whether
you can manage—"

"I shall," I vowed. He would not see me flinch again.
Already he was tearing one of the other shirts into long
strips, and, with a deftness I would not have believed
him capable of (was there nothing he could not turn
his hand to?), he began wrapping those firmly about
my sore feet. I caught my lip between my teeth and bit
hard upon it, refusing to let him know what pain his
ministrations cost me.

Having put one layer about and secured that with
knots at my ankles, he strode back across the small
room and picked up from a stand by the empty fireplace
a small hand axe, together with a billet of wood which
he split quickly, ripping away the bark which still covered what had once been a sizable branch.

I fumbled beneath the cloak, guessing what he was
about, and brought out that cord-wrapped knife that
had been such a threat in Lisolette's hands.

"Will this serve better?"

"Good!" He caught it from me eagerly, and, again
with a skill I found hard to believe was part of the
knowledge of such a man, he shaped the bark into two
patterns, measuring them against my bandaged feet
before he bound them on with more wrappings, sitting
back at last on his heels to look up at me soberly.

"The best I can do—"

"You have done better than I could hope." I resolutely refused to acknowledge the twinges his actions

caused. "I would not have thought of such an answer. Now—do we go?"

He went to that same lookout I had found by the shutter and peered out.

"I would say wait until night, but we cannot do without food, water—and we are far too near to Wallenstein. If they discover Lisolette, she may well tell them all—"

I caught up the clothes he sorted out and slipped from the table. He was already pulling on a stained shirt, drawing over that the leather vest which strained across his shoulders as he started toward the door. When that closed behind him I threw aside the cloak, dropped the torn remnants of the two petticoats which had not survived well the rigors of our flight. The breeches were large and they smelled strongly, but I drew them on, belting them with a tie torn from my top petticoat, while the shirt covered the low-cut chemise. The wreck of the red bodice and my other discards I made into a tight package as I put on the cloak once more. I had rebraided my hair as best I could and tied the ends also with rags, tucking the lengths under the collar of the cloak.

He was back just as I had done, in his hands a wooden ladle, the wood half rotted away, but still sturdy enough to hold a measure of water. I drank feverishly, though the taste was strong of the dead wood which held it. He saw the bundle I had made of my torn clothing and nodded approvingly.

"That we must hide. I do not know if they will bring out hounds—"

His words shook me. The thought of being hunted through this cursed and desolate countryside like some despairing and frightened animal struck home. He must have read that sudden flare of terror in my face, for he smiled and held out his hand to me.

"There are tricks to that, my lady. A few I know well. Also—let us go!"

Outside the hut I found that the day had come fully

upon us. However, there was no sun. Instead the sky was darkly overcast, with clouds piling over the heights, hanging heavily over the sullen and forbidding walls of Wallenstein which was now well above us, for the hut was not too far from the cliff on which the castle had been built.

I had only a glimpse of that prison, for the Colonel urged me into a screen of brush. We reached a dead tree, which still stood, a fire-blackened trunk showing a hole within some distance up. My companion picked up a nearby branch and with the aid of this thrust the bundle of discarded rags well into the hole.

"There is a stream—this way." He came back to me and again put his arm about my shoulders, taking some of the weight from my bruised feet, though I tried as well as I could to manage by myself. We did come to the stream and I waded in as he did, guessing that the water should hide our trail should they indeed bring out hounds to hunt us down.

The dire promise of the clouds was soon fulfilled as rain began; the dead trees and new saplings bordering the narrow ribbon of the brook not furnishing any cover, so that water soaked us from above even as it arose about our feet and legs. I had been miserable in that cell, but never so lacking in comfort of body as I now was when I slipped and slid over the stony bed, my wet cloak dragging down on my body. It might have been a relief to complain aloud, but that I would not do, my pride was strong enough to keep me going in silence.

Our first bit of luck was stumbling upon what must have once been a farm, though fire and disaster had struck here. There were berry bushes laden with fruit which had somehow escaped the general fate, and I crammed their sweet yet tart goodness into my mouth with both hands. The Colonel left me sitting on a tumbled wall and went to poke about in the blackened space between the walls of what had once been a large dwelling.

He came back swinging his arm over his head in

248

triumph and I saw that what he carried was a sword, dull, with spots of rust along the blade. The axe from the hut he had hitched to his belt, but that was a poor weapon compared to his present find. It appeared to me that there was a new confidence in his step now that he held a useful tool of his own calling.

"Fortune would seem to favor us." He made passes through the air with his discovery. "Why this should remain and not be in some looter's hand—"

"So you have a sword—" I feared that that sum of dismal feelings which I had choked down all morning during our rain-buffeted journey now came to the fore. "But where do we go—and what can we do?"

He dropped down on the tumbled stones next to me. "There is this," he said slowly, "I know something of this country, not much, but enough to perhaps take us out to the north. We held maneuvers on the edge there two years ago. There is a road, hardly more than a forest track—but still a road. Beyond that lie some scattered farms. We shall be out of their country where the Von Zreibrukens rule, and so need not fear so much trying to find some aid. Hesse-Dohna is now in a state of uneasiness. The new Elector has not established a firm control. Those at court will be busy playing their games to establish themselves in his favor. I do not think that the commandant of Wallenstein will be too quick to report our escape—though he will busy himself to recapture us."

"Do you have any friends, any who will aid?" I asked bluntly.

He shrugged. "It might be better to believe that my circle of friends has shrunk to acquaintances who may no longer find it politic to acknowledge any closeness past the polite civility of the civilized—" He did not sound bitter, only mocking. "However, as that may be, it would now be wise to move on."

At least we were no longer wading through the stream. The wrappings about my feet were soaking and the rain soon made the rest of me as sodden. That he did what he could to lighten the journey for me I did
249

not question. Beyond the ruins of the farm there was indeed a road of sorts which we followed. Here the brush had grown out over its one-time boundaries, while thick grass spouted between the old ruts.

I would not let myself lag, though my legs ached, and then seemed to go slowly numb. Once or twice I stumbled, so that he put out a quick hand to support me. How far we had come from Wallenstein, even in what direction we now headed, I could not have said.

Suddenly my companion pulled me to a halt. I wavered and frankly clung to him, since my balance was now so insecure. I stared about but could see nothing to alarm. The Colonel's head was up, I saw his nostrils expand as if he drew in a deep breath. When he spoke his voice was low, hardly above a whisper:

"Do you smell it?"

Smell? It seemed to me that my senses as this day had worn on had become so deadened I was perhaps able to see, even hear but little. What was there to smell—the rain?—some heavy odor given off by the ravaged land about us? Some ancient foulness? For I could only couple evil with this deserted country.

"Wood smoke—" he explained. "Come—" His strength both supported and compelled me off the ancient track, into the bushes, where the moisture shook off the leaves to add a further burden of damp to my cloak. "Stay here!"

With no more than that order he pushed me into leafy hiding and slipped away himself with an ease which I would have thought more born of the training of a forester than that of a court-based officer. I remained where I was, my head up, sniffing hard, until I, too, caught the scent which had alerted him.

But who could or would build a fire in a rainswept wasteland? Had we near blundered on another forester's hut, this one perhaps occupied? I sighed and rubbed my grimy hands over my cloth-wrapped feet, trying to ease away some of the chill numbness which cramped my toes. It was summer, yes, but this day felt more like the beginning of autumn. I longed so for a hot drink, even a cup of the lukewarm chocolate which had been so distasteful in Axelburg, for a bed on which I could just stretch out and never have to move again.

Then I cowered closer into the enveloping brush, looked about me for a weapon, any weapon— There was a moss-encrusted stone within arm's reach. I tore that free of the mold and gripped it fiercely as I listened to a rustling in the brush which had certainly not been caused by any wind.

The figure moving toward me, of whom I could only catch glimpses now and then unless I moved, which I dared not, wore a cloak much like my own, save that that of this stranger had a hood pulled up to protect the head. As the form bobbed up and down, I could see that this other was gathering firewood, branches brought down from the dead trees.

Then I caught the sound of a voice, low and sweet— singing—? A woman's singing! So strange had any normal kind of life become to me during the past days that I was as startled as if she had screeched savagely as the Indians of my own home land might have done as they came down on some settlement in a war party's raid. Was she some farmer's wife—or daughter? Had there been some one-time settler courageous enough to return, to rebuild a destroyed home in the waste?

Prudently, I did not set aside my stone. A woman here would surely not be alone. Who knew who might come at her call should she sight me? The Colonel—in spite of all his caution he could well make some slip to betray us both.

I was now a small hunted animal, crouching so close to the thick mat of decaying leaves that my body had forced the beginning of a burrow in that slimy deposit. Still she advanced, while all I could do was will, as fiercely as a person might pray, that she turn aside to the right or left.

Instead, she straightened up to her full height, the harvest she had garnered, held against her body with her left arm, while, with her right hand, she brushed back the hood which had fallen a little too far forward. I could clearly see her face.

See her face? No, this was some trick of mind, some chance resemblance in which I dared not believe. This could not be Truda—here in the forest she had shown such a fear of earlier! Truda, whom I was more than half sure must have also been taken into captivity because she had served me!

Now it was as if she could in some manner sense that she was being watched. For she had stopped singing, had edged back a little into the bushes herself, seeking cover. I saw her look carefully about as a fugitive might when traveling with fear.

The more I looked at her I was forced to accept the evidence of my own eyes. I was not dreaming—not in any drugged state when one can see what is not. This was certainly Truda! The stone rolled out of my hand. Feeling dizzy and weak, I reached out and pulled down the branch which had been my principal screen.

At that moment she tensed, turned swiftly as if to run. I called out, my voice hoarse with urgency and need:

"Truda!"

The wood she had gathered fell out of her hold. As swiftly as she had turned, she swung back, her eyes wide, a look of near terror on her face. Now there was no screen of leaves between us, she could see me as easily as I looked upon her. For a long moment she stared as if *I* were a nightmare figure. Then she sprang toward me, her hands outstretched:

"My lady—oh, my lady!"

There was no mistress, no maid as we clung together when she had knelt beside me and her arms had gone out to gather me to her. Instead she rocked me in her hold as one might comfort a child.

"Oh, my lady—you are truly here! I cannot believe it, but it is so!"

And I could only repeat her name, "Truda! Truda!" and hold to her as if she were a rock standing in a fast-running river down which I had been swept without hope of any safety to be found.

"Truda." At last I managed to make myself think past the first wonder of our meeting. "How did you come here?"

My question appeared to alert her again, for she glanced up and around as if she feared danger.

"Please, my lady, can you walk? It is not good for us to stay—come, let me help you!" She did not answer my question. Instead, as had the Colonel, she took command, and at that moment I was content to follow her urgency.

Somehow I got to my numb feet, tottered forward with her support, in and out among the bushes. We moved between two tall rocks which stood like the pillars marking some manor entrance, and so came into a dell in which there was a tumble of stones, standing walls, but little roof, and graceful pointed windows without any glass.

Through one of the windows trailed a wisp of smoke, while coming swiftly from the doorless opening before me was the Colonel. He strode to us and without a word swept me up in his arms, carrying me on, with Truda hurrying beside him into that place of shelter.

That determination which had kept me going since we had left the evil temple in the cliff cave drained from me as blood pumped from some deep wound. I, who had never been given to the swounds supposed so much a female answer to fatigue or fear, saw walls waver and seem to nod in toward me as I slipped down into darkness in which there was no longer need to struggle.

I awoke reluctantly, because someone was holding up my head, pressing something to my lips. There was a wonderful smell, I heard a murmur of voice which meant nothing. But I drank eagerly, without even opening my eyes, what was so offered me. It was a thick soup with such a flavor I could not believe remained in the world. As that heated liquid trickled down my throat it seemed to bring strength with it.

Now I looked up. Truda knelt by me, holding the cup to my mouth. But I was supported by someone else. And there was a third person moving beyond, but could not make out who that might be.

"Drink, my lady, it is good. Kristopher snared a hare only this morning. And there is barley in it also to give full strength. Here, taste—" She dipped a spoon into the cup and came up with a piece of meat, which she ladled into my mouth. I found myself chewing as eagerly as I had drunk the broth.

My wits came back. I had not been dreaming—this was indeed Truda and—I managed to turn my head a little so I could look up and see it was the Colonel who held me. There was still rain falling, but not where we were—for a projection of broken roof kept us dry, allowed a small fire to burn. Now I could see that other who had stooped to feed more wood to the fire, a young man with a good face, I thought. Kristopher—yes, had heard that name before—some place—some time.

I ate and slept again, then awoke to no more rain but sun slanting warm across me, so warmly that moved to push aside the cloak which served as a covering. At my movement Truda appeared, to kneel beside me.

"My lady." She touched my forehead as one seeking signs of fever might check.

"I am very well, Truda." For indeed I was. At that moment I felt as if some great burden had fallen from my shoulders, and the lightness left in me wanted to bubble up and up. I could have sung—have shouted as does a child in some exuberance of pleasure. I moved to sit up and she was quick to support me. Only I no longer needed that.

"Truda—what happened? Where is this place? And how did you come here?" All that had been in the immediate past flooded back, but memory no longer wore with it a weight or fear and endurance.

"Let me get you food, my lady, and while you eat—then I shall talk."

She settled me with my back against a stone wall and I looked around our refuge with a need to know how we were housed. The roof extended over about a third of the building, which was not large. A little away there was a raised portion like a small dais on which stood a massive block of stone. On the wall behind that was a cross deep carven in the surface. I guessed then that we sheltered in some chapel that had once served the people before the land had become a waste. It was a very simple place, with no other carving besides the cross itself. But the tracing of the windows was well shaped and graceful, if plain.

To one side two packs were placed, one beside the other, and there was also a pile of firewood where Truda was busy tending a small pot standing on a tripod above the flames of the fire. She filled the cup I had seen before and brought it to me with the spoon.

Again it was a soup-stew of some sort which I ate eagerly and, I fear, with greediness. For the moment the food more important than all else. Then I remembered and stopped to ask:

"The Colonel—Kristopher?"

"They go to hunt out a way for us." There was a frown between her eyes. "We cannot stay here. They are hunting—those others."

I resented the return of anxiety, but I knew I could not escape it.

"But you, Truda, you and Kristopher—how did you get here?"

She told me in short, bald sentences, making little of what must have been a time of terror and despair not unlike my own. The night after Konrad's visit she had found herself locked in her room. All her demands to be allowed to go to me had been refused. Then she had been told I was leaving with my "husband," was allowed to witness the passage of a carriage which she was told contained the Baron and his bride. After that

255

she was ordered to prepare to return to Axelburg. But her good sense warned her that if she left Kesterhof it would not be for the capital but rather to her own death.

Before, however, such a journey could be arranged there had come other arrivals to the lodge—soldiers with orders to confine the Gräfin and her household. Among those soldiers had been Kristopher. He was already secretly alarmed at the disappearance of the Colonel, by the many rumors within the city, and had determined not to take part in any wrong which might be intended.

"For he is a good man," Truda told me. "He heard many things which made him fearful—for the Colonel, for me—even for himself. Those sent so secretly could later be charged with the very evil they had been ordered to do. Then, when he saw the second carriage and you put in it—"

"Second carriage?" I was so excited by her story I forgot to eat.

"Yes—the first one—it had been just meant to deceive. The Baron was in it, yes—for I saw him. But the other carriage came the same night that Kristopher was on guard. It was not driven by anyone of the Gräfin's people, rather by a man Kristopher knew of—one who is known well to be the Princess's man—the Princess Adelaide. The Gräfin was shut in her room then, and you they brought out. Kristopher told me first he thought you were dead, but then he saw you move. There was a woman, a woman dressed like a sister, who gave the orders. They took you away so.

"Kristopher, he heard—that they took you to that place of evil—Wallenstein. He knew that you were of the Blood, our Elector's own blood, and there was danger for all of us. So that night also—or rather in the early morning—we two got away. Kristopher had to fight with one of the foresters—if they find him—" She clasped her hands so tightly together the knuckles stood sharply out— "He is now counted a deserter, my lady. They shall hang him if he is taken. But he has
256

listened so much that he was sure that the Colonel was also in that evil place. So we waited—hoping we could find some way— We crept about in the wood— And I prayed, my lady, I prayed very hard. As you see—the Good God heard. If in so much He has helped us—then there will be more. HE will not forget us—"

I set aside cup and spoon and put my hands over hers. "HE will not, Truda, surely HE will not!"

Chapter 19

It was dusk outside and we had put out the fire. There was still light enough so that one could look from face to face and try to read the expressions thereon as we four held a council of war in the ruined church. That we could continue here in hiding was a risk we all knew we dared no longer take. The subject of where we could go, and how, was now a matter of discussion, for the Colonel was not giving orders, he was listening to suggestions, first advanced awkwardly by Kristopher, who gradually became more assured and self-confident when he realized that his opinions did carry weight with the man he had considered to be so far above him that nothing he might think or say would matter.

We needed transportation of some sort, and also disguises which would carry us out of this part of the country.

"There is a market at Gratz. It is also a horse fair—though it is far less than it once was," he said slowly, as if he were thinking aloud, or at least putting one idea to another, as a quilt might be patched piece upon piece. "Farmers go there to pick up work animals. There may be a small garrison there, yes. Perhaps it is also true that now they would police the fair itself. So this would be a risk—"

The Colonel rubbed one hand across his unshaven jaw. Already he had the stubby outgrowth of a beard so dark that it gave his harsh features an almost sinister cast. Eyeing him objectively, I thought that I would rate him one I would not now care to meet on a lonely road were I alone.

We had all been reclothed after a fashion from the bundles Kristopher and Truda had smuggled out from Kesterhof on their flight. She and I both wore the full skirts, small shoulder shawls, and the aprons of country women, all of the garments soiled and a little ragged from our encounters with the thorn brush between the ruined chapel and the spring. There were thick-soled shoes over my bandaged feet, while Truda went bare in spite of my urging—saying that she was used to that in summer, showing me that indeed her feet were hard and calloused.

The Colonel's breeches had suffered so much wear that they could be taken for a soldier's castoffs, plenty of which were sold second and third hand in the rag fairs. His boots, having such hard usage, also could pass as finds from such markets. The shirt and jerkin he wore were like Kristopher's, and his hair was an unruly thatch which might never have known a comb. Looking from one to the other of my companions, I believed that, unless someone knew us well and was deliberately seeking us, we could indeed drift into a village fair.

However, I had a question of my own now:

"We have gold. Would there not be a question as to where we got it if we tried to buy openly?"

Kristopher and the Colonel both frowned as if they immediately saw the sense in that. But Truda leaned a little forward.

"Loot—" she said in a soft voice. "Loot, buried, found— This has happened before. Or even a lost traveler who ventured into the wrong house—held—"

The Colonel gave a short bark of laughter. "Truda, my girl, what kind of company have you kept?"

"I have but listened—when I was serving in the inn. There was that affair of Hirsh, Kristopher—"

He gave a vigorous nod. "Yes, that was well known. Hansel Hirsh, sir. He was near a beggar, lived in a hut one would not put even a chicken to shelter in. Then, all at once, he had money in his pocket and there was the story of his skulking about where the French and the Russians had had a skirmish and both of their troops were badly mauled so they did very little looting after—that was done by someone else. Oh, I know that it has been a long time since the war now. But there was much fighting—and suppose an officer had been lost and died—and his body found? Or loot gathered and hidden never later picked up?"

"My gold is English—and American—" I realized the trouble that might cause.

"Gold is gold," the Colonel returned. "Coins might well have been through a fire—turned to lumps. Yes." Again his fingers rasped in his beard. "That idea is one which might well give us a good story. Frankly, I can see no better way now." He looked at me critically. "That fair hair of yours, my lady—could it be darkened?"

Truda nodded vigorously. "Mine also, and for Kristopher. There are things in the woods I can boil—bark. Also we can darken our skins—seem like the wandering folk, though we do not want to look too much like them, for the soldiers are always suspicious of them. Only—there are also those who have lost their land because of taxes, or—" She shrugged and threw up her hands. "We can surely make up some good tale among us!"

The girl who had so worn the cloak of servility in the houses of the Baroness was a different person. I warmed to her quick mind, as well as to her kindness and loyalty.

"Good enough. We shall journey to Gratz then." The Colonel turned to me. "Give me some of the smaller coins. We shall see what can be done to make them lose their identity."

With a firm plan now in mind we went to work eagerly, not letting even the dark deter us. Hammered vigorously between the stones, the coins were so defaced they could indeed pass as loot which had been badly used during its progress through thieving hands. Truda, while there was still enough light left for gleaning, went out and returned shortly thereafter with a huge double handful of bark, which she cut with a knife into thin shreds. Lighting once more the fire, she put these on to boil, stirring and tending the resulting mess until she had a thickish liquid which was like dark soap, before she set the pot aside for its contents to cool.

In the morning we set about our personal transformations, Truda and I washing each other's hair with a liberal use of the dye from the pot, leaving a portion for Kristopher. I had no mirror to survey the results but judging by Truda, I must now present a far different appearance. What I could see of my own hair as I toweled and dried it in a wind which had spring up in the morning was now a very deep brown, nearly black. Once we had so changed our appearances Truda stood off and looked at me critically.

"We must be sisters, my lady," she told me. "Kristopher can be our brother. You, sir," she spoke now to the Colonel—

"I am her man, of course." His hand fell upon my shoulder. I had an odd feeling for a moment or so that it did belong there, that I found the warmth of his touch as it spread through the thin stuff of my worn blouse comforting and strengthening. "But remember, both of you"—his voice once more held the crack of an order—"no more 'sirs' or 'my ladys.' She is Amelia, and I—my name is too foreign—I shall be Franz—Franz Kilber. No, you had better be Lotta, it is more in keeping," he ended, speaking to me. I agreed with a nod.

We set off on the second day after we had made our plans. The Colonel and Kristopher having, on the afternoon before, made one last swing out of our refuge and a short sortie in the direction of Wallenstein to make sure that no hunt was up. The Colonel admitted that he was puzzled at that continued lack of determined pursuit. His only guess was that for his own safety, the commandant of the fortress was still attempting to keep our escapes a secret.

"Undoubtedly," he commented as we went, he slouching along at a gait quite unlike his usual stride, I, matching step and balancing a bundle on my hip after the fashion Truda had shown, "there is still some intrigue in progress."

I looked down at my left hand. There was a band of angry-looking red flesh about the finger where I had insisted that my companion cut off that ring. I had wanted to hurl it as far from me as I could, but Truda had prudently insisted that it be added to our supply of "loot," pointing out that its mutilated condition and the fact it was an undoubtedly old piece, would add to the story. The iron butterfly necklace I had rolled in a strip of cloth and stowed between my breasts in the safest carrying place I knew. But the swollen flesh of my finger still marked what had bound me.

Was I in truth married? I could not see how that would be so. I had no memory of the ceremony past those few scattered bits. Certainly I had never knowingly responded to any of the traditional words. Yet I was sure that as long as it might be possible that my grandfather's legacy could come into my hands I would not be safe, or free, of the trickery from which I had suffered.

The Colonel's eyes and thoughts must have followed my own, for once more he moved closer to me, and now his arm came about my waist as if he would give me help over rough ground. Truda and Kristopher had moved some paces ahead and perhaps could not hear him as his voice dropped to whisper level.

"Be sure, you will not have to deal with *him* again! Not alone!"

"He wants the treasure. That miserable treasure— I want none of it and never did!" I said fiercely, keeping my voice as low as his. "I do not know the law here, he may claim me as a wife if he finds me, and the law will give him full power over me. He said my grandfather wished our marriage."

The oath my companion spit out did not distress me. Had I known any as potent, I would have been moved to use them myself.

"He lied, of course. There were—" He stopped short. "Your grandfather did strive to make certain provisions for your safety—unfortunately his power did not extend beyond his deathbed. Yes, it is the treasure which they hope to use as a trap."

I laughed without any pleasure. "But it is no trap for me. For I have no wish for it. I have my own treasure—where it belongs—my home—" At that moment I was so struck with a wave of true sickness for the manor, for all the ordered life I had known, that, that I could have broken into the wails of a heartbroken child, had I not held firmly to my control. Yet he must also have known what I longed for, for he said softly, with all the sternness of seconds before gone from his voice:

"It is very beautiful, your home—"

"But you do not know it!"

"I saw it—and you in it. You were right, are right— it is your place. This"—he gestured with his free hand—"is not—could never be."

For the first time I asked him a directly personal question:

"Where is *your* home?"

262

He shrugged. "A soldier's home? Everywhere and nowhere. He flits as a migrating bird where duty sends him. The Fenwicks were rooted once, war tore us up, we became wanderers. I do not own any rooftree, nor even a patch of land as large as this." Once more he held forth his hand. "The Elector offered my father a title, lands. They had been battle comrades once, before the Elector returned to Hesse-Dohna. But—it was not home—the home my father had known as a boy. He wanted no courtier's holdings, though he was shrewd enough to see that a portion of the generous gifts the Elector awarded him were sent to be banked in England. Just as he had me schooled there. So I will not be penniless when I cross the border. In fact—I might even someday fulfill my father's dream."

"That was?"

"To return to the country which thrust us forth. Old hates must have died by now. I think he often planned that he might repurchase—perhaps not Queen's Gift— but some smaller manor on the Eastern Shore. He spoke of it when he was dying—"

"Queen's Gift!" I stared up at him. "But I have seen that! It is the Artley place."

"They were cousins—who chose to desert their king. No, perhaps it is not right that *I* should now speak of the old troubles. There is no king on your side of the ocean, and I am sure the land is more peaceful for it. I have seen too much of courts and rulers— But it remains, yours is a fair land, and, I think, one in which a man can be happy."

I found myself pouring out eagerly then, as I would have never thought I could have done to anyone since my grandmother died, all my memories, my hopes, my love of the manor and the land of my birth. He listened intently, so that I felt that in some way my own feelings reached within him and found there, in a measure, their match. It was an hour which soothed and rested me, pushed aside all the darkness of the immediate past, and brought hope and trust to full flower in me.

It took us two days of tramping through settled land

beyond the borders of the waste to reach Gratz. We slept in two small inns, crowded together in rooms with other fairgoers. On the first night Kristopher, by clever questioning, got the name of a dubious trader who dealt in things bought undercover. With the Colonel he visited this man, making a bargain for a portion of our "loot." They were, the Colonel told me, cheated of full value, but the coins they got in return were such as could be shown openly. Part of that which they so got rid of was the ring, for which I was very glad.

Gratz itself was so crowded that we could not find lodging within any inn, but Kristopher fell in with a horse trader who had a wagon which carried a wife and two imps of children. This man was willing to let us stay at his fire on the outskirts of the town and share from the pots his wife tended when we supplied bread, cheese, and a chicken to help fill the major pot.

Gratz had something beside horses to offer. There was no need here for us to seek out some cheating thieves' confidant to change our gold. There was a small colony of Jews who had been herded here during the wars, settled, and were tolerated. One of them was a merchant of some standing. The Colonel went to see him and came back, nearly unmindful that he must play the shuffling, near-vagabond he was so encouraged.

He had discovered the man to be both prudent and honest, having connections with another such merchant that Fenwick himself had known. Horses could be bought through him, and a wagon. Also there was news.

The new Elector, making a leisurely and triumphant progress, had reached Axelburg, which was now in a frenzy of preparation for a week or more of formal welcome, as well as the state funeral of my grandfather. All the nobility were converging on the capital to see and be seen, especially at court where quick attendance on their new ruler could well, if fortune was kind, bring them into favor. There were representatives also comng from neighboring states and a constant stream of he travelers across the borders.

During this, to slip away, by some smugglers' route, would be far less difficult. We were exultant that night as we gathered together when the horse dealer had gone to drink in some tavern and his wife had bedded down both the children and herself.

"But you, Truda, you and Kristopher, what of your future?" I suddenly remembered that these two might have now as much, or more, to fear inside Hesse-Dohna.

I saw them look to each other. It was Kristopher who answered. He held Truda's hand in his very firmly, but when he spoke there was a difference in his voice and he used the term of respect he had been warned against.

"My lady—we cannot stay here either. If—if you could see fit to take us into your household—we would be very happy there."

"But I live overseas. To go with me would mean leaving your homes, your country, perhaps never seeing your families again!"

"Lady, it is better so. We will be hunted, when there is time and men to do the hunting. Our families must not know where we are. They, too, can suffer if it is suspected that they do. There is no home here for us. We can work—we wish to work—to be together."

I held out my hands, one to each. "You do not come to serve me—but as my friends. There is land for the taking in my country—to the west. If this is your wish—then let it be so."

To my vast discomfort, they took my hands, not to clasp them in a bargain, but to kiss them. I drew my fingers away quickly.

"We are friends," I repeated meaningfully. "As friends only do we go."

We left Gratz far more encouraged and with our confidence at a high level. The cart was small, our two horses (we dared not arouse suspicion by buying more) old and their chosen pace hardly more than an amble.

To which the men allowed them to keep while we were on the main, traveled roads. We did not stay at inns now but slept with our cart as a shelter. Since it was summer, we did not fare badly. Having discussed the route together, the Colonel and Kristopher thought it best to strike across Hanover to Hamburg. Since Hanover was linked to the English crown, the Colonel had those living there with whom he had certain ties, and once we reached the seaport—why, then I, too, had resources through my grandmother's dealings. I could recite easily from memory the names of four highly placed merchants who should have influence to gain us passage on either an American or an English vessel.

We avoided towns, took such wayside tracks as led in the direction we must follow. They were not easy days with all thought given to a traveler's comfort, but they were good. We shared these hours with a happier spirit than I had known since I crossed the sea. If there was any hunt up, we had no knowledge of it. However we did not relax our vigilance for all of that.

Our way took us within a few miles of Truda's inn. I noticed that she was silent most of that day when we made our way along lanes at that pace we could no hurry, though our eagerness to be across the border grew ever stronger. That she should have a chance to see her family was a thought which grew ever strongly in me, perhaps because I had no longer any family to be concerned with me. But when I suggested it twice during the afternoon, she shook her head with determination which was stubborn in its intensity.

"They must have heard that Kristopher has deserted, that I am gone. The inn would be the first place that any seeking us would come to search."

"But perhaps they would never believe that you would be so foolish as to go there—"

She shook her head. "That is just what they would think, my lady. They believe that I am a witless peasant girl, one without any mind to think for myself—that if I was in trouble, I would go running to my family for aid. No, it must not be. When we are safe, then
266

shall write to them, very carefully—for the mails will be watched. But there are words I can use which will let them know from whom such a letter comes. Then they will not grieve for me as dead—or rotting in such a place as Wallenstein." Her eyes were hot and her mouth was a line of strength. "They will know, even if they cannot wish me well—but so they will—in their hearts. Also they will let Kristopher's family know— Only we must be safe first."

So I never got to see the inn which Truda had described with such honest pride. Instead we drew into a small ragged field which had been partially abandoned to growing scrub, in the corner of which was a nearly demolished shed. Into the shed the men pushed and worked the cart, concealing it with the stinking, moldy hay which was heaped there.

At night we started on the last lap of our journey out of Hesse-Dohna. I found myself uneasy, listening to every sound out of the growing dusk. It was as if some shadow now hung over us, darkening the night even more, as a storm cloud could move quickly to blot out friendly and encouraging stars. Our days of travel— had they been far too easy, bringing us now to a trap? I could not think of why I should have these irrational fears growing now—

Kristopher took the lead. He showed a certain confidence which suggested that he knew more of the smuggler trails than he had earlier admitted, though, once we had entered a small wood, he slowed pace and would stop now and then, a shadow among other shadows, looking about him, as if for some landmark.

We went on foot, leading the two horses on which we loaded the gear we had collected little by little, blankets, cooking pans, changes of coarse clothing. In the night we donned dark cloaks, in spite of the warmth, which hooded us well against being sighted, though the forest way was certainly not a highway and could not believe that there was anyone within miles.

There was one bad place ahead against which Kristopher had already warned us. The boundary here was a stream which must be forded, and that ford was not only known to most of the countryside but was also in the wide open. There was a full moon tonight, though here beneath the trees its beams did not catch us. Thus the fording place would be very visible.

Were we indeed the smugglers we patterned ourselves on, we need not have been so cautious, for those had their own spies and lookouts, their warnings. The ford was also known to the border patrol, but I had gathered from what I had overheard of the conversation between Kristopher and the Colonel that there were also profitable arrangements to be made between the soldiers and those using this way secretly. The trouble remained that, for us, it might not be so—and if the patrol was out, we had no such understanding that we were to be considered invisible.

We came at last into a fringe of trees in which we stood for a long moment or two looking at the water silvered by the moon, the land beyond. Pursuit could even follow us here over such a border, since no one would know nor listen to our protests that we had been captured when legally out of Hesse-Dohna.

The land ahead was very peaceful. I heard the cry of a night bird, the constant murmur of the running water. The Colonel made a swift gesture and Kristopher melted away to the right. I guessed he had been sent to reconnoiter. Truda was very close to me, now her hand found mine, and her fingers closed tightly about my own. I could even hear her hurried breathing. Did she also share the burden of apprehension which had been growing ever stronger for me during the last steps of our journey here? I believed at that moment she did.

This was too easy! Somehow I knew that. There was something ahead wrong and foreboding. Yet all lay before us peaceful and untroubled. I heard a slight rustle and was startled into a movement. But it was only Kristopher appearing once more out of nowhere.

"It is clear." His whisper reached us.

Still the Colonel lingered. I could see the white blur

of his face, well bearded now. He was still surveying the way ahead. Finally he nodded and moved out. I saw that he not only wore that sword he had found in the ruined house bare bladed in his belt, its hilt ready to his hand, but he had also the knife we had brought out of Wallenstein.

He stepped aside to bring up the rear, Kristopher leading, we women with the horse ropes in our hands between. Now we did hurry, our steps becoming a trot, while the horses snorted and complained as we jerked impatiently at their leads. I felt very much exposed, very helpless during those moments.

Kristopher waded straightway into the water. Without stopping to kilt up our full skirts or shed our foot gear, we splashed after him. There was firm enough footing, in spite of the pull of the current. It felt as if someone had laid pavement there under the surface— a water-hidden road. The water washed as high as our knees, and our soaked clothing was a weight we had to fight, but we came out on the other side, unchallenged, though I had half expected to be with every step I took. My fear appeared to be shared by all the company, for we did not stop to wring the water from us, or empty our thick shoes and boots of the load they now carried. Instead we quickened pace even more, the horses now lumbering along.

There was an inn not too far ahead which Kristopher knew of—one where they did not ask questions of travelers out of the night, if such could pay their way. This was to be our goal. There was even a rough track which led from the ford in the direction of this dubious shelter. That we followed now as trees met once more over our heads.

Then there was the wink of a lantern through the night. Kristopher spoke in a low voice:

"That is the Groshawk—"

The inn! I was so thankful to see that spark of glass-protected flame that I could have cried aloud. We had made it! Perhaps we would never be free of some part of apprehension until we were safe on board the ship

I had held ever in my mind as the goal to keep me going. However, we were now in Hanover and so out of the immediate reach of those who wanted us.

In the dark the inn was a mere black bulk of a building, crouching close to the ground. That lantern which might have been a signal of sorts to attract its less legal trade, the only light we could see. All was very quiet and again the Colonel waved us to a halt. For the first time Kristopher questioned his authority.

"It is always so, sir. They appear closed. In fact those who use the road we have come do not even enter the main building. We shelter in the stable to the left. There is a man there—to be sure that he gets an accounting—but for the rest, they do not see, so they can never speak."

Still the very darkness of the place brought back once more my own fears. What Kristopher said made sense. However, his argument did not lessen my uneasiness. Neither did I think that the Colonel was too pleased. Finally he shook his head—

"I do not like it. There is something here— I say we go on."

"Where?" Kristopher demanded. I think that he felt the Colonel's choice a reflection on his judgment.

"What do you know of the neighborhood?" The Colonel countered with another question. "Who is the nearest landowner?"

"The Gräf von Mannichen, sir. He has come many times to my father's place when the hunts are on. For the hunts there is no border." It was Truda who answered.

"Von Mannichen!" He was plainly surprised. "Then that is it! Our answer! We need only reach him— How far to his manor?" He asked with a new eagerness.

"Perhaps a half league, sir. But the Gräf—"

"I know him—I have hunted with him—he was a good friend to my father! We can get all the help we need from him!"

"Up." The Colonel turned and pulled at the pack on the back of the horse I had been leading. "Drop all this.
270

You mount, also, Kristopher, take Truda up with you. I shall take my lady. We have but to ride your half league and sleep thereafter in good beds—this again is good fortune!"

Only he spoke too soon. For, even as we had thrown aside all our gear and were mounted, the inn behind us suddenly showed life. There was a glaze of light as a large door was flung open, and men came pounding out.

"Ride!" I heard the shouted order of the Colonel and felt the horse under us respond sluggishly to his urging. My hands were tight on his belt as we headed on into the night, hearing sounds which could only be that of a chase beginning behind us.

Chapter 20

"Turn off at the woods track!" I heard the Colonel's second order even over the shouting from behind us and the heavy thud of the horses' hooves on the track we followed. Why those from the inn had not already mounted and been after us, catching up with ease, I could not understand. It was as if some carefully set ambush had been spoiled, and those lying in wait did not think clearly nor quickly beyond their now-ruined plan.

We were in woods again, a thick growth, and the

track we followed took a looping turn to avoid an out-cropping of rocks. Sounds of pursuit came at last and I heard the crack of a shot, though what that had been aimed at, since we were now out of sight of those behind, I did not know. Yet my heart jumped and I felt sick. They were armed, doubtless well armed, and we had no defense against bullets, nor could we hope to outride them, mounted as we were on these clumsy farm horses.

"There!" The Colonel's cry came loudly. He swung our mount to the right and Kristopher followed. We were in a much more narrow way now, one flanked at its start on either side by pillars of stone surmounted by carven figures of birds, their wings half-mantled, as if they were about to take off into the sky—which I could see when the moon pierced this small clearing.

We could not ride abreast here. The Colonel waved Kristopher ahead. "Watch," he commanded, "for the forester's cottage—we can make that—if we have any luck at all!" There was such confidence in his voice that it almost won me to believe that there was indeed hope lying somewhere ahead of us now.

I do not know whether our abrupt turnoff into what was plainly a private road confused our pursuers any. The way we now followed was a wandering one, with many loops and turns, brush and trees thick on either side. I thought that cloaked, in the dark (for the moon did not touch much here), and weaving in and out of the shadows as we now did, we could not present good targets, though I had no idea how skillful with weapons our followers might be.

"Ahead—sir!"

We did not need Kristopher's call to alert us. Again there was the gleam of a lantern, this time at a doorway which was half open, light shining out enough to show a man's outline. He put the lantern down on the ground, and had a shotgun swung up and ready as Kristopher's near-floundering mount charged close at a failing pace, our own only moments behind.

"Stand where you are!" The order was as assured as

any my companion could have given. The Colonel spun part way around, loosed my hold on his belt and dropped me to the ground, following me by slipping from his own seat a moment later.

"Get to the house!" It was me he spoke to first, giving me such a push between my shoulders that I fell to my knees. "Kasper!" Now he hailed the man in the doorway. "It is Colonel Fenwick— Remember the broken-tusked boar?"

That must have been a password of some importance, for the weapon no longer covered him as he stooped to pull me again to my feet.

"What chances, sir?"

"I do not know, except we are hunted men."

"On the Gräf's own land!" It was plain the forester was outraged. "We shall see to this!"

I was so shaken by my fall that the Colonel had to half carry me to the house. Within I was dazzled by the light after our long time in the night's dark, so that it was a moment or two before I could look around. Truda had joined me on a bench, gasping for breath, and catching instantly at my hand as she dropped down beside me.

There was a younger man by the fireplace, another shotgun in his hands. He was not much more than a boy and he was gazing at the door with startled expression. The door slammed shut and the Colonel, Kristopher, and the forester were together by it, the latter bearing his weapon across his arm.

"The Gräf?" the forester said as he turned and with one hand dropped a stout bar across the door. "He is in London, sir. He has gone from here on with the embassy to the King—"

I remembered then that Hanover was still part of the British Crown, as long as King William should reign. No wonder the Colonel had had ties with this Gräf—

I saw the Colonel frown, glance now at the barred door. But the forester had apparently already perceived our dilemma, for he swung around toward the boy to bark out an order:

"Out with you at the back, Jakob, arouse our men and light the beacon. We shall have no trespassing on my lord's land!"

"Leave that." The Colonel strode across the room and caught the shotgun from the boy. "We may have use for it here—"

The man Kasper was close to middle age, a sprinkling of gray in his dark hair. He had an open face, but now a scowl made him look near as stern as the Colonel.

"Sir!" He was indignant and angry. "They would not dare to do violence here, not in the Gräf's own hunting preserve."

"If they are from across the border, Kasper—they will dare," the Colonel assured him. "They might hope to take us and be away before any help could be summoned. Once we were in their hands, what good would protests from your lord matter? They could weave a hundred tales, even punish a few underlings, but it would not free us."

Slowly Kasper nodded. "There is perhaps truth in that, sir. How many do we now face then? You, Jakob—" He looked around at the boy who had lingered, his attention for the gun the Colonel had wrested from him, as if he were about to snatch it back.

"I go, Herr Kapplemann!" Go he did, into the darker part of the room where he opened a door and then closed it firmly behind him. His master crossed to drop a bar in place there also. He had not yet taken his hand from that when there came a cry:

"Ho, there—the house!"

Kapplemann looked questioningly at the Colonel. "Jakob is good in the woods at night, but he cannot bring in the men for a time. What shall we do?"

"Talk," retorted the Colonel. "Ask who they are, why they come, use such anger as you wish concerning their trespassing, keep them talking—"

The forester wore a dubious expression. "I am no

much with words, sir. But what I can do"—he shrugged—"that I shall."

He opened one of the shutters a fraction, choosing one which would give no view of the part of the room in which we had taken refuge.

"Who are you? These are the lands of the Gräf. No one rides here!"

"In the Elector's name—" began that other.

"Elector?" Kasper interrupted him harshly. "We have no Elector here—this is Hanover and we have a king. What do you want? It is unlawful to ride thus onto my lord's land."

"We want those criminals who came and you now shelter—"

Suddenly I knew that voice. Fear and anger combined brought me off the bench. I shook free from Truda's hold and went to the Colonel. He looked at me sharply and I mouthed in pantomime rather than spoke the words aloud: "Baron Konrad." For that was a voice I would never forget, it was seared deep into my memory.

He gave a swift nod. Then approached that quarter-open window-slit from the other side.

"Von Werthern!" He raised his voice. "You hear *me*, Von Werthern! You do not deal with helpless women now!"

There was silence from without, a silence which held so for several breaths. Then:

"So it is you, Fenwick—you thought to steal my wife? She is there with you—" Then he made a suggestion so obscene that I felt the heat of shame—no, of righteous anger—rise along the whole of my body. The words were utterly vile, meant to be so, I realized in a moment, for the very purpose of bringing some reckless response from the Colonel which he could turn to his purpose.

"Yes, my lady wife—do you hear that, forester? Your master can raise no objection if I regain my own wife from this seducer of flighty whores—"

275

"Von Werthern—" The Colonel was still keeping away from the window crack. I knew that he suspected he might well be shot if he was seen by some one of the men who had followed Konrad here.

"I am here—nor will I go, Fenwick. In your insolence you have far overreached yourself this time. There is no Elector to give you protection. I will have my wife And you—you are an escaped prisoner, to be dealt with like all worthless dogs who dare growl at their betters—"

Baiting—he was baiting, yes. But I was sure he did not understand the temper of the man whom he tried so to force into some action which would give him the advantage.

"How many do you judge, Kasper?" The Baron might have been a spiteful breeze trying to reach us, for all that the Colonel paid attention to him now. I noted that the forester stood with his head slightly to one side, a very intent expression on his face.

"It is difficult, sir. They have spread out a little. think they plan to rush us from all sides if they can But they are not foresters." He smiled coldly. "They thrash about in the brush like untrained hounds broke from the master's leash."

Kristopher approached the other two. "What guns have you?" he asked directly of the forester.

"Mine—Jakob's." He nodded to that in the Colonel's hand. "A fowling piece in the cupboard yonder."

Kristopher turned abruptly and went to the cupboard the man had indicated. A moment later he held a third weapon, turning it about in his hands. "They will not take me," he said between set teeth and I knew what fate haunted him—the death of a deserter.

"They will not take any of us," Fenwick replied calmly.

There was something hostile in the glance Kristopher gave him then.

"How can you be so sure of that?" I noted he added no "sir" to that question this time. The Colonel's pres tige seemed to have suffered a defeat as far as this follower was concerned.

Fenwick made no answer, he did not even look around. Instead he spoke outward into the night as matter-of-factly as if he were entirely in command of the situation.

"Von Werthern, remember Askarburg?"

There was frozen silence. The question might have been one of those momentous ones in some old tale which hold all listeners spellbound. Then came the answer in a voice as cold and clear as Fenwick's, but lacking that edge of contempt I surely had not just fancied a part of Fenwick's tone.

"I remember."

"I heard that since then, you have taken a lesson or two—" The Colonel might have been exchanging some comments upon the darkness of this night. "Do you fancy that such have improved your style?"

Again that long moment of silence. Then, out of the dark, there came a reply, and I could not mistake the heat of rage in it.

"You had but luck—!"

"Was that so, Von Werthern? Luck? Was that what you claimed afterward? Oh, yes, I remember—the sun struck across your eyes at the crucial moment, was that not it?"

"I marked you!"

"You did—and then groveled on the ground for your steel, that sword you did not have the strength to hold. However, you have taken lessons since. From my old master. I understand you spent some time seeking him out to learn all my weaknesses, to perfect your own counter to them. You want me, don't you, Von Werthern? Even though you want your wife, you want me more—*Me*. Not to turn over to your jackals and be dragged back to prison—but to bring down yourself— is that not the truth of it?"

For the third time silence, complete. I saw Kasper

make a gesture with a hand. His lips shaped a whisper which even I, as close as I was, could only half catch.

"They have moved around now, sir. Best for this man of yours to take his place at the back. The windows are shuttered. Let him bar the door. It has the old squint slit above."

Kristopher must have heard also, he waited for no word from the Colonel but whirled and made for the back. Fenwick paid no attention to that withdrawal. Instead he stood very close to the window, his whole stance that of one waiting something which he willed to happen with every fiber of his taut body.

I moistened my lips. From what I heard I thought that I guessed his purpose. He was trying to get Konrad von Werthern to meet him in a duel. But what weapon did he have? Only that rust-spotted sword he had found in the ruins—nothing which would be a real defense. Such action was the greatest folly—or was he merely working so upon the other's pride to win us time?

He made another gesture, this time toward his right—to where a fireplace, now empty for this season, covered a good third of the wall. Above it the light picked out what hung there—a pair of scabbarded crossed swords—no, sabers! Kasper edged away from the window crack, the Colonel, slipping closer to take his place, set down his shotgun and quickly freed both the blades from the coverings which remained fast to the wall.

"Well, Von Werthern—do you wish to see the result of your instruction?" the Colonel called out as the forester rejoined him, the blades in one hand.

Was he utterly without any caution? I sucked in a breath and moved swiftly to catch at the Colonel's arm.

"You can't do it! He will let them fire upon you, or do it himself the minute you show yourself!" I made no effort to keep my voice down, as had the others, and it carried. For, out of the dark came Konrad's answer, even as the Colonel freed himself from me with a quick twist of arm.

"Better listen to your whore, Fenwick. She has little confidence in you—"

It was not the name he gave me which aroused the flash of rage in me, I expected no less from him. I raised my voice again, cutting across the spiteful derision in his call:

"No confidence in *your* honor, rather. You have none worth the naming—"

Perhaps it was that retort which accomplished just the opposite of what I had intended. I could see through the slit of the window now, as clearly as the men I stood beside: Into the circle of the lantern light did come Konrad von Werthern. He had already thrown aside his hat, if he had worn one, and the light flickered over a tight tunic of green, a uniform jacket I did not remember having seen him wear before.

"I am waiting, Fenwick." He brought up a bare saber, executing a flamboyant salute, his eyes narrowed as he watched the door of our refuge. That he would honor the rules for any such meeting was impossible, I believed. Again I tried to catch the Colonel's arm, but he moved quickly out of my reach, looked to the forester, who nodded slightly.

"Yes, sir," the latter said in a low voice. "I hear them—the owls gather."

I had been so intent upon the exchange between the Colonel and our enemy that I had not been aware of something else. Now, in a small moment of silence, I did hear a mournful cry and then a second, sounding through the night.

"They will take him—as they have the others," Kasper spoke with no small satisfaction. "Jakob must have met the night patrol at the spring meadow. We have been plagued with poachers recently—"

"No!" The Colonel shook his head. "This is between the two of us. Handle his men as you wish, he is my meat." He had taken the sabers, swung each in turn, selected one. Now he gestured and Kasper withdrew the bar of the door.

The forester took up a second lantern and, holding his shotgun in the crook of one arm, carried the light with the other hand as he went out to plant the lantern on the top of a cart so the space before the door was illuminated now from two directions. Fenwick followed, the bared saber in his hand.

As Von Werthern had, he raised the blade in salute. I saw the Baron glance at the woods quickly. I waited, my hands pressed hard against my breast, for a shot to sound, for Fenwick to fall, having been reckless enough to play his enemy's game. But there came no shot. Dared I depend upon the forester's belief that his men, slipping through the night woods, had immobilized the force Konrad had brought? It would seem that for the present Von Werthern had no support.

However, he did not withdraw as I had expected him to do. Rather, he thrust his saber point down in the earth with enough force to hold the blade upright while he sought the fastenings of his tight uniform jacket and shrugged that off, casting it behind him. Fenwick made no such preparations. Kasper whistled softly and his whistle was answered from at least six points.

I could not read the expression which flitted momentarily over Konrad's self-satisfied face at those answers. He must have known then that any trap he had planned was sprung uselessly. He retrieved his weapon and they fronted each other.

My legs were suddenly weak. I found myself with one hand on either side of the door, my nails digging into the old wood to steady me. I could not retreat now any more than either of the two men.

I know nothing of the skill of a swordsman, but there was a grim, cruel grace in their movements. Sometimes they circled each other, then came together in a fast flurry of thrusts and parries, like the figures of a stately but deadly dance. I saw a line of red grow along the Colonel's upper arm, soaking through the sleeve, heard Konrad's small crow of triumph. Yet the wound, be it painful, or a mere scratch, seemed to offer little handicap to Fenwick.

280

There was now a steady flurry of attack and defense. I could hear their panting, the stamp of their feet as they moved. Then—

Konrad gave a queer, choked cry. There was steel driven deep into the upper part of his chest. He staggered back a pace or so, so quickly that he took the saber with him. The Colonel's arm had fallen to his side, the whole upper part of his sleeve now sodden with blood which spun out in a flurry of drops as he tried to reach once more for the hilt of the saber.

There was a terrible look on the Baron's face as he wavered on his feet in the full light of one of the lanterns. His mouth became an ugly scar, his eyes held such hot hatred as a devil might show. Paying no attention to his wound, to the blade which was so deeply buried in his flesh, he appeared to draw to him strength enough to come forward again, his purpose plain to read. He was bringing death—

Maybe I screamed, I do not know. Was it that cry which brought his eyes up, around to me? One step— another— Fenwick made no attempt to fall back. He had clasped one hand over his wound, his face impassive as he watched.

"Damn you—!" Was that said to me, or to Fenwick? I would never know. Konrad readied for a fatal thrust at his enemy and—fell forward to his knees.

"No! No!" He denied his weakness, his failure, yet still crumpled limply forward on his face.

We sat about the table in Kasper Kapplemann's lodge. I had tried to tend Fenwick's wound, a slash which had continued to dribble blood until Truda pushed me aside and took over that task with more competence than I possessed at that moment. The Colonel's face was pale beneath the black bush of his dust-streaked beard, and he exhaled the fumes of the brandy Kasper had produced, but he would not hear to any rest.

I tried to keep my thoughts away from the form swathed and tied into a cloak which lay on a farm cart outside. Come light and that and the now disarmed men who had followed Von Werthern would be escorted to the river, seen across it and back to Hesse-Dohna by Kasper's foresters.

Though there still might be pursuit, we had gained some time in which to put ourselves well ahead. Since the Colonel could not use the right hand of the arm now resting across his chest in a sling, I had had to school my trembling fingers to write out three papers which now lay before me on the table. One was of my own indicting, and whether it would win me complete freedom from the past I did not know, but I was the easier for the writing of it. For on that page I made formal assignment of any bequest which my grandfather had seen fit to give me to the new Elector.

The other two were of Fenwick's composition. One was his resignation from the service of Hesse-Dohna. The other was to the Gräf von Mannichen, detailing all which had happened here and that Kasper and his men had had no part in it, save to defend their master's property from unlawful invasion.

Had I really been a wife in name? That fact no longer mattered—I was now safe from any such bonds. There was still the faint stain of pink about my ring finger and it was a little tender to the touch. That unlucky ring had played a second part in the action which had overtaken us here. For Von Werthern, questing after us, had secured it from the trader and been sharp enough to foresee the direction of our flight. This we learned from questioning his second-in-command, a sinister-looking fellow whom Truda recognized as the same coachman who had supposedly driven us on our honeymoon.

I had no grief for the man who lay out there in the cart. From the first I had found him distasteful, while the brutality which had been unleashed upon me on that night when he had tried to force the right to the treasure from me had made me hate as well as fear him. Only his fury had been so useless. I had not ever wanted what my grandfather left. He and the Gräfin
282

could have shared it for all of me. Because they would never believe that anyone could turn so aside from greed, one was dead—and I would probably never know the fate of the other.

That I was safe out of the murky currents that the past had drawn around me was all that mattered. A vast weariness settled on me as I folded the papers, sealed them with wax Truda dripped carefully from a candle, and impressed the Colonel's two with the ring he gave me. For my own I brought out of hiding the iron butterflies. Perhaps no one in Hesse-Dohna would know or recognize their significance, but as a matter of identification I set the impression onto the wax of my document. Two were to be sent by messenger to Axelburg. I wished the new Elector the joy of what was in the tower he could now claim as his own. To me it had been ill-omened indeed.

Kasper escorted us to the Gräf's castle, for castle it was. There the staff made much of us. A surgeon was summoned to look to the Colonel's wound and I slept away two days—at least I can remember very little of that time, though I awoke once or twice, drank what was offered me, only to lapse once more into a blessed dark in which there were no dreams, only peace.

Though Truda labored later with various preparations she knew, the stain on my hair faded very little, so that when I at last aroused into a measure of intelligence again, I fronted quite another person in the mirror of the guest chamber I had been given.

The housekeeper raided the wardrobe of her mistress, in spite of my protests—pointing out that I certainly could not go on in the peasant dress, torn and grimed as that had become. So she set a maid to altering two gowns, provided underlinen, and refused any pay—though I vowed that the Gräfin von Manichen (for whom I left a letter of mingled apology for he liberties taken with her clothes, and thanks for all he courtesy shown us) would in time receive such a gift as would please her.

On the fourth day after we had arrived so secretly

and dramatically in Hanover, the Colonel declared he was ready to travel, though I mistrusted the return of his strength. We were to go as directly as possible to Hamburg and there take ship for Britain—since he was determined to make sure of his funds before he tried his luck overseas.

We had spent very little time together after we had reached the castle. I had visited his room at intervals to see how he did, but never alone. We were back once more among the proprieties, and I think that the house-keeper suspected the worst of our relationship. Men must have talked and undoubtedly the words Konrad had used were not forgotten, nor could I hope that they had gone unrepeated among the staff.

When we set out we had the loan of a coach as far as the nearest town where we could hire some equipage of our own. My gold was proving all that I thought it might be—a saver. Thus we made the journey across Hanover. I spent hours in the coach, sharing one seat with the Colonel, Truda across from us, Kristopher riding with the coachman. Thus conversation was of a most general character. There was no return to that day when we had tramped the road and I found it so easy to talk of my home, though I could not take all the blame for Fenwick's downfall, his exile from the country which he had served so well, I could not entirely rid myself of a feeling of guilt. Certainly it was my involvement which had led to that lantern-lit duel ground and the fact that he not only bore a new healing scar on his body, but that he had to kill a man. I felt very shy and constrained, and he looked as brooding and preoccupied as he had at the very start of our acquaintance.

We reached Hamburg at last without incident. There I was able to claim more funds from one of the merchants with whom my grandmother had had dealings and who, luckily enough, had once visited our manor and so knew me to be who I claimed I was. Truda and I spent some days in shopping, though, as she had warned me, the styles offered were sadly out of date when compared to those of the nobility. But their very dowdiness was a pleasure to me, for I could not always throw off the suspicion that some very long arm of the law from Hesse-Dohna might not extend even here.

My grandmother's friend found us a ship, bound indeed for the port of London, and flying the British flag, under which the Colonel, at least, could claim some small freedom, for he had cousins who had settled in England. So, on a bright and sunny morning we gathered on board, Truda bustling about to see our baggage safely below, ordering Kristopher hither and yon with the pride of a new wife. For that, too, had come about in Hamburg and I had given her a dowry which had left her speechless—for a while.

I turned my back upon the stern of the ship, stood looking out into what was our future. Yet I was not so unaware of what went on about me that I did not know when he came to join me. His scrubby beard had gone, he was dressed again as a gentleman, but not in the bravery of a uniform. His arm was no longer in a sling, though he favored that shoulder a little, as I had witnessed. Now he, too, was looking forward, I saw, as I stole a glance at him from under the rim of a plain straw bonnet which lacked any pretense of fashion.

"A fair wind, a fine day—" he commented.

However, neither wind nor day meant anything to me then. I had gathered up all my courage to face this moment because I had to. I must know.

"You will go on—to Maryland?" A very bald question which held nothing really of what was in my mind— or my heart—for now I knew I had a heart at last, though what it held—I could not be sure—not yet.

I had his full attention at last. Just as his habitually stern face had taken on new lines that time he had laughed when we met in the secret ways of Wallenstein, so did it change now—though it was not laughter which moved him. I gave a little gasp, though in such an open place he did no more than take my hand in his. But the very grip of his fingers was such an enfolding one that he might well have drawn me boldly

285

into his arms and held me so—in peace, yet waking to feelings I once secretly believed never did really exist.

"Is that what you wish?"

I lifted my head to meet honestly the searching gaze he was giving me.

"You need not ask that."

"No," he agreed, "I do not."

"Come." I drew him by the hand which held mine, so we came to the rail of the ship.

Then I brought my left hand from beneath my light shawl. I shook out the handkerchief I had clasped therein, loosing its burden to spiral out and down, falling into the lap of the waves, swallowed up forever. It was part of the life of others, now both dead, both in their time unhappy. I wanted none of that unhappiness to touch what I had found. I do not think mine was then a selfish wish.

The iron butterflies so made their flight into the past forever. His hand tightened on mine and I welcomed its jealous force, its steadiness. Then he did laugh.

"He got his will after all—"

"Who—what—?" I was confused.

"The Elector. He did have a husband selected for you—"

"Konrad!" I was angry to think of his dragging the past into this moment of release and happiness.

"No—me. That was why he sent me to fetch you in the beginning. He could not escape the training of his own caste—an arranged marriage for his granddaughter—one he had sponsored. I could not refuse to go but—"

"But you determined to have none of me?"

He looked then a little embarrassed before he smiled.

"Would you have taken to such a suggestion then yourself, my lady?"

I did not see fit to answer that. Instead I had another question:

"Are you still duty bound, sir?"

286

"My name is Pryor. And there is nothing dutiful in this." He had me suddenly in his arms and I learned the excitement and awe-changing power of a kiss.

A NEW DECADE OF CREST BESTSELLERS